PROMISE OF PLEASURE

Like a dream, she came to him, her hands reaching out to touch him. The softest of skin slid over the roughness of his chest, her slender fingers mingling with the thick covering of hair. She drew closer, lingering over him in taunting beauty. The scent of her filled him, drawing him further into her world of passion. Her silky hair fell on him, tickling his sensitive flesh. He could no longer resist the temptation to wrap its golden length around his hand, pulling her down to him, inching her full, voluptuous lips to his own. All earlier promises were forgotten, leaving only the promise of the pleasure to come.

FELA DAWSON SCOTT

GHOST DANCER

To the men in my life.
First, to David Scott for a husband's love.
To Bill Dawson, for just being my big brother.
And to Billy G. Dawson, who no longer is a part of my life, but remains strong in his daughter's memories.

A Centurion Book®

Published by special arrangement with Dorchester Publishing Co., Inc.

Printed in the United States of America.

GHOST DANCER

THE LEGEND

From generation to generation, the Ghost Dancer's spirit endures, gathering knowledge and wisdom as it passes to the next, chosen one. The Ghost Dancer will live forever.

It is said the Ghost Dancer lives among the Sioux, who make their homes nestled in the Black Hills of the Dakotas. White men dismiss the stories as legend, nothing more. But the tribe of the Nahhe Lahkota—the Ghost Sioux—truly believe. . . .

Prologue

The Black Hills in the Dakota Territory
1853

The village was quiet but not silent as the constant beat of a single drum filled the air, and the Indians performed their daily routines in hushed stillness.

No children played in the compound's dusty yard; even the usual yelping of the dogs was missing. In the distance, horses grazed on tender shoots of grass. For a moment the strange mood was interrupted by a baby's cry that was quickly quieted by his mother's breast.

Without their normal chatter, women prepared their meals, setting their pots to bubble over crackling fires. To keep their minds from the sadness that claimed the camp and its people, they also cleaned hides and wove baskets.

None of the men hunted in the wooded hills stretching out behind them. Tall, almost black evergreens would not hear the yells of the hunters that day, and no prey would be threatened by those warriors. Men sat in groups, their talk low as they busied themselves with their weapons, making and repairing them for another day. Saddened eyes glanced every now and then at the large tepee that stood near the center of the village.

For hours it had been so and it would continue to be until they knew *he* had died . . . only to live again as another. For the death of the Ghost Dancer, they would mourn; for the rebirth of the Ghost Dancer, they would rejoice. It had been so since the First.

"My son."

Black Hawk stood and crossed the darkened tepee to his father's side, taking the gnarled hand that reached for him. There was no warmth left in the flesh, and Black Hawk knew his father, Ghost Dancer, was near death. Smoke drifted above them. The heavy hide walls allowed in no light or fresh air, and the heady smell of the burning herbs was choking and stagnant. The nearby chanting of the medicine man continued unbroken, his hand never pausing in the beating of his drum.

"Many winters have passed since the First was given to our tribe. . . ."

Black Hawk nodded. Like all their people, he knew the story. Still, he wanted to hear it again. Just as his father wanted to retell it. One last time. . . .

"The First was a man, the same as any other. Perhaps a bit stronger, wiser than most but mortal in all ways. It was a time of many wars . . .

a time of grief for the people." The old man's eyes stared blankly, seeing only what his mind conjured.

"The First became a great chief, leading his warriors to victory many times against our enemies. Yet, he was wounded in a battle and knew he would not survive. He worried for his people, knowing they needed his guidance and leadership. If only he could give all he knew to another."

Again Ghost Dancer stopped to gather strength. His heavy breathing grew calmer as the quiet minutes passed.

"The First prayed to the Sun to grant his people its immortal strength, and he prayed to the Moon to grant his people its immortal wisdom. He offered up a scarlet blanket, the last of his strength flowing from his body in blood. As he lay weak and dying, he dreamed of the birth of a child and saw upon this babe's right palm the symbol of the Sun, and upon his left the symbol of the Moon. Immortal strength and wisdom had been granted by the Ones Above, and so they still bless us . . . and the Ghost Dancer lives forever."

Black Hawk strained to hear the words. With every moment that passed, his father's voice grew weaker. He heard the rattling breath the old man drew as he paused in his tale. Patiently, Black Hawk waited for him to continue.

"I had a dream . . . and I saw the future."

Black Hawk nodded, his heart beat quickening in anticipation of the Ghost Dancer's words. Now he would know who was chosen.

"Our people will not understand. . . ."

Black Hawk's brow wrinkled. "Why, Father? Is it not to be as it always has been?"

"Yes . . . the Ghost Dancer shall live on in another."

"Then what is it we will not understand?"

Ghost Dancer sighed tiredly. "In my dream, I saw the chosen one. It will be a girl child."

Black Hawk knew that to be unusual, but it would be acceptable, and he said so.

"The Ghost Dancer will be a child of the white man, my son. She will have eyes the pale color of the sky and hair, the yellow-white of the moonlight . . ." Faded eyes sagged in weariness.

Black Hawk was truly shocked. "It cannot be!"

It took a moment for his father to speak again. "It is so . . . my dream has . . . shown me what is to be . . . and we shall . . . not question."

Black Hawk lowered his head in submission. Never had he doubted his father's dreams. He would not begin now.

"Four winters will pass . . . before you find this child."

Raising his head to meet his father's aged gaze, Black Hawk sought understanding. "How will I know this girl child to be the Ghost Dancer?"

As if recalling the vision, his father's eyes closed. "I saw her standing among fire and broken arrows. You will not question her existence, my son. This fair-headed child is our future."

"The child shall be as my own. None will doubt her." Black Hawk's promise was sincere; he would die before dishonoring his father.

A bony hand reached out to touch Black Hawk's cheek. He watched a single tear roll down Ghost Dancer's leathery skin, following the trail of sun-baked lines which told of the many years his father had seen.

"You are a good son and my heart fills with love when I gaze upon you. My wife and the children of my younger years were taken from me. But I was blessed by *Wakan Tanka* granting me a son so late in my life."

"I shall miss you, my father."

"And I shall miss you . . . my son."

Black Hawk could see the shadow of death creep over Ghost Dancer. The light in his eyes dimmed, then slowly faded. His father's breathing became more shallow and uneven, his words the softest of whispers.

"I see her." His hand reached into the air. "I hear her cry." His arm fell limp by his side. "I see our future. . . ."

The drumming stopped.

Ghost Dancer breathed his last as Angelique drew her first.

Chapter 1

1873

Cameron Wade was going to die in only a matter of minutes and he knew it. The young Cheyenne warriors who had pinned him behind the rocks were satisfied for the moment to play with him, wanting to prolong the enjoyment of the kill just a little bit longer.

One by one, they came at him, their shrill war cries filling the air. They tested their courage and some died, but for each warrior who fell there always seemed to be another to take his place. Cameron's ammunition was running low and too soon he would have none. His back was to a wall of solid rock, preventing him from escaping, but it also kept any Indians from sneaking up behind him.

He was in a tight spot, unable to move far without exposing himself. Each time he managed to get off a shot, he was barraged with arrows and rifle fire. He had been nicked a few times by the sharp arrowheads, but these were minor injuries.

Cameron looked upward. The sun was bright, high in the sky. Darkness would be a long time coming. Perhaps too long. . . .

Perspiration trickled down his forehead, and he wiped the salty sweat from his eyes. He waited, wondering how he'd ended up in such a God-forsaken country, miles from the fort.

A few days ago, when Colonel Dawson asked him to check Sam Smith's shack in the Black Hills, it had seemed like a good idea. Or at least it hadn't seemed to be a bad one. The colonel had hoped some information about the old man's family would be found. Someone somewhere would want to know of Sam's death, and perhaps, would also want a few of the old prospector's personal things.

Now, as Cameron considered his plight, he decided the colonel's notion had been a damned poor one. The old man was dead, and probably no one cared. And now, he himself would soon join him.

Another warrior's yell ricocheted off the cliffs, and Cameron's gaze jerked up. An Indian came flying through the air toward him, his dark face a mask of hatred. His catapulted weight knocked Cameron off his feet, and the two men grappled in the dirt. Cameron managed to clamp down on the brave's wrist, grateful his strength kept the knife from descending. Barely an inch shorter than Cameron, the Cheyenne warrior was not quite as agile or strong. Within seconds, Cameron was able to turn the Indian's knife on him and deal a killing blow.

Before he could relax, Cameron felt a flash of searing pain rip through him, knocking him off his feet. He felt as if a hot poker had been stabbed into his shoulder as the fire shot across his chest, stealing away his breath. His fingers went numb. His pistol fell to the ground, useless. He rolled back into his protective hole. Arrows rained down on him, like hail in a storm. He could feel the warmth of his blood spreading across his shirt and down his arm. Brilliant red turned the dry ground black.

Another warrior charged him, his savage face painted black and red, and this brave's size was a match for Cameron's. Warily, they eyed each other, judging the other's strength and power. Cameron felt his strength draining from him with each passing second. His sight began to blur, his breathing became ragged.

"Come on, you black-eyed son of a bitch. Come on!"

The Indian obliged and leaped at him, catching Cameron in the stomach. The force of the blow jerked his shoulder back. Never had he experienced such pain. The world spun about him, the ground shifting like the ocean. Cameron's sense of helplessness made him madder than hell. His anger gave him the strength to hurl the warrior from him in a cry of fury.

When the savage leaped to his feet with a knife in his hands, the look in his dark eyes was one of a man ready to deal out death.

Cameron braced himself, hoping his body still had the strength to obey his mind's commands.

The warrior sliced the air with his knife, its edge whistling as it cut an invisible arch. Slowly, the Indian approached him, striking with the quickness of a snake. Cameron jumped back. Not far enough though. The blade scored a path across his chest, slicing deeply, drawing a river of blood. He winced in agony, both from the sudden movement of his shoulder and the knife's deadly path. Again and again, the warrior leaped at Cameron, a look of pleasure lighting his savage face at each slash he made across Cameron's chest and arms.

Cameron knew he wasn't a coward, but he couldn't think of a worse way to die. The foe he faced intended to draw out his pain to the fullest and to provide his companions with as much enjoyment as possible. It was a game . . . a game of death, and the Indians were making the rules and holding the winning hand.

As Cameron lay battered and bleeding on the hot ground, the warrior raised his knife, taunting, teasing above him. Maybe the game would end sooner than he'd thought. Then an arrow skimmed through the air and buried itself deep in the Cheyenne's throat. A look of horror twisted the redman's face. Death froze the look in place before the Indian hit the ground.

Cameron rolled to his side, his eyes turning to the direction from which the arrow had come. A lone rider emerged from the rocky crags that surrounded him, and the Cheyenne, too, had stopped to watch the rider's approach. Cameron's interest was no longer on them, but on the image that moved down the hillside toward him.

The sun glistened off the pale gold of her hair, the long, silky length gently blowing in the breeze. The fairest skin and the most perfect face taunted his failing sight. He blinked to clear his eyes and felt a sudden wash of anger. By damn, unconsciousness threatened to take the beautiful vision away. Yet he was unable to stay the blackness that finally blocked the soft blue of her eyes.

"Damn," he cursed, sliding into oblivion.

Ghost Dancer had a last-minute flash of uncertainty when she neared the man in blue. She had watched the Cheyenne attack him, and common sense had urged her to leave the soldier to his fate. But something had kept her from abandoning him. Perhaps it had been pity. Death at the hands of the Cheyenne would not be merciful. Or maybe a sense of fairness had made her kick her horse closer so that her aim would be true; the numbers against the white man were too many.

Now she was committed; her arrow had been accurate, deadly. She stared down at the white man's still form before sliding off her horse and kneeling beside him. He was a larger man than he had seemed from her perch above. His shoulders were so broad, his muscled body long, hard. Was he dead? She heard his low groan and breathed an unexpected sigh of relief.

For the moment, she forgot the Cheyenne warriors and the danger she was in as they stood in stunned silence, watching. They seemed unimportant as she gazed down at the stranger. His face had not been foreseen in her dreams. Her brow wrinkled in confusion, and she wondered what had drawn her here. Surely if this man was of importance to her, she would have known.

A sharp, demanding word from one Cheyenne drew her attention. She stood and faced the five young warriors. Unafraid, she looked from one to another, her icy stare never faltering. From the fear she read in many of the dark eyes, she knew they had guessed who she was. They were Cheyenne, and Cheyenne claimed not to believe in the Ghost Dancer, but they were still apprehensive.

"You will go," Ghost Dancer said softly in their own language. "You will leave him."

A few stepped back, mumbling in fear, glancing at each other for support. When her pet wolf, Wolfdog, appeared to stand by her side, teeth bared, only one brave stood rigidly before her.

"No," he spat, his face twisted into a mask of fury. "He is ours to take. You will not interfere, woman."

Ghost Dancer took one step toward him, showing she did not fear his anger. "I will not let you take this man."

The young Cheyenne cocked his head, his eyes becoming narrow slits. "Who are *you* to dare such a thing?"

"I am Ghost Dancer," she said simply. Yet she knew she struck terror deep within his heart.

The warrior hesitated, then grabbed her hands roughly and turned them over to see if she truly bore the markings of the sun and the moon. When he was satisfied, he flung her hands from him.

"It does not matter that you are the Ghost Dancer. You are a woman . . . a *white* woman, and I say that he is ours."

"It would not be wise to defy me," she said almost sympathetically. The braves who had stood back from them fled, having taken her warning to heart. The warrior now stood alone.

He seemed to be thinking about what to do next, but she knew he had come too far to back down. Calling upon the force from within, Ghost Dancer used a hypnotic stare to draw the man into her world of dark magic.

She sensed that the power he felt angered him, and he lunged forward, his tomahawk raised to strike. Ready, Ghost Dancer grabbed his wrist, stopping the angled blade from descending on her head. As hard as he struggled, he could not break her hold. His look of surprise turned to one of despair at the strength in her arm. She could see the change deep in his eyes as his instincts told him he was dealing with much more than a woman . . . much, much more.

Ghost Dancer drew him inside her, drowning him in a dark blue sea. The beads of perspiration on his upper lip told her of the sudden flush of heat he was experiencing. His body began to sway as his world started to spin, followed by a deafening roar and blurring vision. Hidden fears began to touch his mind like the blade of a knife drawing blood, planting terror in his heart.

He turned away from her to look up at the tomahawk he held. Slowly, he saw the weapon turn into a snake. Frozen in place, he watched the serpent twist about his wrist then slither down the length of his muscled arm. With a guttural cry of unleashed horror, he flung the creature from him and stepped back from Ghost Dancer. Darkness swallowed him, taking his fear away.

Ghost Dancer knew the Cheyenne warrior's pride was saved, for to battle an evil spirit so bravely would spare any shame of loss. No doubt, for many years to come, he would retell an exaggerated version of the story for his family and friends.

She turned from him, giving the Cheyenne no more thought. She had more important matters at hand.

Chapter 2

Black Hawk crossed his arms in a stern pose, his ramrod-straight appearance forbidding. His sun-darkened skin stretched tight over the angular bones of his face. The only sign of age was a smattering of gray at his temples. "I do not think it was wise for you to bring the white soldier here."

Ghost Dancer looked up at her adopted father. His face showed stony disapproval, although his brown-black eyes still held the warmth she knew so well. A bit of uncertainty was in her voice as she tried to explain. "It was not a matter of being wise. I could not leave him to die."

In despair, he raised his arms, and the still-firm muscles of his arms and chest rippled. "What does this man have to do with you? Over the years I have learned to accept many of the things you do, but to bring home this stranger was foolish."

"I do not feel that he is a stranger, my father." She smiled shyly.

His look turned serious. "You have had a vision of this soldier?"

"I have never seen this man before." Ghost Dancer paused a moment as she felt a blush warm her cheeks. "Yet I feel drawn to him, and I do not understand why. My dreams have not failed me before. He is a mystery, and I have no idea what has brought him into my life."

A relieved sigh came from Black Hawk. "This man is a danger. You have placed us all in jeopardy with your actions."

Her father's look was once again harsh, and she was aware of his disapproval. "He does not seem so dangerous."

"He is white. That is enough."

She tilted her head. "I am not of the tribe."

"Your skin is white, my daughter, but your heart and soul are Sioux."

Ghost Dancer considered his words. "Perhaps, I should not have taken such a risk. But it is done."

"Yes," he agreed. "It is done."

She looked into his scowling face and experienced a surge of panic. At that moment she regretted her impulsiveness. Yet she could not keep silent. "You would not take him away?"

"It would be best if I did." The hard resolve faded from his eyes. "But to abandon him to die now would be wrong."

Relief replaced dread. "Thank you, Father."

"You have always saved the birds that fell from their nests." Black Hawk's face softened. "I cannot stay angry at the gentleness you possess in your heart."

"Father?" Ghost Dancer drew Black Hawk's darkened eyes to her. "It will be all right, Father. You will see."

He reached out to caress her cheek, the strong hand giving only the gentlest touch. "Take care of your fallen bird then, my daughter. But remember he is not of the Sioux and cannot be trusted."

Cameron heard the soft humming while he was still deep in a healing sleep. It intrigued him, even then, his groggy mind wondering from where it came. It was a beautiful sound, soothing in its tone, drawing him closer and closer to the world of consciousness. Slowly, he came awake, his mouth forming the words of the familiar tune.

"Hush little baby . . ." There was no sound, only his lips moved. " . . . don't you cry . . ."

He listened closely, his mind singing along with the hum that filled the air. "Mama's gonna sing you a lullaby." Cameron smiled in remembrance.

Determined to find the source of the song, he opened his eyes. Wherever he was, it was dim, but even the small amount of light hurt his eyes. He had to wait several minutes before he could focus.

A powerful thirst dried his mouth. His tongue was so thick he found it difficult to swallow. His chapped lips moved to speak but still no sounds emerged. He could hear the crackling of a fire and smell the burning wood. Against his cheek, he felt the softness of fur, and slowly, he turned his head to look.

All about him lay skins of many kinds, each worked with painstaking care. He moved his hand to touch his shoulder and found it tightly bound with bandages. He could feel the many lacerations crisscrossing his body in haphazard patterns. Ointment must have been worked into each cut to ease the tightness that usually came with healing.

Bits of memory came back to him, reminding him he should be dead. Instead, he seemed to be very much alive and securely tucked within a tepee. Curiosity prompted him to turn his head a bit farther, so that he could examine his surroundings. In the center was the fire he could hear, cheerfully eating up the wood laying within its bed of rocks, its smoke snaking upward to drift out the carefully positioned tent flaps. Furs on the floor spread out from the inner circle of fire, and woven baskets, beaded bags, and decorated pouches were neatly arranged along the walls. An inner lining of rawhide stretched around the tepee, elaborately painted with stories of old. Drums, pipes, and waterbags hung from the poles, and various kitchen utensils and pots were near the door, a small stack of firewood on the other side. These surroundings gave him a surprisingly comfortable feeling.

Finally, his eyes came to rest upon the source of the humming, and again, he wondered at the vision he saw. It was the woman he had seen earlier in the hills just before he had passed out. She sat demurely at the end of his pallet, leaning against a back rest, obviously concentrating on the shirt she mended. He continued to stare as she carefully sewed the many rips in his shirt, restoring it to its original shape and form as best she could. It gave him a strange feeling of warmth to watch her, a feeling he couldn't remember experiencing for a very long time. Content for the moment, he said nothing. He wanted this special sensation to last.

Ghost Dancer was well aware that the white man was staring at her, but she waited for him to speak before raising her head.

"Where am I?" His voice crackled with dryness.

She considered his question before answering, studying his face. She had only known one other white man in her life, and he was much older. This man's face was extremely pleasant to look at. But it was his marvelous eyes that kept her attention, sparkling with the light of the fire, making them dance with life. "You are safe," she replied in English.

Instantly, she read the confusion in his handsome face, and she went on to explain. "I brought you to my village, not far from where I found you. The Cheyenne are gone, and you are safe."

She could see he wanted to speak, but he coughed instead. Ghost Dancer stood and brought him some cool water to ease the rawness in his throat. He leaned forward to drink from the horn cup, wincing slightly with pain. When he had settled back in the bed, she remained by his side.

"What is your name?"

"I am Ghost Dancer." She sat on the floor next to the bed, receiving a strange pleasure from being close to him.

"No, what was the name your mother gave you? Your Christian name?"

"Christian name?"

"Yes, your Christian name." Cameron's look turned impatient. "Your white man's name. Your *real* name. Not the name they've given you here."

She gave this some thought, not really understanding the urgency in his voice. "Angel. She called me Angel."

Obviously, it still wasn't what he wanted to know. "Was that your given name? Angel?"

Ghost Dancer looked beyond the wounded soldier and into the past, concentrating on his question. She cocked her head as she tried to recall memories of long ago. "Angel . . . Angelique." She smiled proudly. "My *given* name was Angelique. It is all that I can remember. Except for the song."

He smiled in return. "It's a beautiful name." Then he tried it out. "Angelique. May I call you that?"

Cameron watched her face closely, wanting to read some sort of pleasure in his using her real name. Instead, he was almost certain he saw indifference.

"If it pleases you."

"It does," he replied, trying to figure her situation out. "Doesn't it please you?"

Ghost Dancer considered this, not having thought about it before. "Yes. I think it does." She did like the way he said it, almost caressing the word with his lips. It did make her feel strange inside, but nice. Having decided, she repeated with more confidence this time, "Yes, it does please me."

"My name is Cameron Wade."

"I know," was all she said. Last night, in his sleep, he had revealed his name to her.

It seemed that curiosity would not leave Cameron be, and he asked her another question. "How is it you came to be here?"

"My adopted father, Black Hawk, found me. The wagon train my parents and I were in was attacked. I was the only one left alive."

"How long have you been here?" An uneasy feeling was creeping over Cameron. She seemed unafraid, her look remaining calm as he continued to question her. He thought it odd that her recollections of her capture held no fear.

"I have been here a very long time."

Long enough to forget all but her name. Dread accompanied his uneasiness. "Am I free to leave here, when I'm well enough to ride?" he asked with an abrupt change of subject, wondering if he would be here a very long time, too.

A shy smile flitted around the corners of her full mouth, turning up the corners mysteriously. Her delicate brows raised ever so slightly over her large eyes, the color of cornflowers. "Of course. You are not a prisoner. I only brought you here because you were hurt."

Cameron realized how ungrateful he must have sounded. "I forgot to thank you."

"To thank me?" she whispered as her thick-lashed eyelids lowered, blocking the vivid eyes he studied so closely.

He nodded. "For saving my life. How did you get me away from the Cheyenne? They were bent on killing me." Cameron noticed the soft rosy hue that came to her cheeks, and the color of her full lips, only a shade darker. "Then, out of nowhere, you appeared."

"You should eat and gather your strength." This time, she changed the subject.

He got the message, but added, "When I go back to Fort Laramie, you can go with me."

Her confusion showed. "Why would I want to go to this Fort Laramie?"

"Why?" It was worse than he thought. "To be with your own people again. I'll take you home, Angelique."

Her laugh was sweet, like musical notes of mirth as her smile revealed even white teeth. "This *is* my home, and I *am* with my own people."

Ghost Dancer stood to get him some food but as she turned toward the fire, Cameron reached out and took her hand, stopping her. Ghost Dancer felt the shock of flesh meeting flesh, but he dropped her hand just as quickly as he had taken it.

"You can't be serious?" he asked, his mind rejecting what she had said. A white woman living with Indians? It was wrong. Plain and simple.

Ghost Dancer's brows raised. "I am very serious."

Cameron just stared for the longest time as he seemed to consider her reply before asking what he refused to believe. "You are happy here, among the Sioux?"

She nodded and again, she smiled. Her hand still tingled and disappointment flashed over her that the contact had ended.

The subject was dropped, and Ghost Dancer thought no more of his strange notions. Never had she given any thought to leaving her tribe. But then, Cameron Wade could not understand that she was the Ghost Dancer.

Cameron watched Angelique through half-closed eyes. She busied herself with getting his meal, ladling a thick stew into a carved wooden bowl. He found himself wondering about this woman, many questions drifting though his thoughts in haphazard fashion. Her answer shouldn't have surprised him. After all, he was now aware that she had known no other life. But that really didn't change things. He wasn't going to leave her here. It wouldn't be right. He would see her safely among her own kind. Perhaps she even had family somewhere.

He knew nothing of her, only her first name. Yet he was intrigued by her and even more, he felt a need to protect her, to rescue her as much from herself as from the Indians. It was his sworn duty as an officer and a gentleman of the Army to save her from this barren existence, and, by damn, he would, too.

His decision made, Cameron relaxed. Slowly, he found himself paying careful attention to what she wore. The traditional Indian dress was actually quite becoming on her and he felt a sense of betrayal as this thought came into direct conflict with his beliefs. Still, his emotions remained in control. The dress was made of doe hide the color of a fawn, and looked as soft as a baby's skin. Only long fringe adorned it, and it was elegant in its simplicity. Angelique was barefoot, and her golden hair hung loose about her shoulders, reaching well below her waist. He found himself wanting to touch the silken length, to twist it about his hands and to run his fingers through it.

He admired the gentle curve of her hips and the fullness of her breasts beneath her bodice. He imagined the long, muscled length of her legs as his exploring touch discovered their firmness. When she turned her back in his direction, their gazes tangled, green finding blue, freezing them both into place. He strained to gain control of both his imagination and his emotions. Beads of perspiration broke out on his upper lip. The fever that had broken earlier was now replaced with another heat.

His look was bold and arrogant, and she returned his gaze. She didn't turn away, and only the slightest blush stained her cheeks. Surely, she understood what he wanted; it was clear. Then, just as suddenly as the desire had come, shame washed over him, dousing the blaze inside him. He was the one to turn away.

Had he no honor? Was he going to repay her kindness by seducing her?

Damn! he thought. *It hasn't been that long.* He was an officer and a gentleman, and he *would* act accordingly.

Determinedly, he brought himself under control. When Angelique handed him the bowl of stew, he accepted it gratefully. With her help, he sat up, comfortably positioning him against a back rest. As she tucked the furs around him, he realized that he was naked.

"Are you all right?"

It was almost too much for him, to stare so closely at the luscious curve of her lips. He fought the strong urge to take her in his arms and claim her mouth for his own, to drain the sweetness from within. Instead, he drew back.

I must be losing my mind. How could this bit of a woman, a woman he had never seen before, torture him in ways far more cruel than any Cheyenne brave? Was she a witch? Had some mystical spell been cast upon him while he slept? How long had he been there? How many days had passed since he was wounded?

He handed the empty bowl back to her. "How long have I been here?"

"Not long. Only three days," she replied.

Another question came into his head and he spoke without giving it much thought. "How is it you speak English so well? You said you didn't remember much before you were taken, yet you speak as well as I do."

"You ask many questions, Cameron Wade." She turned back to the fire. "If your strength is to return, you must rest."

Twice now she had put him off. This time an impatient spark of anger burst forth. "You're good at avoiding questions, Angelique. Why? What are you hiding?"

He hadn't bothered to mask his annoyance and when she turned back to him, he could see the hurt he had caused. Suddenly he felt like a cad.

"Oh, Angel." He hardly realized he'd used the familiar endearment. "You didn't deserve that and you're right. I do need my rest."

Angelique's smile made his heart lighten. Never before had he witnessed such beauty.

"You are forgiven."

Ghost Dancer stood for the longest time, just watching him sleep, his even breathing reaching her ears. She longed to touch his face, to learn every inch that made him Cameron Wade, to feel the firm jaw and each handsomely formed feature. Again, curiosity overtook her, and she could no longer resist the urge to touch the soft length of dark hair that curled at his neck. Then, taking courage, she felt the line of his lips but pulled back at the chaos it caused in her body. She recalled the sparkle of his eyes, but mostly, she remembered the look that lit them when he watched her. She had seen that look before, among the men of her tribe, but never before had it affected her in the way it had today. It had stirred feelings deep inside her, hidden emotions that burst forth in a stream of desire. Still, her innocence mixed evenly with her fear of the unknown.

What had made her bring him here? Her dreams always prepared her, seeing all in the nightly visions granted her by the Ones Above. Why had she seen nothing of this man? Nothing at all. Why did his soft voice send shivers through her, and his sharp green eyes create havoc in her stomach? Or his slightest touch steal away her breath? It was so unlike her to react in such a way, and she carefully examined this.

But Ghost Dancer found no answers to her questions and, discouraged, moved to her own bed to seek the evasive sleep she needed. She only knew one thing—that she would never again be the same.

Chapter 3

Cameron waited for a moment before he tried to sit up and a groan slipped out at the pain it caused his bruised body. But a familiar urgency lent him strength.

"You should not get up."

Cameron lifted his eyes to see Angelique standing before him, her arms extended to help him. He felt as weak as a kitten and welcomed her strong support. "Let's just say that I feel the *need* to get up."

She did not seem to understand the need he referred to.

"Where's my pants?" Cameron felt uneasy under her look of concern and glanced about for his clothes. She still made no move. "My pants," he repeated. "Where are they?"

She handed the trousers to him, though her eyes made it clear that she did not approve.

When she continued to watch him, he added, "Do you mind?"

Her large eyes blinked in confusion. "Do I mind what?"

Cameron could not help but chuckle at her complete innocence. "Would you turn away while I put my pants on?"

He could tell by the look on her face that she still did not understand, but. she complied. Cameron pulled them on as quickly as his wounds would allow, his teeth gritted against the pain. Patiently, he explained his request. After all, she would need to know these things when he took her back to civilization.

"You see, Angelique, a gentleman does not dress in front of a lady he doesn't know real well. Actually, he wouldn't be undressed in the first place. It's just not proper." When he was finished, he added, "Okay. You can turn around now, I'm decent."

When she faced him, he could see she was thinking over what he had said.

"So," she began hesitantly, "it was not proper for me to undress you after I brought you here?"

Cameron actually felt the blood rush to his face. He laughed at his own embarrassment and the whole silly situation. "I guess." He cleared his throat, feeling the awkwardness of the situation. "Under the circumstances, you had no choice."

"Then it was proper?"

Her look was so serious, he felt he should ease her doubts. "Yes." He nodded. "It was proper."

His reply made her smile and that made him feel good. "Now, I must go out, Angel."

Angelique's smile faded. "You are not strong enough."

Cameron held up his hand, stopping further argument. "Trust me, I *must* go out."

"Then I will go with you," she insisted.

His head moved back and forth. "No. There are some things a man must do . . . alone."

He could see that, this time, she understood and was embarrassed. Without another word, she lit a torch and handed it to him.

"I'll only be a second." He grinned sheepishly, then disappeared beneath the fur that covered the tepee's door.

In fact, only a second or two passed before Cameron nearly fell back inside.

"Christ Almighty!" he hollered. "Where's my gun?"

"What is the matter, Cameron Wade?" she questioned. Suddenly fearful, she followed him about the tepee as he searched frantically for his weapon.

"Damn it!" After flinging a few furs aside, he turned and demanded, "Where is it?"

Wolfdog picked that moment to stroll into the tent, his golden gaze turning in their direction. Cameron instinctively put himself between the wolf and Angelique, his large frame overshadowing her smaller one. "Jeezzuss," he whispered in awe. "That's the biggest son of a . . ." He stopped when the animal moved across the floor and stretched out by the fire, seemingly disregarding their presence.

Ghost Dancer peeked around Cameron's back and looked up at him. "I see that you have met my pet." A very meek smile came to her lips.

"Pet?" He almost barked the word, his body aching terribly from his sudden movements. "That monster animal is your *pet?*"

She nodded. "His name is Wolfdog."

"Ha!" This time it was a bark. Small beads of perspiration marked his forehead and upper lip now. "How original." Cameron instantly regretted his sarcasm. "I'm sorry. You didn't deserve that." He pushed back his hair.

Angelique seemed to become even more confused by his apology. "I am sorry he startled you."

Cameron looked away from the silver beast and back to her, his anger gone as fast as it had come.

"I am certain that there are no more *monsters* to block your way." Angelique offered another timid smile, its warmth easing the difficult moment.

Cameron laughed, the deep rumble filling the tepee with its mellow sound. It didn't matter that the shaking of his body hurt him. "Well, then, I'd best finish what I started. Before I embarrass myself . . . for the second time tonight."

Cameron awoke several moments before he opened his eyes, but his anticipation of seeing his blue-eyed rescuer was cruelly taken away when his heavy lids lifted. An Indian sat by the fire, his dark visage prompting Cameron to sit up, even though it caused him great discomfort. Quickly, he scanned the tent for his gun or anything he could use as a weapon.

"Sometimes my daughter does not please me, but I cannot fault her kind heart."

Cameron turned his attention to the man claiming to be Angelique's father. "I've got to agree with you there. She has a big heart. I owe her a great deal for what she did."

The dark head nodded. "She is curious."

It seemed a strange statement, and Cameron took a chance to pursue it further by asking, "Curious about what?"

"You," stated Black Hawk with only a slight hesitation.

"Me?"

Again, he nodded, his expression remaining hard and unreadable. "She has known so few men of your race, of her own people. Naturally, she is curious."

Somehow, Cameron got the distinct impression that this man, obviously her adopted father, was none too pleased by this turn of events. "And you . . . you are not."

His firm lips leveled into a straight line. Neither a smile, nor a frown. "I find nothing in your world to hold any appeal. You bring only pain and destruction to my people, in the name of glory and greed. Why would I want my daughter to know of these things?"

Cameron bristled at his visitor's one-sided assessment, or perhaps it was the fact that the older man's words rang with a certain truth that bothered him. Anyway, he thought it wasn't the time to argue the point, whatever it might be.

Black Hawk continued, "Should I be feeling joy that Ghost Dancer, the daughter of my heart, finds you interesting?"

Cameron took offense at the older man's honestly spoken statement. "Now, I'm not all *that* bad, Chief. I mean no harm to you or to your daughter. Besides . . ." He paused, choosing his words carefully. "Don't you think she has the right to know where she comes from? To be with her own kind?"

"Ghost Dancer is fully aware of how she came to be here, among the Ghost Sioux. She has no loyalty to your world, so do not interfere."

The words were plain enough, but it was the tone that made the chief's feelings completely clear to Cameron.

Cameron raised his hands in submission, deciding to let the issue drop. For now. "I wouldn't dream of it."

"You may stay until you are well enough to ride. Then you must go and forget that you have seen the Ghost Dancer. She is my heart, and I will not abide interference. Especially from a white man."

It was an odd statement; at least it struck Cameron that way. He also was taken aback, never having expected such honest affection from the Indian chief for a white captive. Cameron watched him as he left the tent, then slumped back down onto the soft furs, suddenly overwhelmed with fatigue.

"So, my angel is curious," said Cameron aloud, feeling pleased with himself just before sleep drove all thoughts from him.

Cameron stretched the stiffness out of his legs and arms, yawning widely at the same time. He shook his head to rid himself of the sluggishness that still claimed him.

"All I do is sleep," he mumbled. The tepee was

quiet, and he sensed he was alone even before his eyes confirmed it with a quick skimming of the tent.

Suddenly, he couldn't lie there any longer. The bed seemed to cause more discomfort than comfort. Slowly, carefully, he moved to a sitting position. Encouraged, he stood. That was a bit more painful. Cameron eyed the flap that was propped open, letting fresh air in. He looked straight up and squinted at the light that came from the open smoke flaps.

Noises began to work past his thoughts, and Cameron started wondering about what lay outside the hide walls. Small, somewhat unsure steps took him to the opening. He seemed even stiffer than the last time he was up. A soft laugh slipped out as he recalled his heroic behavior, and he felt foolish at having tried to protect Angelique from her own pet.

He mumbled again to himself, "Wolfdog," then shook his head in wonder. Even when he was short and ill-tempered with Angelique, she was so unaware of it, making him laugh outright. This slip of a girl made him feel good.

Bending down, he ducked under the flap and stood outside, grinding his teeth at the pain. But the fresh air and sunshine that greeted him made it worthwhile. Curious, he looked about. The scene before him was a peaceful one, almost serene in its setting, backed by the magnificent black mountains in the distance.

The chatter of women drifted on the gentle

breeze. He couldn't understand the words, but the tone was one of a common language. He saw some working just to his right, hanging strips of meat and fish on the large racks to dry for winter storage. A variety of fruits and berries were also evident, and he found his mouth watering with hunger.

The cries of children's laughter caught his attention and he saw Angelique's golden head. Ghost Dancer . . . Wasn't that her Indian name? She walked along beside the small group, her own laughter musical and soft, her skipping step almost childlike as she began singing, and the children's voices echoed hers.

It was such a pleasant sound, and it brought a large smile to his face. The tune ended in a peal of laughter, infectiously spreading to everyone within hearing distance and soon caught hold of Cameron, too. As the children ran off to play, Angelique stood a moment, watching them, her head cocked to the side.

"Perfect," whispered Cameron as he continued to watch. "Perfect."

Like a gaggle of geese, the young Indian girls moved across the compound to where Cameron stood, their laughter pulling his stare away from Angelique to them. Their shy, dark brown eyes studied him intently, their obvious interest showing in various ways as they moved closer, prodding each other and whispering in each other's ears.

Cameron smiled, bringing even more giggles from them, their white teeth flashing against the smooth, cocoa skin of their cheeks. They dared to inch a little closer.

"Wechasha," one girl said, pointing to Cameron. Then pointing to herself, she added, *"Weenyon."*

"I . . . I don't understand," he replied, aware that she, in turn, would not understand him.

Again, she pointed a slender finger to him. *"Hegnahkoo,"* and back to her, *"tahwechoo."*

Cameron lifted his shoulder and hands in a gesture that told them he didn't know what she was saying. This brought even more giggles.

"She said," Angelique interpreted, joining them, "man and woman."

"She said something different the second time. What was it?"

All the laughter had stopped, and the young girls braved a look at Ghost Dancer, the frown on her face telling them she wasn't happy with them.

"Husband and wife."

A choked laugh came this time, and the girls scattered like a flock on the run, each taking a different route to safety.

Cameron winced as the laughter grew within him, causing him pain. "A bit forward, aren't they?"

"You are something strange and different to them. They are still children and are only playing. Nothing more."

"You don't approve?" he asked, interested in her reaction.

Her delicate brows puckered in thought. "You do not seem to mind their attention, so why should I?"

He smiled and shrugged his shoulders. "I don't know. Why don't you tell me?" Cameron could see the confusion starting to sneak into those damn beautiful eyes of hers. "It did bother you, didn't it?"

"Yes, it did, Cameron Wade," she confessed, unable to lie.

Her admission created a great sense of satisfaction in him. "I'm glad it did."

"And why would you be glad?" she asked, now curious.

Cameron chuckled again, the sound deep and warm. "It does my ego good to know that a beautiful woman is jealous over me."

Her brows shot up in surprise. "I am jealous?"

It was so innocently put, but even more so was the astonished look on her face. He was enthralled. "Yes, I believe you were."

"Oh," was all she could say as she seemed to consider this new twist.

Another question popped into his mind and out of his mouth. "Am I strange and different to you, too?"

"Yes, you are."

At least she didn't hold back. "But you're not a child at play. You're a woman."

"Yes, I am."

He grinned and laugh wrinkles appeared at the corners of his eyes. "That, you are."

Silence descended between them like a wall, neither able to scale its height or to break through it. So they just stood, entranced by each other's stare.

When the old woman tugged at Ghost Dancer's sleeve, both turned to her. She smiled shyly and only chanced a quick look at Cameron. She handed a small object to Ghost Dancer then, as quickly as she had appeared, she disappeared.

Ghost Dancer looked at the delicately quilled wrist band, and touched it lovingly.

"What's that?"

Her misted gaze moved back to him and she smiled. "A gift."

"It's very beautiful. Is it a special occasion or something? You're birthday, maybe?"

"No." Her smile grew larger and more brilliant. "It is just a gift."

"Do they give you gifts often?"

"Yes. I have told them it is not necessary, but it pleases them to do so."

Cameron thought about what she said. "They seem to love you very much."

"As I love them."

A sudden feeling of wrongness claimed him fiercely, and he had to turn away from that special glow on her face. How could she love the very people who had taken her captive? "It's all so strange," he said more to himself than to her.

"Why is it strange?"

He looked back at her, the sunlight making her hair look alive with golden sparkles. "You being here. The way you are treated. It's all wrong."

"It is wrong to be loved by your people?"

Now, he was angry and he wasn't even certain why. "These are *not* your people. It's wrong for you to be here. You just don't fit."

The high color that tinted her cheeks told Cameron of her reaction, even before she spoke. "I am where I belong. It is something that I know. It is something you do not understand, so you must not say such things."

"What is there to understand? You're a white woman living among the Sioux. It's wrong. Plain and simple."

"I *am*," she stated quite firmly, "the Ghost Dancer. It is the way it *must* be." She turned and walked away.

Cameron instantly felt ashamed of himself. He was pushing this on her too fast. "Angel," he called, then started after her. "Please stop."

She did.

"I'm sorry. I had no call to do that. I apologize."

"You seem to speak in anger, then must say you are sorry."

He was rightly feeling the fool. "What can I say? I'm hotheaded."

This brought a sudden smile. "I think I know what you are saying and I agree. You are hotheaded, Cameron Wade."

Cameron laughed again. "You are catching on quick, Angel. Real quick."

"Yes, I am."

Chapter 4

"How about a walk, Angelique?"

Ghost Dancer looked up from her work, and her eyes crinkled slightly at the corners when she smiled. "Do you feel strong enough?"

Cameron felt a warmth spread in his stomach at the beauty he saw. Her flawless, honey-colored skin covered her high cheekbones, tinted with the slightest hint of pink. Her small delicate nose turned up in perfection in the center of her heart-shaped face. Her eyes were large and almond-shaped, long lashes fringing them with the darkest brown-gold. Her luscious full lips, the shade of a dewy red rose, tempted him, and when they curved into a brilliant smile, he felt his heart succumb to her magic.

"I'm feeling better by the minute, and a walk with such a pretty lady just might work wonders on this poor, broken body." He returned her smile with a warm one of his own.

Angelique's laughter was soothing and Cameron had a sudden desire to hear it often.

"Then we should go for a walk," she agreed with

enthusiasm. "If only for the sake of your health."

It was a warm autumn day, but both seemed to enjoy the heat against their faces. Cameron drew long breaths of the fresh, clean air, having grown tired of lying in the darkness of the tepee. It was true, his strength was returning quite fast and, with Angelique's constant mothering, he knew it would not be long before he could ride again. Whatever she had used on his wounds was miraculous in its healing power. He would have to remember to ask her what it was.

His thoughts traveled to his return to Fort Laramie, and a new sensation grabbed him. A deep wanting filled him, and he hoped for time to stand still, to prolong his enjoyment with her. He wanted to know more about this woman called Ghost Dancer who quietly walked beside him, and logic told him that once he took her back to the fort, it would not be the same as it was now. Regret for what he knew he must do overwhelmed him, making him doubt, for just a second, his decision. Still, he confirmed his resolve. It was the right thing to do.

So many questions rambled through his mind. Yet he remained silent, keeping his thoughts to himself. The few times he had asked a question, especially about her, she had carefully side-stepped him. There was something else that held him back. On the one hand, he wanted to get to know her *very* well, yet on the other, he was afraid to know her *too* well.

"Cameron."

Her soft voice broke into his dangerous, often

confusing thoughts. "What is it, Angel?"

She stopped walking and focused her full attention on him. "Are you still in pain?"

Cameron had to turn away from the sultry eyes that made his blood pound hard within his veins, but even the concern laced in her sweet words made it difficult to concentrate on what she had asked. "No. I'm feeling much better."

Hesitant, yet unable to resist, Ghost Dancer reached up, and with gentle strokes rubbed the furrows from between his eyebrows. "Then why are you frowning so?"

Her touch nearly undid him. "I was just thinking about when I have to leave." He grasped her hand, filling his large one with her tiny slender one, the warmth of her flesh melting into his.

"And this made you sad?" she wondered out loud.

Cameron felt himself lost in her azure gaze, and he turned her palm to his lips, brushing them against the delicate inner flesh. "I suppose it did," he whispered softly, the tone saying more than the words. Purposely, he had not mentioned that he would be taking her with him, and that was what made him frown. His mind was certain that she would want to come, despite her denials, he couldn't think any other way. It was his heart that reacted, making him wonder, but he easily put all other feelings aside in the face of his overwhelming determination.

They seemed frozen in place, unable to move and not really wanting to. Suddenly, the spell was broken.

A child's giggle brought them both back to reality, and they found themselves the center of attention as many children gathered around them.

"Chontohgnahkah," chanted one little girl, and the others joined in, quick and eager. *"Chontohgnahkah. Chontohgnahkah."*

Cameron's smile grew big, and he asked, "What are they saying?"

Ghost Dancer blushed clear to her toes and looked away from his probing eyes. *"Chontohgnahkah* means love." She shooed them away, their cries of laughter trailing behind them as they scattered. "They mean no harm."

"Of course not," he agreed. "They're only children."

"Perhaps we had best go back. You look tired."

If the truth be known, he wasn't. The mention of love had shaken him to his very core. He turned toward her tepee and mutely walked beside her. How could one little word shatter him so totally? Even more, how was it that one little word could make him wonder if that was what was happening to him?

No, he answered his own question. *Not me.*

This thought brought on a flurry of memories. Some happy, too many sad. Hadn't he promised himself that if he chose Army life he would never marry? Hadn't he broken his mother's heart to follow in his father's footsteps, just as his older brothers had? The Army. It seemed to be the choice of the men in his family. Only his mother, Clarissa, had never known that dedication.

He had known Clarissa wanted him to stay in

Boston, but he couldn't. They had all left her, one by one, to follow their heart's longings. First, his father, unable to choose the sedate life of the rich. Then, as each son entered manhood, they joined their father. Cameron tried to please his mother and remained in Boston but this broke his spirit. Finally, her love for her son greater than her own loneliness and pain, Clarissa released Cameron and told him to go.

At that time, Cameron had vowed that if his career was to be in the Army, then he would serve alone. He would never marry and cause a woman such loneliness and pain. Only a year after he had joined up, Clarissa had passed away, and he had never quite forgiven himself for leaving her.

How odd, Cameron thought. After all these years, the grief over his mother's death was still so strong. Even the death of his father and two brothers in the Civil War did not hurt as much. Perhaps it was his guilt for having chosen the Army, just as his father had. If only he had known, if only. . . .

Cameron shook his head as if to free himself of the dogging memories. He could not change the past, but he could control the future. And that meant staying well away from Angelique. At least emotionally. He did not need any ties to the girl. It just wouldn't work.

"What am I to do?" Ghost Dancer asked as she gently stroked her horse's neck. "He is a white man and I cannot love him. It would be wrong."

She plainly spoke the answers, but her heart did not listen and she felt the pain of its dissention.

"My Ghost Horse," she sighed sadly. "You know your purpose in life, to be beside the Ghost Dancer. Until Cameron Wade came into my life, I knew without pause my own. Now, it is all so unclear. Even my dreams have given me no respite. They tell me nothing of this soldier I have brought back from the dead."

Ghost Dancer spoke no more, her mind heavy with the burden of who she was. She did not hear anyone approach, and when he spoke her name, she jumped, startled at his appearance. Especially when he was the very person her mind dwelled upon so intensely.

"I didn't mean to frighten you."

"I did not hear you," she whispered, still struggling to bring her jumbled emotions under control.

Cameron reached out and rubbed the animal's velvet muzzle. "He is a magnificent horse. Is he yours?"

She nodded. "He is the Ghost Horse."

Ghost Dancer was well aware of his efforts to keep the grin down to a polite smile.

"Ghost Horse?"

"I dreamed of the great white and my brother, Red Bear, found him for me and brought him back to me. He is most devoted."

Cameron moved on to another topic. "It must have taken your brother a long time to break him."

She saw the admiring gleam in his eye, his appreciation of fine horseflesh clearly written on his handsome face. "There was no need. The

Ghost Horse allows me to ride him but no other. As it should be."

His look bespoke his disbelief but all he said was, "Where is your brother now?"

"My brother and many others are on a hunt. They will return when they have found the buffalo."

"Oh."

A strained silence descended upon them, neither seeming to find anything else to talk about. Unable to bear it any longer, Ghost Dancer said simply, "Good night, Cameron Wade."

"Good night, Angel."

Cameron lay awake that night, too aware of the woman who slept only a few feet from him. He was letting Angelique get to him, and he knew he shouldn't. He was curious about her, and that was normal. After all, there was something really mysterious, almost bordering on strange, about Angelique—Ghost Dancer. The whole tribe treated her with utmost respect, to the point of placing her on a pedestal. Somehow, he had a feeling that it had little to do with her being the daughter of a chief. Yet there was an immense love among them, love given to her so unselfishly, so pure in its meaning. In turn, Ghost Dancer's love for these people bound her to them, an invisible tie that seemed unbreakable. Cameron felt as if there was something about her that he didn't know, something that only the Indians understood.

Then there were the emotions that were building inside him, like an engine gathering steam.

His very first sight of her had prompted passion within him, and with each day that passed, it grew. The more he knew of her, the more he wanted her. As he thought about this, Cameron realized something quite shocking. He could no longer deny that his feelings were running much deeper than just physical attraction. Yes, he desired her. What man wouldn't? It was something else that was weaving its way firmly into his tapestry of feelings. How could he grow so fond of someone so quickly?

Well, he thought to himself, *I'll forget her just as quickly when we get back to the fort.* He would see to it that she was deposited at the right doorstep. The Baptist Church in Laramie would probably take her in, maybe even locate some of her family. Once she was out of his sight, she would be out of his mind. He was sure of it.

His plans made, Cameron tried to sleep, but couldn't. His shoulder ached and his mind played games with his will. Back and forth, his emotions warred, leaving him frustrated. Finally, he rose and stood by the fire.

Quite involuntarily, he found himself staring at the woman sleeping a few feet away, the one who was keeping him awake, and his thoughts settled on a single, very prominent feeling. Desire. It began to flutter inside him like a butterfly crawling from its cocoon, until it was larger than life and nearly out of control.

Cameron took a step forward, his hand reaching out to touch the tempting smoothness of her cheek. A low growl sounded from Wolfdog who lay snuggled at her side. His eyes were still closed, as if asleep, but his warning was all too clear.

Taking heed, Cameron moved away in silence, once again seeking some rest.

"Are you all right?"

Cameron's deep voice penetrated Ghost Dancer's sleep, and her eyes opened to meet his, filled with concern. She sat up.

Again, the sensuous sound came, bringing her further back to reality and leaving the nightmare behind. "You must have been dreaming."

She nodded, but still she did not speak. He remained a respectful distance from her, his gaze never leaving her. The covering of furs had slipped from her body and lay about her waist. Her breasts were bared to his heated gaze, even though the shadowy darkness allowed him only a hint of her nakedness. But it was enough to tease his already barely controlled passion for her rare beauty.

She could hear the sharp intake of his breath, but she still said nothing. A wet nose nuzzled beneath her hand, and Ghost Dancer unconsciously stroked her pet, her loving movement reassuring Wolfdog. When Cameron stepped forward this time, the animal did not growl, feeling no alarm from his mistress.

"You are so beautiful."

A chill washed over her, robbing her of her breath. She closed her eyes against the image of this man, his tall, lean body reflected so vividly in the fire's ashen glow. When his hand touched her face, Ghost Dancer felt a sudden weakness and trembled. Slowly, she raised her eyelids and instantly met his bold stare that sparked like lightning in the ebony sky.

Finally, it was Cameron who looked away. "I'm finding it extremely difficult to act the gentleman, Angel." He brought his attention back to her. "And it doesn't help when you are so innocently tempting."

There was little modesty among the Indians, but somehow, Ghost Dancer understood his meaning and shyly covered herself. "Forgive me," she whispered. "Our ways are so different. I did not think."

Cameron instantly felt bad at making her uncomfortable. "No, it's my fault. I am a guest in your home, I should be stronger."

"You are very strong, Cameron Wade. And sometimes . . ." Ghost Dancer paused, her confusion apparent. "Sometimes I wish that you were weak."

Without further confession, she lay down and turned her back to him, ending the conversation. When she heard him return to his own bed, she allowed the tears to fall.

Chapter 5

The meadow grass was knee high, and the wild flowers were sprinkled among the green, the splashes of yellow and purple a picture of perfection. They had emerged only moments before from the dark interior of the forest where the spruce and fir trees were so thick the light did not reach the damp, needle-covered floor. Within view was a huge grove of cottonwood, birch, and willow, touches of yellow among the green, a stream meandering nearby.

As Cameron and Ghost Dancer walked, they nibbled the wild berries they had gathered, those spared by foraging bears. Even farther beyond lay the granite mountains, jagged crags rising in splendor and beauty. The tall, gray peaks were framed by the bright blue of the sky. Puffy, white clouds hid the highest points, as if in passing the cottony billows had been snagged by the stony fingers.

"It's beautiful." Cameron stopped to look around him, then took her hand into his before continuing. "Do you come here often?"

"Yes," she said, smiling. It pleased her that he liked this place, but even more, she felt excitement quiver inside her at his warm touch. "It is a special place. I come here often when I feel the need to be alone."

Again, he paused in their journey, his brows furrowing together in concern. "You come here alone?"

"Of course. Is it not proper?"

"No . . . I mean yes. What I mean to say is that it is not safe for you to wander about alone."

Ghost Dancer was confused. "Not safe. In what way?"

Cameron's arm swept out in a wide circle, emphasizing his words. "It's dangerous. There are wild animals in these forests and then there's the chance that you could run across some Cheyenne warriors. I did."

Again, she felt pleasure, this time at his honest concern. "But I do not fear the animals or the Cheyenne."

"They could still do you harm." His expression became extremely serious. "Why does your family give you so much freedom? You even live in your own tepee. I thought daughters stayed with their families until they married. Yet you live alone. Why?"

"I live alone because I am the Ghost Dancer. It is also the reason that my family does not fear for me." She hoped that her answers would appease him, but guessed that they would not.

"I sure as hell don't know what that means!"

Cameron appeared so distraught that Ghost

Dancer took pity on him and tried another, simpler explanation. "It means, that in the future, I will be more careful."

"I wouldn't like it if something were to happen to you, Angel."

With loving tenderness, his hand cupped her chin, tilting her face up to him. Ghost Dancer felt the heat in his eyes, like a smoldering fire burning its way over her warm cheeks, stopping only when it arrived at her lips. His fingers moved to touch their softness, the tips running over the rosy flesh. She continued to watch as he lowered his head and his lips claimed hers. Her eyes fluttered closed, and he pulled her to his hard, muscled body.

Ghost Dancer offered the sweetness he sought, and Cameron accepted it freely. She felt the warmth inside her burst into a burning flame, sweeping through her body like wildfire. It consumed her like dry kindling thrust into an orange-and-blue blaze. She had never felt her heart beat so hard or so fast, and feeling fear, Ghost Dancer pulled away.

"Angel?" Cameron muttered when she withdrew so quickly from his arms.

Like a child, she ran from him. At first, just to clear her mind, then with the mischievous intent to tease him.

Cameron pursued her, close on her heels. Then he stopped his chase to call to her. "Are you playing games with me?"

Ghost Dancer stopped, too, and turned back to him, her laughter dying in the air. Uncertain, she bit her lower lip and considered what she was doing. "Children play at games."

"Yes, they do. They play tag, the same as we are." Then he grinned widely, a devilish glint sparking in the depths of his eyes. "But when I catch you, I guarantee it will no longer be child's play. Be warned, Angelique."

She understood all too well his meaning and felt her knees weaken. With an unusual boldness, she returned his broad smile. "Then catch me if you can."

In a flash, she was off, running through the meadow with the grace of a deer, her peals of laughter like a melody, leading Cameron to her. But when she turned back, she could not find him in the gently swaying green carpet.

"Cameron," she called, moving back to where she had last seen him. "Cameron."

Suddenly, he was there, like a giant rising from the sea, stealing her into his arms before she could turn and flee. Ghost Dancer screamed from surprise and from pleasure as he pulled her down into the bed of wild flowers, their perfume heavy in the air.

"Got you," he whispered, gazing into her wide eyes, his hand brushing the stray hair from her face. "You're mine, Angelique. All mine."

Cameron's lips covered hers once again, more urgent than before, taking and devouring the treasure that he had captured. His tongue flicked over the full, delicious line of her lips, then plunged farther to explore the delight within. One hand moved over her hip and down the length of her long, muscled leg, while the other cradled her head, his fingers lost in the mass of pale, golden curls.

With agonizing slowness, he moved to her throat, his lips discovering the curve where her neck met her shoulder. He nibbled and nipped, knowing the havoc he created inside her already trembling body. He could feel her heart beating wildly, but this time he saw no fear. A deep wanting claimed him with a fierceness he could no longer deny, for it was urgent and extremely powerful.

Cameron pulled back and caught her passion-filled eyes with his own gaze. "If you want this to go no further, say so now. One more kiss, Angel, and I'm lost. Then there will be no turning back."

Ghost Dancer knew she was shaking, but wasn't certain if it was from doubt or anticipation. Her mouth seemed dry, as if his kiss had robbed her of its moisture. More than anything, she wanted to feel his lips once again. More than anything she wanted. . . .

Wolfdog pounced onto Cameron's back, his howls of delight filling the silence. Playfully, he tugged at Cameron's trouser leg, growling in a non-menacing manner.

The look on Cameron's face caused Ghost Dancer to burst into laughter, building until tears were streaming down her face.

Finally, maintaining some semblance of control, she sat up to watch and between giggles said, "He likes you."

Cameron scowled. "Lucky me."

As always, she took his words to heart. "He does not normally like people, except for me. He abides them, but has no true affection for humans. You *are* lucky."

As always, her smile melted away all doubts, all questions, and only the loveliness of her face mattered to him. It amazed him how she could turn his sarcasm into a positive comment, but then, that was one of the things he loved about her. "Then why does he stay with you if he doesn't like people much?" Cautiously, he roughhoused with the wolf, careful to keep his fingers safe.

Ghost Dancer shrugged as she looked at her pet a long while. "I do not know. He comes and goes as he pleases. He will leave for days, sometimes weeks, but he always returns to me. Perhaps he longs for the affection I give him." With that last comment, she patted Wolfdog fondly on his head. Content now, he took off, chasing a butterfly like an overgrown puppy.

Cameron gave her a perplexing look, no longer interested in the animal's actions. "And what of the affections that I long for?"

Blushing, she turned away, the heat still churning inside her. No words would come.

Feeling awkward, Cameron stood and added, "It was an unfair question. Forget I asked it."

Ghost Dancer wanted to forget, still, she knew the answers must be found. Not only for his sake, but also for her own.

All the way back to the village Cameron berated himself, each step drawing him closer to his own conclusions. He had come close, too damn close, to taking her in the meadow.

Have you lost your mind? He'd asked this of himself before. But now the question was more urgent. Certainly, it would be the most foolish, rash thing he could do to make love to Angelique. He'd be leaving soon and didn't need any ties to this woman he planned on returning to civilization.

For heaven's sake, his mind chided, *she's a virgin! That's obvious.*

Yet, with clarity, he recalled her passionate response and the willingness he saw so plainly in her eyes. Doubt began to nip with persistence at his resolve.

No, he continued to argue with himself, standing firm in his decision, *I would still be wrong. Even if there was no resistance, it would be wrong. It would be wrong. . . .*

I will be strong, he promised himself.

"I must rub some more ointment into your cuts."

Cameron's self-imposed lecture abruptly ended at the sound of her soft voice. His gaze met hers, his immediate thoughts contrary to the ones of only a second before. He shook his head to control his wayward feelings.

"No?" Ghost Dancer asked at the movement of his head.

"Yes." Then seeing the confusion in her eyes, he added, "Yes, you can put some more medicine on my wounds."

"Oh," she mumbled, somewhat shaken from

what had happened in the meadow. Timidly, she sat down beside him, her bowl of ointment in her hand. "You must take off your shirt."

Cameron shifted and did as she asked. "Of course."

Ghost Dancer closed her eyes for a brief moment, willing the tremor in her belly to go away and the sweating of her palms to cease. When she opened them again, he was watching her, his eyes the color of the grassy meadow, the sparkle that lay within their depths like a sprinkle of wild flowers. Her mouth became dry and she licked her lips nervously. A strong blush heated her face as she started to work the salve into his lacerations with her trembling hands.

It would be wrong, repeated Cameron over and over to himself. Her touch became torture, not to his injuries—the cream she applied was quite soothing—but to his emotions, and even more so, to his body. The passion was there, like a bear awakening from its winter's sleep to an overwhelming hunger. So was his lust for her.

Yet, with extreme determination and control, he maintained some semblance of calm. It was the hardest thing he had ever done, but he kept his promise in mind.

Ghost Dancer finished and stood, needing to get away from him, his nearness destroying her self-control. In her haste, she stumbled over his feet and he caught her in his strong arms before she fell.

As if she had landed in a bed of hot coals, Ghost Dancer jumped up and scrambled away. "I . . . I am sorry. I can be so clumsy." Embarrassment flooded through her, bringing her near tears.

"It's all right, Angelique." He sensed her dismay, knowing it had absolutely nothing to do with her clumsiness.

"No," she whispered. "I can do nothing right."

Cameron stood and crossed to her, his finger running over the pink tint of her cheek. "No, Angel. You do everything right. That's the problem."

He left the tepee, giving her the time she needed to collect herself and him a moment to cool the heat that scorched him inside.

Cameron felt the emptiness of the tepee, wondering where Angelique had gone. Unable to bear it any longer, he went in search of her special warmth, desire deep inside him urging his step to quicken. He didn't want to take time to consider what he was doing and why. All he wanted was her company.

"Nothing wrong with that," he mumbled, making excuses to himself as his mind scurried over the real issue. "Nothing at all."

Reassured that he was right, he carried on his search for the woman he'd been thinking of. When he found her, she was sitting in the shade of a giant oak, its limbs stretching out in a protective umbrella of greenery. Her head was resting against the wide trunk, and her eyes were closed. In her arms she cradled a baby, and her lap was filled with a sleeping toddler's head. The sweetness of her voice carried to him, the gentleness so soothing he stopped dead in his tracks.

The childish chanting he had heard before was just that, and what he heard now was pure heaven. It set off a small alarm in his heart.

He should leave. Right now. Before it was too late. But he didn't move. He just continued to stare, like a lovesick fool, soaking in each honeyed note that fell from her lips.

Suddenly, he knew why he was so drawn to this woman. It was the love and caring she had for these people. This thought ran headlong into his belief that she was living in the wrong world. Even more surprising was that Cameron admired her determination to stay. He didn't understand it, but he did admire it. Never had he met a woman with such purpose, and she never seemed to doubt her life at all. Not even in the face of his own determination to take her away. She never questioned being here among the Nahhe Lahkota. Why? This ate at him, twisting his mind and his already confused emotions.

She seemed guided by a strong sense of honor and duty, just as he was. Cameron's father and brothers had given their lives for those same beliefs as would Cameron, if need be. Was Angelique—Ghost Dancer—as driven by the love for her people? Of course not, he decided quickly. This was mad! How could he possibly consider thinking such a thing? Even worse, how could he even consider the question's answer?

When the chanting stopped, Cameron lifted his eyes to Angelique, quieting his wandering thoughts. She was looking at him now, and the fire started anew. He moved closer to her, anxious for her companionship.

"I missed you."

This brought a smile to her full lips and he felt as if he'd been rewarded. Then a sudden feeling of foolishness overwhelmed him, stealing away his pleasure. Why had he said that?

"Do you want to sit?"

"Yeah." He stretched out on the grass next to her. "Who are your friends?"

An even wider smile brightened her face, a proud smile. "These are my brother's children. They are most precious."

"You love children, don't you?"

"Of course. They are *Wakan Tanka's* greatest blessing. I hope to have many someday."

The radiant glow that shone on her face showed Cameron her heart, and, again, he felt a strangeness touch him. "Why haven't you married?" Another question he regretted with all his being.

"I . . ." Angelique seemed to have difficulty finding the answer and then finally gave up. "I do not know. I would suppose it is because I do not love any man enough to be his wife."

Cameron did not like this subject of conversation, but could not keep silent. And, after all, he had started it. "I would think all the men of your tribe would be lined up for your affections."

A petal-pink blush caressed the silk of her cheeks, drawing his eyes, and awakening a longing to touch them. Her long fingers gently stroked the baby's head and Cameron found himself wishing they were entwined in his own hair.

Ghost Dancer found her voice and whispered, "The men who stand in line, Cameron Wade, do not hold my interest."

"And what of me, Angel?"

She did not answer.

Cameron could see the distress this created. "You don't know, do you?"

"No," she admitted. "I do not know what it is I feel for you. Only that you frighten me."

"Now, why on earth would I frighten you?" he asked, surprised.

Ghost Dancer glanced away. "Because you have confused me, and I do know that I care too strongly for you."

He reached out and touched the very cheek he had admired only a few moments before. "Is that so bad?"

"Yes." Ghost Dancer pulled away from him. "Yes, it is. You are not of the Sioux."

"But I am the same as you," he argued despite his wish not to.

"No. Our skin is the same, but our hearts are not. You do not understand me or my people and it is wrong that I care for you."

Cameron found himself wanting to convince her that she was wrong. Yet common sense halted him, keeping him from pursuing the subject further, except for one more question that he could not control. "Why do you care?"

"Why?"

"Yes, Angel. Why do you care if it's so damned wrong?"

She gave this her full concentration. "I like your

ways. You are strong, yet in your heart I see a great kindness. I do not see the hatred in your eyes when you look upon my people. When you saw these children, I saw only the gentleness within your soul. And, most of all, when you look at me, you do not see the Ghost Dancer, but a woman, and I feel warm inside."

Now he wished fervently that he hadn't asked.

Chapter 6

A dingy shaft of light filtered through the small opening in the door, glinting off the smooth steel of the knife. Death moved in silence, the razor-sharp edge finding its mark quickly, efficiently.

Ghost Dancer came awake, instantly alert to the sounds around her. From a distance a lone wolf's low howl touched her soul with its song. Her pet had gone to be with his own; perhaps he was the one who called to her in the night. As sleep worked its way from her mind, she recalled the dream she had just had, and fear and sadness quickly replaced her slumbering thoughts. Visions danced before her mind's eye, vividly portraying the images of her nightmare. She had seen her old friend, Sam Smith—and he was dead. She had felt danger days before, and her premonition now confirmed its truth. But she was confused by what she saw. The four-fingered man was somehow involved. Since she was a child, she had dreamed of him. She had never seen his face clearly, only his eyes, their wicked blackness frightening in their strength and power. The man presented danger at its most horrifying. This Ghost Dancer knew.

Some other feeling drew her from her bed, and she quickly pulled on her doehide dress, careful not to disturb Cameron as he slept. Within minutes, she was on her great white horse and headed toward the old miner's cabin. For years he had lived in the hills with the Ghost Sioux, digging in the earth for the yellow stones.

Black Hawk had liked him and saw no harm in his work. So the tribe had left him alone, leaving him to his lonely existence in the dark caverns of the granite mountains. Now Ghost Dancer was positive that something awful had happened to him, and she felt the grief pulling at her heart as the tears filled her eyes. She, too, had liked him, and would miss his odd ways.

She had gone only a short distance from the village when she heard the call of her wolf, and paused long enough for him to appear from the shadows of the trees. When she urged her mount forward, Wolfdog followed obediently behind, content to be with his mistress in the ebony night, the time of the wolf.

She traveled on and stopped only a brief moment to experience the short time when the sun and the moon shared the heavens. Ghost Dancer watched the splendor of the sunrise, its glory and strength shared by her spirit. The blackness began to glow with the brilliant red of the sun, chasing away the darkness and setting afire the world. She could feel the warmth and light it brought with its dawning. The moon began to fade into the distance as its counterpart gained momentum, and eventually the symbol of the night disappeared from the pinkened sky.

Cameron followed Ghost Dancer as she rode, grateful that the moon had provided enough light for him to keep her in sight. Now, as the day lightened, he knew he would not lose her. What had made her take off in the middle of the night? That she had done so without even considering the danger angered him beyond measure.

"Damn woman," he grumbled, sorely put out by her odd behavior.

When she arrived at Sam Smith's old cabin, he was really confused. He rode up and dismounted, then went inside where she stood.

"What are you doing here, Angelique?"

With anguish, she faced him. "He is dead."

"Yes," said Cameron softly, suddenly feeling uneasy about this whole thing. "He was found dead over a week ago. That's what brought me here to begin with. I'm surprised that the fort hasn't sent out someone to find me."

Ghost Dancer moved to touch a book that lay upon the dust-covered table. "I sent word of your injury. They know you will return when you are able." Sadly, she picked it up and placed it among the other volumes that lined a crooked, board shelf.

Cameron looked around him, taking in all the clutter and mess. "I came all this way to see if the old codger had any family, but from the looks of things he had no one."

Ghost Dancer crossed the dusty floor to stand beside him. "No, he was alone in this world."

"You knew him?" he asked.

She nodded. "I have been coming to see him since I was a child."

Suddenly, Cameron knew the answer to one mystery. "Sam taught you English."

She nodded again.

Cameron tossed the old tin cup back onto the cluttered table and raked the dark hair from his eyes. He felt a frustration tugging at his heart. It was obvious the old man had nothing worth killing for.

"So why was he murdered?" mumbled Cameron to himself. He found no answers, only more questions. "What are you doing here, Angel? What on earth made you leave in the middle of the night?"

Cameron turned to her and waited for an answer.

"I felt a strange violence pull me here, the same as I felt before I found you. I had to come, if only to be near his spirit. Perhaps to better understand why he was killed."

Cameron's brows drew together in a frown of confusion. "I didn't say anything about *how* he died, Angelique. What do you know of this?"

"I know many things, perhaps even more than you." There was no cockiness in her statement, just truth expressed by her simple, straightforward words.

"What do you mean?"

Ghost Dancer sighed sadly. "I have seen his murder."

"That's impossible." Cameron felt his patience fleeing faster than he wanted. She could be so . . .

so mysterious. It was like pulling teeth to get straight answers from her. "He was killed at the fort, and you were here. It would be impossible for you to have seen him murdered."

"I did not say that I was there."

His hands flew up into the air in aggravation. "Then what is it you *are* saying?"

Ghost Dancer worried her lower lip. "I do not think you will understand. Perhaps it is best we do not go on with this conversation."

"Not a chance." His finger pointed at her, and his temper began to rise. "You started this, so finish it."

"You are angry," she stated, her lips pouting in sudden doubt and hurt.

"You're damn right I'm mad." It was true. He was losing control, something he did not do easily. Her calmness seemed to irritate him even further, and he had to resist the strong urge to shake the story from her. "Explain."

His commanding tone brought a slight flush to her cheeks, and she seemed to consider his order very carefully before she spoke.

"As you wish."

Cameron felt a small victory and waited in silence for her to continue.

"Four nights before I found you, I had a nightmare. I saw a man dead, and . . . I also saw the man who killed him. I knew it in my heart. Last night, I dreamed again. It was Sam."

Ghost Dancer was right. He did not understand. As a matter of fact, it struck him as humorous. "This is a joke?" he asked as a slow chuckle erupted from within his broad chest.

He watched as her eyes narrowed dangerously, and the pink blush on her face deepened to red. He should have taken heed.

"My visions are no joke, Cameron Wade."

"Visions?" This time he broke out into laughter. But when an object struck him directly on the head, he sobered in an instant.

"You think," she hissed, her own fury finally showing, "that because you do not believe it is a joke?"

Ghost Dancer moved closer, her steps denoting her mood. Her eyes became dark, and when she stood before him, her hands planted firmly on her hips, Cameron wondered at the woman he saw, so unlike the gentle angel he had mistakenly thought her to be.

"Angelique . . ." he began.

"I am Ghost Dancer."

She seemed so insistent that he gave in to her on that one point. "Ghost Dancer, everyone has dreams. Perhaps, somehow, you did have some sort of premonition. Women do, you know. But you honestly can't expect me to swallow this whole bit? Who is this man, and what makes you so sure he killed Sam?"

"It is something I know."

He stifled his laughter, but could not hold back his smile. "From your dreams?"

She nodded. "My visions last night showed me clearly the face of the dead man. It was Sam."

"I'm sorry, but it's not enough." Cameron expected another burst of anger, but none came.

Only pain lingered on her face.

"Was it not enough that I found you because of my dreams?" This seemed to grab Cameron's attention, so Ghost Dancer went on. "That first nightmare brought me here, to Sam's place. I waited several days, but he did not come. I feared the danger in my dreams was true. I wanted to go, but other dreams kept me here. They made no sense, but I felt a certain danger and a strong sense of death. Those feelings drew me to where you were. I did not know why until I saw you. Was that not enough?"

Cameron's look lost all humor. "You dreamed of me?"

"No. Not directly. I only felt the danger you were in." Then quietly she confessed her other thoughts. "Somehow, I believe that our futures are entwined, that this was all meant to be. Why else would our two worlds have been brought together?"

Cameron shifted uneasily. "I came to check out this shack, nothing more."

Ghost Dancer reached out to lay her palm upon his chest, the beat within quickening at her touch. "Sometimes the thoughts of our minds are not the reasons within our hearts."

"You speak nonsense," he whispered, his soul drawn into the dark blue pools.

"I speak the truth." Her voice was soft, deepening from emotion. "Can you deny the connection between us?"

"You're a beautiful woman, Angel, and I can't deny that I desire you. But there's nothing more, got that? Nothing." He felt like he had lied. But his mind only flitted over the possible reasons, the distraction of her closeness breaking his concentration.

She pulled her hand away and the warmth left Cameron, leaving only a cold emptiness to take its place. He felt a twinge of disappointment that she was giving in so easily.

"As you say," was all Ghost Dancer said, walking from the dingy shack and out into the bright light of day.

Reluctant, yet resigned that it was best this way, Cameron followed. "You know, sometimes you're a real pain in the ass, lady. And sometimes, mind you, a real strange one t' boot." He was pushing her, he knew it, but even anger was better than that hound-dog look of hers that made him feel like a heel.

She just ignored him, making him feel even worse. After she had mounted her great white, she turned sad, disappointed eyes to him. "You are afraid to speak the truth, Cameron."

"There is no truth to speak. There is no *we* to this whole thing. You're reading much more into this than there is."

"Do I frighten you?"

The question was so brusque that the word no came to his lips instantly, but it never surfaced. Instead, he gave serious thought to her question, his ego forgotten for the moment. "I suppose, in some ways, you do. You're a mystery to me, Angelique. A damn unbelievable mystery."

"If you believed," she began, nudging her mount forward, "there would be no fear."

Cameron opened his mouth to reply, but there was no sharp retort forthcoming, so he snapped it shut in aggravation, if not in self-pity. What did she mean by that? In his mind, there was nothing to believe. This vision nonsense was just that, nonsense. And he was much too intelligent a man to buy it.

Black Hawk and Cameron sat together in the shade of the tepee, an uneasy peace between them. Ghost Dancer had all but abandoned him with her father, and Cameron felt awkward, if not a bit nervous. In the silence, Cameron's mind buzzed with thoughts as he watched the people of the village go about their daily chores. In the week that had passed, he had observed the tribe and their ways, learning much of the Ghost Sioux. It all seemed so normal.

Funny, he thought, a touch of sadness underlining it, he had never considered anything about Indians to be normal. Indians had always been . . . well, Indians. Supposedly a savage breed, to some not even quite human, at least not in the same way as the white race was. But now, as he mulled all this over, they seemed much the same. Their way of life and their beliefs were still unlike anything he had ever known. Yet they loved, laughed, and labored just as he did, and, surprisingly, he found a definite appeal to it all. Cameron was at ease and he liked it here.

Even Black Hawk's distrust of him did not cause the reaction that Cameron would have expected from himself. Only a few days ago, he would have felt insulted and angry. But today, he felt saddened by the injustices done to such an honorable people.

Hadn't the Army, the very same institution he had devoted his life to, ridden into villages much like this one and massacred the Indians indiscriminately?

Suddenly, and for the first time in his life, Cameron doubted everything he had always believed in. Then, just as suddenly, he stopped himself.

How could he even think such a thing? His own father and brothers had given their lives for the Army. Cameron himself had disappointed his mother with this obsession that had possessed the Wade men. How could he betray their memory with such slanderous thoughts? Shame flooded him with such force it shook him mentally as well as physically.

"What weighs so heavily upon your mind, Cameron Wade?"

Black Hawk's question brought Cameron from his self-imposed torture. "Is it so obvious?"

The dark head nodded but he said nothing more, merely waiting for the younger man to speak.

"I've found my stay here very enlightening, Black Hawk. But, it has also been confusing, to say the least. I'm no longer sure which way's up and which way's down."

"If there is confusion"—the Indian chief looked directly at Cameron—"then you should seek the truth."

Cameron's question came out of nowhere, perhaps fed by the desire to know more about the Ghost Sioux and more specifically, Ghost Dancer. "What is the truth about Ghost Dancer?"

"There is more to my daughter than you can see with your eyes. You think that because she is white, as you are, that she does not belong among us. You must look with your heart, and you will see the truth."

Confusion clouded Cameron's thoughts. "Look with my heart?"

Black Hawk nodded again.

"Christ all mighty!" Cameron exploded. "I sure don't understand you people. Can't you ever just explain something clear and simple? Instead, you make a giant puzzle out of everything."

Black Hawk took sympathy on the young man, and his chiseled features softened slightly. "It is because you do not understand about Ghost Dancer."

"You're damn right I don't. So why don't you just start explaining it to me . . . clear and simple?"

Cameron could almost see the memories flickering in the back of Black Hawk's mind, as he recalled a time long ago. He did not prod, but waited for the chief to start Ghost Dancer's story. Strangely enough, he was excited.

Black Hawk began with the legend of the Ghost Dancer, then followed with what Cameron waited to hear. "It had been as my father had said. I was not to find Ghost Dancer until four winters had passed. We were following the buffalo when our hunting party saw the smoke. But we came upon the wagon train too late to save it from the Cheyennes' attack. All the men and women were dead—the children had most likely been taken hostage. The burnt remains were the only remembrance of the white families' lives."

Cameron felt a sadness lay heavily on his heart from Black Hawk's words. Still, he remained silent.

"Yet, among all the death and destruction was the girl child of Ghost Dancer's vision. As I rode closer, I could see she stood among the fire of a burning wagon and in her hands she held the pieces of a broken arrow. I knew then that I had found her."

Again, Black Hawk paused, the emotion of that remembrance making it difficult for him to speak. "Haunting blue eyes watched me approach, unfearing and wise. Then she reached out as if she had been waiting for me. From that first moment I took her into my arms, I have loved her as my own."

It was all so far-fetched and Cameron was bombarded with too many questions to be silent any longer. "You mean to tell me she remembers all that your father had learned in his lifetime?"

"Yes," Black Hawk confirmed. "The Ghost Dancer carries the wisdom of ages within her soul. She is much like my father, and his strength became her own. Yet, with as much knowledge as is passed on to her, she is still a human being and innocent in many things."

"Such as?" This was getting more and more unbelievable.

Black Hawk turned his wise gaze to Cameron. "Such as the ways of men."

Cameron felt a warming of his blood and became uneasy. He decided to change the subject. "What about these dreams she's spoken of?"

"It is the blessing of *Wakan Tanka*—the great mystery. It is how she protects the Nahhe Lahkota from danger. She foresees the future in her visions and once she has seen the future, it cannot be denied."

"So"—Cameron was trying to be patient and sort it all out—"if she says she knows who killed Sam Smith, I can count on it to be true?"

"It is the truth."

"This is crazy! No one can tell the future. That's for fortunetellers and mystics in carnival shows, and then it's all fake. I'm sorry, Black Hawk. It's just too much for me to believe that Angelique is an immortal spirit or something." Within the dark recesses of his mind, Cameron could not, perhaps would not, believe it, because he feared the truth of it.

Black Hawk hid his anger. White men could be such fools. "You are not of the Sioux. It cannot be expected."

Cameron's pace was fast, his long strides taking him within minutes from the busyness of the village to the rugged quietness of the river's bend. The wide spot seemed to slow the current, creating a pond in its elbow curve. As darkness neared, most of the Sioux were in the village and the banks were deserted. Cameron was grateful. He needed some time to himself. Time to sort out the thoughts that seemed to clutter his mind.

He could hear the gentle bubble of the current, and the birds chattering as they settled down to sleep. The sounds seemed to calm him.

What in heaven's name was he to do? Everyone knew that Indians believed in all this malarkey. But he was a grown man, a man of good sense, a man of wisdom. How could he be expected to think it was anything but nonsense?

Still, he felt a strange guilt.

Cameron had a sudden urge to bang his head against the trunk of the tree he was leaning against. Frustration began to build a strong foundation for other emotions to grow upon.

It was all nonsense!

Suddenly, he felt his words were a lie, a bold-faced lie. On and on his mind argued, back and forth, like a tug of war between children.

Still, he had reached no decisions nor was he any closer to understanding Ghost Dancer and who she was or what she was. Finally, Cameron decided it best to leave it for another day.

Again, he reconfirmed his notion that once he was gone, he would easily forget her. He turned to seek out Angelique's tepee, when something stopped him. A few feet off the grassy bank swam the very woman he'd been torturing himself over.

He wanted to leave her to the privacy of her bath, but, as hard as he tried, he could not force himself to move. Instead, he sat down on the soft, green knoll, the cottonwood casting him in its darkness and keeping him hidden from view.

Angelique—Ghost Dancer—disappeared beneath the crystalline water, only to appear several feet away, breaking the ripple-free surface. Her hair billowed out behind her in a fan of gold, the clear depths revealing only the shadow of her body just beneath. Again, she dove down into the pool, only this time, she did not reappear as she had before.

Concern crawled into Cameron's mind, and he moved closer to the river's edge. Then, slowly, her head emerged, only an arm's length in front of him. Her darkened eyes were barely visible above the smooth surface, their color the same blue-black as the water. She rose, inch by inch, revealing her nose, then her wet lips opened slightly so her tongue could lap up the droplets of moisture that clung to them.

Cameron could not breathe, or *would* not breathe for fear that she might disappear if he moved even the slightest bit. Finally, her chin was revealed to his gaze, then her long, sensuous neck and shoulders. She stopped, the water barely hiding the rounded cleavage of her breasts, the hint even more devastating than if her breasts had been bared.

The heat within Cameron was unbearable. He waited, but she did not move. An eternity passed, leaving him nearly shaking from the intensity of emotions that warred inside him. When he could take it no longer, he turned and left.

He kept the promise he had made to himself.

Ghost Dancer watched him go, her eyes showing her sadness. Her confusion was complete as her mind weighed disappointment against relief, twisting with the slight anger which lingered. She longed for the simplicity she had known only a short time ago. Yet, she realized, if given the choice, she would choose the unfamiliar feelings he so easily stirred inside her. Even if it meant confusion, anger, and hurt would be her constant companions.

Ghost Dancer sighed as she combed the wet knots from her hair; the delicate scent she had rubbed over her body danced lightly in the air. As hard as she tried, she could not put the argument of that morning from her mind. She felt saddened by Cameron's words and cutting laughter. Ghost Dancer could not expect him to believe easily, but to act as he had created much pain and unhappiness. She was not yet prepared to run the gamut of her emotions which he was bringing forth in full force. Still, she would not flee from them.

Standing, she began to pace a tight path around the fire, her mind trying to sort out everything. If she were to face the truth, she would have to admit that she was in love with him. The emotions within her were too strong to forget or to put aside. She stopped and returned to her pallet.

Wolfdog raised his head and his golden eyes watched her movements closely. She rested her hand on the animal's large head, her fingers working into the thick fur to provoke a contented smile on his face.

Ghost Dancer loved Cameron, and he was not of the Sioux.

This knowledge created guilt and distress, mixing uneasily with the gentleness of her new-found love. In the morning he would be leaving to return to the Army post. Deep within her, she harbored a fear of this, her mind warring against her heart. Centuries of tradition clashed with her newly discovered feelings, arousing doubt and anxiety. Still, the love that grew within her heart and soul was strong, pushing her apprehensions from her mind.

She knew what she must do. She must touch his spirit with her own. Their hearts must beat as one, if only for this one night. She would give of her flesh, of her blood, and of her tears. It was the way of the Ghost Sioux.

Cameron watched Ghost Dancer intently. He found himself drawn to her even more since his talk with Black Hawk, his eyes watching her as she moved about the tepee. He really couldn't take it all seriously, but there was something about her. It was clear she was different from other women, and he wasn't just considering her Indian upbringing. It was something else . . . something that went much deeper.

Ghost Dancer had said nothing when he entered the tent, and he figured she was still mad at him. Cameron tried to pretend it didn't matter, telling himself it was best this way. *After all, I'm leaving in the morning and once she's off my hands, I'll never see her again.*

This thought made him extremely uneasy, and it downright scared him to think that maybe, just maybe, it did matter. A whole lot.

No, he argued with himself, denial a more secure route of reasoning. Yet way in the back of his mind lurked the stark, untold truth. But with great determination, he kept it from surfacing. It was easier this way. No commitments, no emotions cluttering up his life.

Ghost Dancer sprinkled a generous amount of dried leaves into the orange-blue flames of the fire and within seconds the whole tepee was scented with the heady perfume. She lifted her head so that their eyes met, pulling him into the ardent depths of her own. Slowly, sensuously, she moved toward him, her look causing his heart to beat wildly.

Cameron caught his breath at the intensity he read in her eyes and his heart nearly stopped when her doeskin dress fell unheeded to the floor. She stood naked before his heated gaze in a provocative display of beauty. The flames within him burst, spreading through his body like hot ashes on the wind.

The firelight danced about her in shadows of dark and light, sliding over her subtle curves, bathing her creamy skin in gold. It drew out the silver highlights of her hair, and with each step she took, it swished about her bare hips, forming a cape about her shoulders. Her sweet, red lips were parted as her breathing quickened. Her tongue darted out to wet their sudden dryness, and her innocent gesture nearly destroyed Cameron's reserve.

Too easily he was consumed with a driving need for her, the hardness beneath the fur cover evidence of his desire. He could hear the beat of his own heart, loud and constant in his ears. Like a dream, she came to him, her hands reaching out to touch him. The softest of skin slid over the roughness of his chest, her slender fingers mingling with the thick covering of hair. She drew closer, lingering over him in taunting beauty. The scent of her filled him, drawing him further into her world of passion. Her silky hair fell on him, tickling his sensitive flesh. He could no longer resist the temptation to wrap its golden length around his hand, pulling her down to him, inching her full, voluptuous lips to his own. All earlier promises were forgotten, leaving only the promise of the pleasure to come.

How he ached for her, every inch of his body on fire. His nights had been filled with dreams of Angelique, and now she was next to him, his to take . . . his to enjoy. He tasted her mouth, taking of her sweet offering, demanding its juicy plunder. Cameron felt the fullness of her breasts against him, flesh against flesh, and like a brand they seared his body, creating a trail of wildfire.

With deliberate slowness, Angelique lowered her body onto his, the covers pulled away to expose his full length. Cameron felt a warm flush wash as the tender skin of her stomach united with his, then her softness caressed his hardness as she lay atop him. He felt himself trembling with anticipation. He had never known such ecstacy before and, somehow, knew he would never know its likes with any other woman.

Cameron's hands explored her curves, lingering over the roundness of her buttocks. His kiss moved from her luscious mouth to her neck, then lowered to capture the fullness of her breast. As he suckled, the pinkened nipple became hard and firm within his mouth, her squirming with delight creating other sensations within his body. When he lifted his head to watch her, he could plainly see the desire that glazed her eyes, darkened by passion's fire. Her hips moved against him, as nature began to guide her in its love song.

Never before had an innocent seduced him so expertly, and never before had he felt such pleasure. Sensing the urgency growing within Angelique, he carefully lifted her hips so she could guide him within her at her own ease. Without hesitation, she did so. The pain his entrance created seemed to send her further beyond control. Once he was fully inside her wet warmth, she began to move, slow and easy at first, building as the sensation within them grew.

Their passion created a euphoric plateau as Cameron and Ghost Dancer rose together, each giving, each receiving love. The ancient dance was performed, the moment of supreme savageness arising within them, tamed only by the sharing of their hearts and the love nestled tenderly within. Cameron felt his release at the same instant Ghost Dancer found hers.

Subtly, without his knowledge, she touched his soul with hers and their hearts began to beat as one.

Ghost Dancer watched Cameron saddle his horse, cinching the straps tight and secure. When he turned back to her, she felt her stomach tighten as he gazed deep into her eyes.

"Come with me, Angelique." His words were the softest of whispers, his tone sad, mirrored by the look in his eyes.

"I cannot go. This is my home." To deny him was the hardest thing she had ever done.

Cameron was disappointed, he had wanted more than anything for her to come with him of her own accord. "Even after what we shared last night?"

A rosy blush colored Ghost Dancer's face and she looked down to the ground, unable to meet his gaze any longer. "I love you Cameron Wade but I cannot go."

"And I cannot stay any longer, Angel." He hesitated, then added, "Will you ride with me a way?"

She nodded, the sudden tightness of her throat preventing any words. Ghost Dancer accepted his offered hand and allowed him to pull her onto his horse and into the comfort of his arms. Soon, there would be no arms to hold her, and her eyes misted at that thought.

"I must go back now," Ghost Dancer said softly after they had traveled a great distance in silence.

He did not stop.

She turned to look up at his grim and stony face. "I must go now, Cameron."

Still, he did not draw his horse to a stop.

A small tremor went off inside her, and she wiggled against his strong hold. "Please, my Cameron. I must go. We must say good-bye."

"We aren't saying good-bye." His voice was pure steel. "Not yet anyway. I'm taking you home, where you belong."

The tiny warning grew into full-blown panic. "You cannot take me. I will not let you."

His grip tightened. "I *will* take you back. I'm bigger than you."

"No," Ghost Dancer cried out in agony. "No! No!" she continued to scream, tears blinding her as she struggled against his strength, causing them to fall from his mount. A terrible pain ripped at her heart and disappointment flooded her mind.

"Angel . . . please. Listen to me. It's for the best, I know it is."

With a yank, she was free of his iron grip and Ghost Dancer scrambled away. "You lie." She sobbed. "To yourself and to me."

"No, I swear. It's not right for you to stay here."

"And what I want," she demanded sadly, "means nothing to you?"

His hands came up, his shoulders shrugging in the same movement. "You can't possibly know what is best for you."

"Do not patronize me, Cameron Wade. I do know what is best. I am not a child and know better than you. I *am* the Ghost Dancer and I belong with the Ghost Sioux. I had hoped that you would respect that."

"Don't you"—he pointed that ever-accusing finger at her—"patronize me! You're a white woman living among Indians, and I'll be damned if that *is* right."

Ghost Dancer felt weak from emotion. "Please go," she whimpered. "Go."

"Not without you, I won't. I *am* going to rescue you, whether you like it or not!"

She heard the resolve in each word he spoke. "You have no choice, you must go without me." Never had she felt such agony of the heart.

"I can't," he insisted, taking a step toward her.

Wolfdog appeared from nowhere, blocking his way, his fangs bared in a protective stance. "You must," she repeated.

Cameron looked from the animal to her distraught face. "I'm only trying to help you. Can't you see that?"

"Yes," she agreed. "I do believe you are and I thank you for this."

"Hell!" Cameron whirled around and grabbed his horse's reins. With quick, jerky movements, he slammed into his saddle and turned one last time to Ghost Dancer. Sadness clung to him, rendering him almost helpless as his supportive anger slipped away. Finally, he said, "Perhaps we'll see each other again someday."

The strange smile that came to her lips made him shift uncomfortably.

"Perhaps," was all she said.

Ghost Dancer knew now what it was to love a man. When he rode away, she felt the pain of her heart breaking and her soul wept.

Chapter 7

Four fingers reached for her and fear pierced her soul.

Ghost Dancer's sleep was shattered just as the disfigured hand touched her, bringing her from its horror. Wolfdog's ears perked up at her quick movement, and he lifted his head to watch her closely.

"It's all right, boy," she whispered in answer to his silent question. Content, he laid back down and closed his golden eyes.

Images bombarded Ghost Dancer's mind as she hugged her knees to her chest. Her dreams of the four-fingered man had changed in the last week, and they had become more and more frequent. Almost nightly. She saw brief visions of fire and the ringing of a child's screams mixed with the war cries of men. She recalled the symbols of her people, yet she felt them to be a lie. Then there was the black-eyed man with the small finger missing from his right hand. His evil presence in her nightmare always brought the stifling feelings of death and destruction. They were too strong to ignore. He was near. This she knew and this she feared.

It was time to speak to her father.

When Ghost Dancer rose and left the tent, her faithful pet was by her side. At Black Hawk's dwelling, she paused and softly rattled the elk knocker to awaken her father and mother, then waited for them to beckon her inside.

"Wait here, Wolfdog."

He obeyed and stretched out by the tepee's flap.

"What has brought you here at so early an hour, Daughter?" Black Hawk asked pulling a skin tighter about him before moving to the fire. Wild Flower remained in their bed, leaving father and daughter to speak.

"I wanted to tell you of my dream."

Black Hawk placed two pieces of wood on the dying fire. Red flames rose casting a shadowy light about the tent, bathing them in its weak glow.

"What has been troubling you, my daughter?"

Ghost Dancer settled down on a buffalo-hide rug and told him of her recurring nightmare and of the four-fingered man. When she paused, Black Hawk did not speak, his silent conclusions much the same as her own.

"He is coming. I can feel it."

"Yes," he agreed. "It seems that your dreams are warning us of the danger he will bring. I will take care."

His assurance relieved her. "Then I will leave you to your sleep, Father. I am sorry to have disturbed you."

His smile was kind, and a loving tenderness filled his voice when he spoke. "To tell me of a dream never disturbs me. You, my daughter, are welcome at any hour."

Standing, Ghost Dancer gave her adopted father a quick hug, then turned to leave. "I have also dreamed of Red Bear."

"Has your dream told you when my son will return from his hunting?" The slightest note of humor touched the question.

Her smile widened at his attempt to tease her. "Soon, Father. Very soon."

Ghost Dancer disappeared through the tepee flap and she could hear the smallest of chuckles on the night air, followed by her mother's soft voice.

"Come to bed, Black Hawk. Morning will come soon enough."

As she returned to her own bed, Ghost Dancer felt the warm joy of family and never doubted that her adopted parents had given her as much love as her white parents would have. The color of her skin had never made a difference in Black Hawk's heart.

She felt the excitement even before she heard it. The cries of the children became shrill with glee, the sharp barks of the dogs persistent.

Without benefit of sight, Ghost Dancer knew that Red Bear was home. She headed toward the gathering crowd at the center of the village.

The hunt had been successful. The Indian ponies were burdened with fresh buffalo meat.

As Ghost Dancer neared, a path was respectfully made to clear her way to her brother.

"Welcome home, Red Bear. It looks as if you have sufficiently seen to our needs once again."

"Little sister"—he grinned from ear to ear—"I missed you." Red Bear slid off his horse, landing agilely on the ground beside her, then pulled her into his arms in a great bear hug. "I missed those blue eyes!"

Everyone crowded forward, some to greet their husbands, fathers, or sons, some just to be a part of the contagious happiness that always seemed to go along with the end of a hunt.

"Red Bear." Black Hawk greeted his son, pride showing in his eyes at the success of the young men's long journey. "It is good that you have returned to us safely."

Ghost Dancer stepped away from her father and brother, content to leave them to their stories of brave hunters and stubborn prey.

"Ghost Dancer," Red Bear called, stopping his sister.

Turning back, she waited for him to catch up to her. When he reached her, he stood for a moment, a puzzled look etched on his handsome features. "What is it, Red Bear?"

He shook his head. "Something is different."

"What do you mean?"

"You are different, little sister. Something has happened since I left."

Of course, the first thing to pop into her head was a vision of Cameron and that brought a dark blush to her face. Quickly, she turned away, avoiding his probing eyes. "I am the same."

He knew better. Reaching out, he ran a long finger over her cheek. "You cannot keep secrets from me, my dancer. I have not been gone so long that you would turn shy with me? I *know* there is a difference about you."

"My husband."

The appearance of Little Deer and their children saved Ghost Dancer from further explanations. When Red Bear turned his attention to his family, she took her chance and disappeared into her tepee. She felt guilty for dodging her brother, but she needed time to collect her thoughts. Something told her that he would not be pleased that she loved a white man. Red Bear would feel that a Sioux would be more deserving of the Ghost Dancer's love. One particular Sioux came to mind, and with that thought came guilt.

When she heard the scratching at her tent, she knew that he had followed. "Enter," she called, having nowhere else to run.

Red Bear's head showed through the skin flap and when she motioned for him to enter, he did so, his tall, muscled frame filling the tepee. Then behind him came Lone Wolf, his face clouded with emotion.

"Have I angered you?" her brother asked.

"No," she answered in a soft tone.

He walked to her pallet and plopped down onto the soft skins, his weariness showing for the first time. "Come, sit." He pointed to the spot beside him and then motioned for his friend to sit across from them. Lone Wolf did so, still saying nothing.

Ghost Dancer also sat, mostly because she knew Red Bear would not be put off. She said nothing, waiting for him to speak and casting a wary glance at Lone Wolf and his stony face.

"Little Deer tells me that you nursed a white soldier back from the dead."

Ghost Dancer heard the slight hint of worry, but it was true and she nodded.

A strange look came over his strong Indian features, a look that hovered on the edge of pain. His full lips stretched into a hard line and a muscle in his jaw moved unconsciously. "He stayed here? In your tent?"

Again she nodded. This time she caught Lone Wolf's sharp intake of breath and when she dared to look, she saw raw, unsheathed anger in his eyes.

"Our father said nothing?" Red Bear's question brought her gaze back to him.

She felt his concern and sighed. "Our father tries not to interfere in my private life."

A spark of indignant anger sprang into the dark spheres that stared at her. "It seems someone needs to watch over you. To do such a thing was foolish. What man from this village will want to marry you now?"

Ghost Dancer felt a flush run over her like a warm shower of water. Her heart began to beat faster and, for the second time in a very short period, she was angry. "There is no man in this village that I *want* to marry. You and Father cannot rule me or my life. There are greater things that guide me and you should not doubt the path I choose."

She knew her brother had referred to Lone Wolf. Hadn't he been matching them up since she was a child? She had special feelings for her brother's best friend, but they were too much the same as the love she had for Red Bear. Guilt suddenly overcame her, making her regret her anger and, even more, her hurtful words. She knew that Lone Wolf loved her and his offers of marriage had confirmed it. He was a good man, and she should be honored to be his wife. Yet she had turned him down. Her excuse now rambled across her confused thoughts.

I have had no dreams to tell me that Lone Wolf is my future. I must wait until they tell me which path I am to take.

Then she recalled Cameron's face, his eyes filled with passion as he pulled her down to him. No visions had prompted her to his bed, only her own love and desire.

"I cannot believe that you would betray your people with a white man. What has possessed you, my dancer?"

Reaching out, she placed her hands on each of his smooth-skinned cheeks in a loving manner. "I have not betrayed my people. I would die before doing so."

"I know this," he whispered repentently.

Never before had Ghost Dancer lied, and as difficult as it was, she did. "He is gone, Red Bear.

But I know that Cameron Wade is my future, and I must follow my heart." She was careful to hide the doubts she was experiencing at her untrue words. It was best that her older brother not know of the fear that lurked within her heart.

Disappointment rang clear in Red Bear's words. "Your heart is weak, and you must ignore its calling. He is a white man, and he will only betray you, my sweet little sister. For all your powers, you cannot keep the hurt from destroying you. Cast him from you now, before it is too late."

"I . . . I cannot."

Lone Wolf stood, unable to contain himself any longer. "Have you had a vision of this man?"

His question was so direct it took her by surprise. She tried to form words, but they did not come.

He stepped forward, towering above her smaller frame, his height suddenly intimidating. He reached down and pulled her up, his touch gentle, but firm. His eyes were filled with pain and anger. "I must know, Ghost Dancer."

Tears came to her eyes and she felt her heart tighten with sorrow. "I . . ." How could she shame him with the truth? "I have seen Cameron Wade in my dreams, Lone Wolf. As I said, he is my future."

He reeled as if she had physically struck him.

"I am only a man, and you are the Ghost Dancer. I cannot compete against your dreams. I know this. But I, too, say he will only betray your love. He cannot know what it is to love the Ghost Dancer. I do."

With this, he left.

"You would be wise to go after him."

Red Bear's statement brought her mind from Lone Wolf's agony. "I cannot, my brother."

He stood. "You are a fool, my dancer."

Before she could say more, he ducked beneath the tent flap, leaving Ghost Dancer alone in the darkened tepee.

The sun was bright and it took a moment for Red Bear's eyes to adjust. His mind recalled the angry blush that had come to his sister's cheeks and the sparks that had lit her eyes, turning them into blue fire. He had been taken aback by her outburst. His sister had always been so quiet and shy, choosing to be by herself more than he liked.

During their youth, the other children were in awe of her, so he had been her only close friend. In a way, and only in his heart, he had wished she wasn't the Ghost Dancer. He had wanted her to be like the others. But that would never be, and sadly, he knew it.

His next thought took him to the stranger, a white man named Cameron Wade. He felt a stab of anger. To share his little sister with a man other than Lone Wolf did not settle well in his mind. His protective instincts prompted him to object, to interfere, and should this soldier come back, he would certainly do so. Confidence surged through him. Most likely they would never see Cameron Wade again. And he was confident Lone Wolf would get over his anger. After all, *she* was the Ghost Dancer.

* * *

Ghost Dancer could no longer hold back the tears. In despair, she turned her face up and lifted her arms to the heavens in prayer.

"*Wakan Tanka,* why are You forsaking me?"

"And what makes you think He has forsaken you, my daughter?"

Ghost Dancer looked at her mother standing just inside her door. Wild Flower moved to stand next to her adopted daughter, taking Ghost Dancer's hand in sympathy.

"I have prayed and He will not show me the answers," answered Ghost Dancer.

"Perhaps the answers you seek are within your own heart. What does it tell you?"

"In my heart," she whispered, "I feel a powerful love. A love that has brought me tremendous joy and the greatest of pain. It makes me do things I do not understand. It has made me keep the truth from Red Bear and Lone Wolf."

"You have allowed Lone Wolf to save his honor with your untruth, and as for your brother, well, sometimes it is best to appease him in this way. It is difficult for him to allow his sister to become a woman. Just as your father, he bears no trust of any white man."

"And what if I am wrong?"

Her mother smiled, a loving glimmer highlighting her ebony eyes. "You are the Ghost Dancer, my child, but you are also a human being. The Gods have given you the greatest blessing to carry within your heart. It would not be as precious a gift if you were given all of its secrets through your visions. I think they are allowing you the pleasure of discovery as a woman, not as the Ghost Dancer. Do not think it a curse, but accept it with delight and anticipation."

Wild Flower dried her tears and gave her a light kiss. "My daughter has grown into a woman. I, too, feel joy and pain."

"I love you, my mother."

"And I love you, my daughter."

Chapter 8

Jack Bender looked down from the hill just beyond the village, a sneer of distaste on his lips. Bender was well aware of the warriors, knowing that they had been close behind him since he had entered unceded Sioux territory. But they were of no concern to him.

"I should just bring in my men and kill them all. Every last filthy savage," he muttered.

A breeze stirred the dark hair that curled from beneath his hat, while the wide brim shaded his eyes from the sun's harshness. But he knew to kill them might bring unnecessary attention to this area and to the secret wealth it possessed. He didn't want that. For now, diplomacy was the route to take.

"Diplomacy," he almost laughed the word. It was something the Army worked at, yet seemed to fail at more often than not. The same Army that had taught him to kill so easily, without thought or conscience during the war. The same Army that had taken everything from him and given him nothing in return. He'd given over a dozen years of service, and now he would take what he wanted. No, what he needed. And certainly this small tribe wouldn't be much of a problem, even if they refused to cooperate.

His four fingers tightened around the leather reins, pulling his mount's head up and making the beast stir beneath him. Absently, he rubbed the side of his hand against the back of the other, the bump of his missing little finger a constant reminder of his deformity. An involuntary flinch screwed his face up and a sweat broke out on his upper lip. The missing finger was the only visible reminder of the torture he had endured at the hands of his Indian captors. The three days at their sadistic mercy had created deeper, hidden scars on his mind, constant reminders of his determination. Nothing would stop him from having what he wanted—nothing.

That thought prompted Bender to kick his spurred heels into his horse's side. It was time to tend to business. He glanced around when he approached the village. Soon, it would all be his. One way or the other, he would rid these dark hills of this tribe, the ones called the Nahhe Lahkota.

"Ghost Sioux." The words were spit out with contempt lacing each syllable. "You'd best be calling on that Ghost Dancer of yours, 'cause you're going to need your mystic to keep me from the gold."

His eyebrow quirked in amusement at his own words. A chuckle rumbled from deep within his broad chest, but his black eyes never lost the hard edge that glinted in their depths, making the smile that split his face a lie.

She heard it, like a word whispered on the winds that stirred the air. Its evil intensity touched her, and the hair on the back of her neck stood on end. Her movements ceased. She had heard laughter, but it held no humor.

Ghost Dancer stood and turned in the direction of her village. The roots she had been digging dropped to the ground forgotten.

He was here.

She began to run.

Jack Bender looked at the grim-faced chief and angrily pointed a finger in his direction. "You'd best be thinking my offer over, Black Hawk. It's a fair offer, and I'll not be denied what I want."

The threat hung in the air like a bad odor, and despite Bender's imposing height and muscled frame, Black Hawk seemed unaffected by him or his words. "You have my answer. It will not change with the passing of time."

Bender drew a deep breath, sucking in air with a hiss, much like the sounds of a snake ready to strike. Ebony eyes locked hard with brown ones, the clash of two strong-willed men in their depths.

"You don't want to cross me, Chief. It wouldn't be pleasant." Bender's attempt to be subtle disappeared and veiled threats became open ones.

"Whatever your desire in our land is, it will go unsatisfied. Return here and you will die. And I promise, it will not be a quick death, but a slow, painful one."

Black Hawk's statement was calm and even, but his rigid, cross-armed stance told of his own hostility.

His black eyes narrowed into dangerous slits, and a muscle twitched in Bender's jaw as his teeth ground together in aggravation and hatred. "You've been warned."

Black Hawk merely nodded and watched the big man swing up into his saddle. Bender whirled his horse and headed back in the direction of Fort Laramie. His posture was stiff and unbending, telling as much as his words had.

By the time she reached the outskirts of the village, the four-fingered man was leaving. Nearing her father's tepee, she saw only the broad expanse of his back as he rode off.

Ghost Dancer watched the tall stranger until he disappeared. She shivered and knew they had not seen the last of him. His evil ways would plague them, much like the fly that pesters a horse.

A nagging fear began to crowd her mind and she turned away, her eyes meeting the faded, brown ones of the old medicine man. She could not deny the contempt she read in them; it was clear and unchecked. Ghost Dancer did not need to be a reader of minds to know his thoughts, for behind the sharp, though age-faded, eyes lay a stubborn, unbending mind. From the day she had come to live among the Ghost Sioux, Broken Arrow had hated her. She presented a change he could not and would not accept.

Ghost Dancer had learned to live with his open hostility and returned his stare, eye to eye. He despised her strength, and even more, it ate at his pride that her powers were greater than his. For these reasons and more, she had never trusted him.

A strange smile lifted one side of his straight-lined mouth. She wondered that any movement, even so slight, wouldn't crack his withered face, furrowed deeply with wrinkles of age, much like the dry, caked earth the sun's heat had robbed of all moisture. The eyes that watched her were no longer white, but a dirtied yellow, the centers a weak, watered brown. A bulging, hooked nose protruded from his round, sagging face, making the normal width of the spheres seem too narrow and the size too small. His large ears struck out from his long, grayed hair, its coarseness easily seen as it hung to his shoulders in strings.

She continued to watch him as he turned to enter his tepee, his bent form supported by his buffalo-bone cane, a knotted hand gripping it firmly. He was ancient and Ghost Dancer was amazed that he had not died years ago. Perhaps his hatred for her kept him going, when others would have gone on to live with the Gods in the heavens above, their bodies left to nourish the earth.

As quickly as he had come into her thoughts, the medicine man was gone, replaced by a new threat, a more sinister one with a four-fingered hand and eyes as black as night.

* * *

The fire cracked and hissed as it devoured the dry wood hungrily, the fiery teeth chewing up the pulp and spitting out the ashes. Orange and yellow flickered and flashed, emitting a shadowy light about the tent, causing undefined figures to dance like mannequins on the darker hide walls. Light blue eyes stared into the darker cobalt flames, yet the vision she studied was only in her mind's eye. What lay before her was unseen by Ghost Dancer.

Clear as day, she conjured the face of the man she loved, every inch of his bronzed features committed to memory—the strong set of his jaw and defined cheekbones. The sparkle in his eyes set her heart aflutter, but it was his sensuous smile that created the warm feeling deep inside her, the heat spreading as quickly as the fire she stared into. Dark shanks of hair lay in soft curls down the back of his neck and she found herself longing to run her fingers through it, to. . . .

Ghost Dancer closed her eyes against the memories she recalled so easily, trying to shut out the anguish they brought. She fought the pain and the terrible loneliness that threatened to stifle her. Her fears of the day were still fresh in her mind, and created havoc with her sensitive emotions. The evil of her visions had come to life in the stranger. Now, he was a real, living man. No longer a dream, but a man to be feared.

Confusion reigned free as a myriad of thoughts clamored in her mind. Ghost Dancer was unaccustomed to these feelings. She had experienced little fear in her life, and her dreams had only teased her with their power. Today, terror had seized her, and like a strong grip, it squeezed the breath from her. With this fear came a new longing, the need to be with Cameron. She wanted the comfort and safety he seemed to provide. Yet, as her thoughts had turned to him, another more viable urge emerged. Her body came alive with its own wanting. Ghost Dancer desired his touch; she cried out in despair for his love. She craved the green light of his eyes, the heated exchange that brought a tingle to her toes and a burning in her soul. Her lips ached for his kiss as she struggled with the building passions of a woman, innocence gone forever.

"Cameron," Ghost Dancer whispered in agony, her hand reaching out to touch what she imagined. Her fingers met only the heat of the flames, and she felt her heart break in misery and loneliness.

Cameron jerked awake. "Who's there?"

No answer came, but he knew he had heard someone call to him. Sitting up, he threw his legs over the side of the bed and pulled himself up. Yawning, he ran his fingers through his sleep-tangled hair, discovering he was damp with sweat.

He had been dreaming.

"Angelique," he whispered to the silent walls.

He went to the small washstand and poured some water into the porcelain bowl. After splashing cool water on his face, he straightened and wiped the drops of moisture with a towel.

That's better, he thought and moved back to his bed.

"It was only a dream," he concluded out loud. "Only a dream."

Chapter 9

The child's cry ended in a shrill scream, terror clear in its high-pitched note. Too quickly, there was silence, death abruptly ending all whimpers and yells that had, in the preceding moments, filled the night air. Then, as the orange flames gathered strength, the roar of fire replaced the cries of the dying, its sizzling fingers tearing and ripping the canvas and wood of the wagons. Some of the victims would never find a resting place in the dark earth as the destruction moved on to claim them, leaving only ashes and bone as a marker of their fiery grave. Yet, in the grim silence, it no longer mattered.

Ghost Dancer came awake screaming, horror and fear heavy in her heart, the dream still clear in her mind. She saw the flames as they stretched long, twisting arms into the blackened sky. Smoke choked the air, stagnant with the smell of death, its acrid taste bringing the bitterness of bile to her throat.

He was there, sitting his horse, unaffected by the death he had created. Remorse never touched him. Only an evil delight lightened his black eyes. This man had no conscience, gave no thought to the death of so many innocent people. He thought only of his own purpose.

Tears spilled down her cheeks as she grieved for the people in the wagon train, their hopes and dreams taken from them by a man she knew only from her visions.

Red Bear found his sister huddled in the middle of her bed, sobbing hysterically. Without speaking, he went to her and pulled her into his strong arms. His hand smoothed her tangled hair and he comforted her, his heart moved by her pain.

"The four-fingered man killed them all," she whispered into his chest, then lifted tear-filled eyes to him. "Even the children."

"God Almighty."

Cameron's words seemed to echo every man's thoughts as they came upon the massacred group. The scene before them was a grisly one, the smell of death causing some of the soldiers to pull out their bandannas to cover their noses.

Nudging his horse forward, Cameron surveyed the destruction, his mouth set in a grim line. A muscle in his jaw twitched when buzzards flew up in numbers, his appearance disturbing their meal as they picked at the bodies that had not burned. He felt his throat tighten, and thankfully so, as it kept the sickness he felt from rising. This was something he never got used to. Never. It was hard for his mind to comprehend what he saw, and at that moment he hated those who had done this. Evidence that the small party of travelers had been attacked by Indians was everywhere, but Cameron was unable to believe that it was true.

He dismounted and walked among the skeletal wagons, the remnants charred and blackened. Everywhere he looked he saw death, but it was the small bodies of the children that caused the terrible pain in his chest.

"Captain," called the soldier behind him.

Cameron turned to his sergeant, relieved to take his eyes from the tiny, china doll that a little girl still gripped in her hand. He tried to reply, but had to clear his throat first.

"Yes, Sully." His voice still came out shaky and weak, but no one seemed to notice.

"Should I start the men to digging, sir?"

Cameron nodded. "Yes. That's a good idea." Then he added as an afterthought, "And keep those damnable birds away from the bodies."

The sergeant agreed. "We'll do that, all right." Then he walked off to start the men to work, his weapon at hand and ready.

"I don't know," Cameron began, pacing the wooden floor directly in front of Colonel Dawson's desk. "We found all of these things that bear the markings of the Ghost Sioux, but . . ." He didn't finish.

Colonel Dawson's eyes followed Captain Wade as he moved back and forth, the younger man's movements showing obvious agitation and worry. "But?" he prodded.

Cameron stopped. "But I just can't believe what these things tell us." His arm swept out in the general direction of the weapons that cluttered the giant oak desk. He felt angry and his mind reeled. He recalled the peaceful scenes of the Sioux village and it clashed with the violence of the scene he had recently left. It just couldn't be.

The colonel's white head moved in disagreement. He wasn't a tall man, but his bearing was formidable. Years of commanding a fort kept a hardness to his body that age might otherwise have softened. His square face was dark from the sun, the white of his hair stark against his tanned skin. A mustache filled his upper lip, the white length soft as it curled over his mouth which was stretched into a grim line. "And why not? They state quite plainly who did this."

"The evidence," added Major Bender, his look revealing nothing, "is quite damning."

The men's eyes fell to the evidence. The lance bore the rawhide images of the sun and the moon and the arrows the tribe's feather markings. The tomahawk was painted red, their tribal color, the same sun-and-moon symbols in black on its handle.

"We found imprints of shod horses among the Indian pony prints and"—Cameron pointed a finger into the air—"the scalping was too messy. Indians are more skilled than that. Even the children were killed."

The colonel considered everything Cameron said before he spoke again. "It's not like them to kill the young ones. Most Indians would take them to raise. Their greatest victory is to take our children and make them their own." Absently, his fingers ran over the sun-and-moon carvings in the wooden handle of the tomahawk. "And it's also not like a warrior to leave such handsome weapons behind."

There was a long moment of silence. Then Bender argued, "No one else would do such a thing. There is no reason."

"And what," Cameron asked, feeling anger rise inside him, "reason do the Ghost Sioux have to attack and kill the wagon train?"

"Indians don't need reasons, they're godless savages."

Cameron was near exploding, and Colonel Dawson interceded before he lost control of the situation. "Major! Captain!"

Both gazes turned to his authoritative voice. "I see that you're quite adamant, Captain Wade. But I need more than your gut feeling on this."

"The Ghost Sioux have been at peace for hundreds of years, sir. Why would they start trouble now?"

Silver brows drew together in concern. "That is true. We've had no trouble from them."

"Yet other tribes have killed for less," commented Bender dryly. "We can't let them get away with this, Colonel. That's why we're here, to protect our own."

"Of course we are. But our main purpose is to keep the peace," Cameron ground out, a terrible fear churning inside him. Over and over in his mind, he envisioned the peaceful tribe—and

Ghost Dancer. "Would you chance all-out war with the Sioux by going into the Black Hills? It's still unceded territory."

"You feel strongly about this, don't you?" the colonel asked.

"I believe they are innocent."

Colonel Dawson mulled this over before he made his decision. "Then you have two weeks, and I think you'd best start by taking another trip into the hills."

"Yes, sir." Cameron saluted his senior officers and turned to leave. He caught Bender's dark look and knew he was not pleased.

Ghost Dancer stood, stretching her cramped legs slowly, easing the nagging pain. The beauty of her homeland was lost to the worry that filled her mind. She didn't see the black-green of the pines, so dark against the gray of the rocky buttes that interrupted the lush forest. She didn't smell the clear, clean air of the mountain, and didn't hear the soft sounds of nature. The turmoil within her heart clashed violently with the quiet surroundings.

After her terrifying nightmare, she had come here on a vision quest. Ghost Dancer had fasted and prayed, seeking answers to the dream, but no answers had come.

Her gaze turned in the direction of her village, too far to be seen, yet she continued to watch the view. The Sun Dance would be in its third day, the tribe's vows and prayers offered in support of her own. Still, no answers had come.

As she stared at the scene before her, she felt her eyes drawn to the southwest. Ghost Dancer felt her heartbeat quicken, its drumming pace steady and strong.

"Cameron," she said quietly, as whisper-soft as the breeze that stirred the leaves on the canopy of trees above her.

She felt his coming.

Chapter 10

The moon was full, lighting the way for Cameron with its silver beams. He pulled his chestnut-colored stallion to a halt. The drumbeats vibrated the earth, their sound deep and steady. Slowly, he moved his mount forward, the pace of his heart matching the heady thumping, the mystery drawing him to its bosom. Within minutes, his eyes feasted on the light and color of the spectacle, its glory matching the sounds he had followed.

As he drew nearer the Sioux village, he began to make out images and forms. In the center of the gathering, he saw the tall, straight cottonwood tree. The soft breeze stirred its leaves and the light of the torches turned the green into silver-gray jewels in the darkness. At its top were four, seven-yard long banners, one red, one black, one white, and one yellow, their brightness catching his eyes. Another flag of each color marked the entrances to the four directions, north was red, south white, east yellow, and west black.

Without being told, he knew the markings of

the great Sioux tradition—the Sun Dance. Excitement surged through him, and the blood in his veins ran hot with anticipation. Few white men had ever had the chance to witness a warrior's vow to the sun.

As he drew closer, a few spectators turned his way, but unconcerned, their eyes returned to the participants inside the Mystery Circle. Cameron had the distinct feeling that they were expecting him and suspicion stirred deep inside him.

He dismounted, his brow wrinkled in dismay at the direction his thoughts were headed. But the frown disappeared when his eyes found Ghost Dancer. Never before had he felt such a surge of joy, its suddenness making him react without thought. In three long-legged steps he was there, lifting her into the air and whirling her about.

"God, I've missed you, Angel!"

His heartfelt confession brought tears to her eyes, and she placed her hands on his face, the memory of their parting gone in the excitement of their reunion. "And I have missed you, Cameron."

Realizing what he had just said made him feel foolish. As quickly as he'd grabbed her, he set her down, trying to think of something else to say. Actually, he had already said much more than he had intended to. What on earth had made him do that? he asked himself in frustration. His heart was telling him the answer, but he chose to ignore it.

"I have been expecting you," she said, interrupting his thoughts.

Again, suspicion's ugly head rose, and Cameron

almost choked on the emotion. "I . . ." He swallowed to ease the dryness of his throat. "I wondered why no one seemed to pay me any mind." The uneasiness in his voice was apparent.

"Cameron, I will always know when you are near. Our souls are united, and our hearts beat as one. You are a part of me, and I am a part of you. I shall always sense your coming. For when we are together, I am whole again. I am complete."

Her words made his heart pound hard. Yet his mind clamored in rejection to her notion. How strangely Ghost Dancer affected him and how strongly. Determination to think of other things made him change the subject abruptly.

"I've come to speak with Black Hawk."

It was a simple statement, clear in its meaning. Somehow, Ghost Dancer saw so much more, her face paling as a frown of concern marred her forehead. Cameron could not have known the visions that plagued her mind at that very moment.

"What has happened, Cameron?"

He hadn't meant to alarm her. "I merely wish to speak with your father. It's nothing to fret over, Angel." The comforting words were the practiced ones he would have used on most women, but he forgot that Ghost Dancer was unlike most women.

"What has happened? What has caused these horrible dreams to visit me nightly? Tell me!"

It was Cameron's turn to pale. "What dreams?" he asked, not really certain that he wanted to know.

"Perhaps," Black Hawk's commanding voice

drew both their eyes to him, "it would be best if we went to my tepee to discuss this."

Cameron's gaze moved from Black Hawk to the younger man standing at his side. No one needed to tell him that it was the chief's son, the resemblance was well written on his face. He nodded in agreement and followed the two men, his hand holding Ghost Dancer's elbow.

Ghost Dancer stared at Cameron, his gruesome tale finished. A loud ringing filled her head and the tepee became unbearably hot. Slowly, everything began to move, then the blood drained from her in a rush.

Cameron caught her as she sank to the ground in a dead faint. With care, he lifted her and placed her on the pallet. Her father and brother hovered at his side.

"Angelique," he called to her, unaware of the looks exchanged between Black Hawk and Red Bear, the younger one's dark eyebrows pulled down into a frown, the elder one's lifted in slight amusement.

Hearing her name called, Ghost Dancer stirred, and her eyes fluttered open. Confusion filtered in, then surprise. "What happened?"

"It seems that you fainted."

Embarrassed, Ghost Dancer pulled herself up and straightened the soft skin of her dress. When she looked about her, she saw the concern on her father's face and the scowl that still lingered on her brother's. "I am all right, Father."

Cameron took her hand into his. "I didn't mean

to frighten you, Angel. I'm sorry."

"Frighten her," Red Bear snorted, drawing their attention. "You come here and accuse us of butchering white settlers, and you dare to apologize to my sister."

"I didn't accuse you of killing them. I merely told you what we found." Cameron stood to face Red Bear, showing no fear of the other man's anger.

Black Hawk stepped between them. "You do not believe that it was the Nahhe Lahkota?"

"No," Cameron conceded. "I do not. I believe that someone tried to make it look like you massacred those people."

Black Hawk motioned for them to sit. "Why would someone do such a thing?"

Cameron sat beside Ghost Dancer and again received a dark look from Red Bear. "To make trouble for your people."

Worried blue eyes commanded Cameron's attention. "If . . . if they attack again, what will happen to us?"

"The whites in this area would be up in arms, demanding that something be done to punish the Sioux."

Ghost Dancer felt terror grip her. "If you believe we have not done this, why would not the others?"

It was Black Hawk who answered her question. "Other whites would think that Cameron did not see the facts clearly."

"Because of me?" She knew the answer even before her father's confirming nod. Looking at

Cameron, she studied him closely. "What is it that you are not telling us?"

His sigh reached her, touching her with his sadness. "I was given two weeks to prove you didn't do this."

"And if you cannot prove our innocence?"

"The army will retaliate—with force."

Ghost Dancer blanched, but Red Bear jumped up and shouted, "Let them come! We have faced our enemies before and have triumphed. We will do so again."

"No," Ghost Dancer cried. She turned pleading eyes to Cameron. "You would not let this happen? You know that we are innocent."

A feeling of helplessness struck Cameron. He wanted more than anything to take away her hurt, but he could not. "All the evidence says that you are guilty. Where am I supposed to begin?"

A grim silence fell over them. Finally, it was Ghost Dancer who spoke. "I know who has done this horrible thing."

Ghost Dancer's words were soft, almost unheard.

"Angel, how could you know that?" A strange sense of *déjà vu* touched him. He didn't want to go on, but he did. "You mentioned a dream."

She nodded hesitantly. "I had a vision, perhaps the very night you speak of. I saw the string of wagons and heard the cries of the people. Fire . . . It consumed everything. The sun and the moon were present, but I felt the untruth of that."

The expression on Cameron's face told her that

he wanted to believe her. "I've told you those very things, Angel."

His tone sounded disappointed. She must make him believe. "I saw a child."

Cameron's head snapped up, and a small muscle in his jaw flexed. "What child?"

"A blond girl child." Ghost Dancer saw him shiver as her words struck him. "She held something in her hand."

He looked as if he wanted to say something, but couldn't get the words out. She continued. "A doll . . . She held a doll." Ghost Dancer concentrated on a single thought. "The face was cracked."

Cameron swallowed hard, the vision of the child's china doll still vivid in his memory.

"Yes," she whispered. "A broken doll."

There was silence once again.

"That still doesn't tell me who did this." Cameron felt deflated, confused, uncertain of what to believe.

"It was a man I have seen only in my dreams."

"You're not serious?" he demanded.

Ghost Dancer felt tears fill her eyes. "I saw him, as clearly as I see you."

Cameron wanted to make the sadness disappear from her earnest face. "Okay. Say that you did see him in your dream. It still doesn't mean that he did this. Come now, Angel. I need *real* proof."

"Such as the damning *proof* that was left to accuse us?" Red Bear asked, his tone angry and impatient.

"Yeah," Cameron acknowledged grimly.

"It seems," Ghost Dancer began, her mind seeking solutions, "the answer lies at Fort Laramie. This man we seek is there. He is the one we must question."

A sad smile curled the corners of Cameron's mouth. "It doesn't work that way. Not in our world. Say this man does exist, and we start asking questions, he would know that we suspect him. He'd make certain we didn't find anything to prove his guilt."

"Then we must go to the fort, watch, and wait."

"Wait for what?"

"We must wait for him to show us his guilt."

The way she said it seemed so simple, so logical. "I can do that, Angel."

"*We* shall do it."

"We?"

She nodded. "I shall return to Fort Laramie with you."

Everyone spoke at once, the tepee filling with the boom of male voices, angry and loud. Ghost Dancer raised her hand, halting the melee. "I am going, I shall not be told any different."

She saw shock mirrored in their faces.

"It is not safe, Daughter," Black Hawk objected.

"I am the Ghost Dancer, Father. It is my purpose on this earth to watch over my people. This is something I must do, for the sake of our tribe."

Red Bear stepped forward. "Then I shall go with you."

She smiled patiently. "You would not exactly fit in, Red Bear. I can walk among them unnoticed.

I will let them believe that I am merely a white woman, nothing more.

Cameron choked. "You cannot be serious!"

"I am most serious Cameron Wade. Perhaps this is the reason for my being, that I may seek the truth among the white man."

"Well," Cameron growled, "I agree with your father and brother. It's a rotten idea."

"What you think, what any of you think, is not a matter of consideration. I will go."

Black Hawk smiled weakly. "Sometimes I forget who you are, and think of you only as my daughter. It is difficult."

"Well, I'm not your father and—" Cameron broke off. It occurred to him that Angelique wanted to go to the exact place he thought she should be. Once she was at the fort, among her own people, he was positive she would never want to leave. "I suppose I could accompany you to the fort and stay by your side during this . . . this charade."

Red Bear stepped forward. "I do not trust him."

Ghost Dancer was appalled. "I do. It is enough."

"No," he objected. "He is not of the Ghost Sioux."

"Red Bear"—she lowered her voice in warning—"you must not interfere."

His head shook. "*I* must know that he can be trusted. My dancer"—his voice became husky—"you are precious to me. I must know you are safe."

"What do I have to do to earn your respect, Red Bear?"

Red Bear stood before him, equal in height, equal in strength. "You must make a vow to the sun."

Ghost Dancer gasped in horror. "It is unfair to ask such a thing."

Cameron gently moved her aside. "This, Angel, is something *you* have no say in."

Honoring his decision, she stepped back.

"I will participate in the Sun Dance to prove my worthiness as a protector for Ghost Dancer."

Black Hawk and Red Bear nodded their approval.

Chapter 11

Anticipation and uncertainty gripped Cameron. He stood with Angelique inside the Mystery Circle, the Sacred Tree looming above them in the night sky. He sensed Angelique's pride as she explained what they saw surrounding them.

"The Mystery Circle symbolizes that which is eternal to us. It encompasses all creation and its relationship with the Great Spirit."

"How is it suppose to work?"

"We stand within a circle of power and it has no limits, except those we place upon our own minds."

Cameron was fascinated. "Where does this power come from?"

"*Wakan Tanka* gives it to us through the sun, the four directions, and the Tree."

The tree held his attention. "What are those rawhide things hanging from it?"

"Images of a man and a buffalo. The man represents the children born and yet to be born, the continuance of the red power."

"Red power?"

Ghost Dancer smiled, pleased by his interest. "Red power is the most important gift of life given to us from the Gods Above, a gift to all living creatures. Without red power we die, for the red power flows through us as blood."

"And the other image?"

"The buffalo was one of the greatest animals God provided for the Sioux. It is our source of life. Such as the bundle of cherry branches put crossway on the Tree."

Cameron reached out to touch one of the rawhide ropes that dangled from the strong cottonwood that towered above them. Then his fingers moved on to feel the red clay strip that ran from the base to the top.

"The red line represents the narrow path we are told to follow as we walk through life."

She raised an arm and pointed to the west. "The altar is always placed there and the pipe rack is put at the head of the buffalo skull, its nose pointing east. The eye and nose sockets are filled with sage and the skull rests upon a bed of sage."

"Why sage?"

"To purify."

Cameron reached down and touched a small bag tied to the trunk. "What's this?"

"It is the flesh offerings."

His brows knitted together. "That has an ominous sound to it."

She smiled. "It is our sacrifice to *Wakan Tanka*. We pray to Him and give an offering of our faith. We give of ourselves. It is all we truly have to give in this life—flesh, blood, and tears."

In his mind Cameron recalled the scarred arms of Black Hawk and Red Bear, even the women of the tribe bore the markings. "You have no scars on your arms." Of which, he was secretly thankful.

"As the Ghost Dancer I am not expected to give of my flesh."

"Why not?"

"It just is not expected."

It was not as complete an answer as he would have liked, but he let it be. "Will I be expected to give a flesh offering?"

"The piercing is a flesh offering, Cameron. Tomorrow you will give flesh, blood, and tears to the Great Spirit." Her eyes met his. He saw the seriousness on her face and the fear in her eyes. "Tomorrow, you will endure great suffering and pain."

"I know, Angel. I know."

It was still dark when Black Hawk came for Cameron. His night had been spent in preparation, fasting and praying. Now it was time for purification in the sweat lodge, cleansing the pledger of his sins and ignorance. When they exited from there, sweat glistened off their bare chests, arms, and legs.

Red Bear led the men who were to be pierced, following the "intercessor" into the preparations tepee. It was there they dressed for the Sun Dance. For the Sioux warriors, it was the traditional renewal of their faith, but for Cameron it would be an absolute test of his courage and stamina. To fail was unthinkable.

The pledgers were left bare with only a breech-cloth to cover their sex. Wreaths of plaited sage were placed on their heads and buffalo fur bands were put around their ankles and wrists. The men were barefooted, and all but Cameron let their long, dark hair hang free about their shoulders.

Cameron touched the medicine pouch that hung about his neck, a gift from Angelique . . . Ghost Dancer. When his thoughts turned to her, he felt a burst of renewed faith and knew he could face what lay ahead. Beside the magical pouch hung an eagle-wing bone whistle, feathers, and quill decorations that tickled his skin.

He stood quietly while the Intercessor painted a large circle on his back with a dot marking its center. Then he drew zigzagged lines in black down Cameron's arms and on his chest, he marked in red the images of the sun and moon. Cameron was ready.

They entered the Mystery Circle. The altar was reestablished in its traditional place of honor by the holy men, and the first prayers were offered.

Cameron could not understand any of the words, but the feelings ran deep and were contagious. Then the pipe of each participant was presented to the Keeper of the Pipes and leaned against the cherry rack at the altar, just above the sacred buffalo skull. Black Hawk came and stood beside Cameron, and the singing and chanting began.

"My daughter has asked me to interpret the prayers for you. She thought if you understood their meaning you might gather strength from them as the others do."

Cameron nodded in appreciation. "She has explained much to me, but I still have a question."

"What is that?"

"Why is Ghost Dancer not expected to give a flesh offering?"

"Ghost Dancer has already sacrificed the ultimate to the Gods Above."

"Ultimate?" Cameron swallowed hard, somehow knowing it would be another answer he would find hard to accept.

Black Hawk's head moved up and down as he spoke. "Yes. Ghost Dancer's spirit has been given to the one who guides us. We merely offer our flesh and blood."

Cameron could find no words, his mind trying to sort out all that had been said.

At the end of the songs one of the holy men began to pray, facing west and the black flags marking it.

"The west," Black Hawk began, "is the source of rain. Good things always follow the rain. It is also the home of the Thunder being a huge bird that flies in the midst of storms, his wings making the thunder and the lightning flash from his eyes. The messenger of the west is the black eagle."

Cameron waited eagerly for the holy man to move to the north and the red flags. His need to know more of Ghost Dancer's world was like a great thirst that was unquenchable.

"Winter's home is here," Black Hawk continued. "Its power brings health. Those who have strayed turn to it for guidance and wisdom to find the right path again. Its messenger is the bald-headed eagle."

It was at that moment Cameron saw Ghost Dancer, her velvety gaze touching him, gentle and sweet. His heart beat faster. She almost looked like a spirit. Dressed in the whitest of doeskin, its fringe long and delicate, she seemed not of this world. Her hair was loose, catching the rays of first light, turning it into spun gold. Eagle feathers dangled from her ears, the white markings of the sacred bird in keeping with this holy occasion. Cameron heard the strong heart beat within his chest and wondered, if indeed, their hearts did beat as one.

The strangeness of her costume made her seem foreign. Nothing about her reminded him of a white woman.

Black Hawk's voice broke into his thoughts, bringing his mind back to what was happening around him.

"The power of the east is born of the sun. The Morning Star, the star of wisdom, is in the east and related to the sun. Its messenger is the brown eagle."

The holy man moved to the last direction to pray. "The sacred power of the south shows us the path as we walk toward the place of life after death. It is in the south that life begins, and its messenger is the white crane."

Even when the prayers were done Black Hawk went on. "We pray to the heavens, the dwelling place of Grandfather—the Great Spirit, the One above all other spirits and powers. All paths lead to Him."

With a start, Cameron realized their religion was similar to Christianity.

"Now would be a good time for you to seek His help, Cameron Wade. Pray for strength." Black Hawk turned and left the circle.

As the sun rose high in the sky, the pledgers danced, gazing directly into the sun to bring down its power. Sweat poured from them as they endured, their faith giving them strength.

When Cameron's calf muscles cramped, the sweat rolled down his body, and his throat was raw with thirst, the piercing began. They led him to the Sacred Tree. He was lain on a buffalo robe covered with the silky, gray-green sage, his head to the north and feet to the south. A holy man stood over him, an eagle claw in each hand. There were no songs or prayers now, only silence.

The claws pierced deeply into the flesh above each breast. The warm stickiness of blood ran down his sides. Rawhide ropes were tied securely to his skin and to the claws before he was "helped" to his feet.

His gaze met Red Bear's, the challenge in the young warrior's eyes clear. Cameron clenched his teeth. It was the look of anger in the eyes of the man standing beside Red Bear that made Cameron determined to withstand his test. He had heard of Lone Wolf's pursuit of Ghost

Dancer and of her rejection of the Indian. The fact that she had chosen him, a white man, and not one of the tribe, made Cameron feel proud. Though it cost him, he stood straight and tall.

Suddenly, with great exuberance, the music began, the beat of many drums drowning out the cries of the on-lookers. Ropes tightened as the pledgers pulled back, keeping time with the surge of sound. An attendant placed the eagle-bone whistles into their mouths, and they began to blow, adding to the clamor of noise, their twisting and jerking more violent as the tempo quickened.

Like a man possessed, Cameron fought the tongs to be free. The pain was excruciating, but became secondary to something more powerful. Over and over, his mind chanted all he had learned, the chant filling his head, his heart, his soul, until nothing else existed. Red Bear's words became reality.

My dancer, I must know.

More than anything, he wanted Ghost Dancer's family to trust him.

Ghost Dancer's spirit has been sacrificed to the One who guides us. We merely offer our flesh and blood.

Flesh and blood. Flesh and blood.

Again and again, it reverberated in his pain-ridden mind. Flesh and blood. Flesh and blood. . . .

Cameron could no longer see as sweat poured into his eyes, burning and blinding. He pulled even harder, gritting his teeth to keep from crying out.

Angel!

Ghost Dancer felt his mind cry out to her, his agony becoming her own. Yet, she remained quiet and her eyes closed as she prayed for him, seeking the sun's power for the man she loved. She knew Cameron would have to survive the painful ordeal alone, for he did not have the divine faith of the warriors who struggled at his side. As time passed, she continued her prayers for him.

Something prompted her to open her eyes. She saw a subtle change come over Cameron and fear slithered into her mind. But it was something else that diverted her gaze, a feeling so strong and powerful it couldn't be ignored. In silence, she followed the drawing need, its urgency quickening her steps.

Ghost Dancer stood before Broken Arrow's tepee, his chants drifting to her attentive ears. Her eyes narrowed in anger and her fists clenched at her side. Without scratching, she went inside the medicine man's tent.

The heat was sweltering, the fire in the pit hot as it burned high. The old man had not heard her enter over its roar, and did not see her until she moved within his sight. His chanting stopped.

Evil, her mind cried, and out loud she hissed, "*Shecha!*"

Slowly, he rose to his feet, leaning heavily upon his bone walking stick. When he turned wilted eyes on her, she saw the immense hatred that burned in their depths. Wrinkled thin lips pursed, making each line even deeper, and his lips disappeared altogether beneath the folds of leathery flesh.

"He cannot be allowed to finish the Sun Dance." His words were gruff and the jerking movements of his knotted hands matched his indignant anger. "He is not of the Sioux. *You* are not of the Sioux. You are not of the people and do not deserve such a blessing from *Wakan Tanka.*"

Never before had Ghost Dancer felt such hot fury, its scorching fingers smothering all sympathy she might have had for him lingering within her heart. "You have gone too far, Broken Arrow, and this time there is no forgiveness within me."

His fear mingled with shards of hatred, but it was true, he *had* gone too far to back down. "You cannot stop what I have done. He will not complete the piercing."

"You dog," she muttered, her eyes narrowing dangerously. "You dare to threaten me?"

"You cannot stop what is started," he cried, uncertainty causing his words to shake.

With deliberate slowness, she moved toward him, her intimidating steps creating havoc within him. He backed up, but stopped when there was no place to go, no place to hide.

"I am Ghost Dancer, and my powers are much greater than yours. What you have begun, I shall stop."

His head shook back and forth in denial and he cried, "No It cannot be."

"Look"—she smiled, making him shiver at the coldness of it—"and you shall learn the power of Ghost Dancer."

Picking up the skin of drinking water, she doused the fire, the sizzling loud in the painful silence. Then she found a feather fan and began to stir the heated air, creating a cooling breeze. Lifting a full horn cup, she took a drink, parching her thirst. Broken Arrow understood, without seeing, that Cameron's own dry throat was wetted, his skin cooled in the sudden wind.

Broken Arrow knew the bitterness of defeat. But when Ghost Dancer pulled the knife from her belt, he felt the sudden pricklings of terror. His watery brown eyes could not turn away from her crystal-blue stare, hypnotizing him in place. Ghost Dancer read a myriad of emotions in his eyes as she moved to stand in front of him, but her heart gave no quarter.

"You will leave our village, never to return. Should my eyes ever see you again, it shall be your last moments upon this earth."

She lifted her arms to the heavens and her eyes closed. The medicine man cowered before her, unable to flee. Before his mind could comprehend what she was doing, she turned the knife to her own bared breast. Deftly and quickly she cut two small marks into the soft flesh, the droplets of blood so stark against the whiteness of her skin.

They both heard the roar of the spectators as a pledger broke loose from the leather tongs. Broken Arrow slumped to the ground, his spirit trampled, yet the burning hate remained in his eyes.

Again, he did not need the confirmation of sight to know that Cameron had completed his vow to the sun.

"Is it true that you are going with the white man?"

Ghost Dancer raised her gaze to meet Lone Wolf's. A twinge of guilt pricked her conscience, the sadness she saw all too plainly on his face the cause of it. "Yes, it is true."

"He will betray you."

"No, he will not. Cameron Wade is risking much for us, and we must trust in him."

Lone Wolf shook his head, "He is a white man, he will expect you to stay with him. This Cameron Wade will never give up his life for yours. And he will never understand who the Ghost Dancer is."

Even loving Cameron, Ghost Dancer knew Lone Wolf spoke the truth. "Perhaps not. Still, I must go, Lone Wolf."

He was silent for a long moment. "Why could you not love me?"

"I do love you." His hopeful look made her rush on. "But it is too much the same as the love I have for Red Bear."

"I am not your brother, but a man. I would be good to you, my Ghost Dancer."

Again, she knew he spoke truly. Still, her heart could not agree. "It is not enough."

"When he has betrayed you . . . when you return to us with a broken heart . . . when you are alone . . . it will be enough. And . . . I will be waiting."

He turned to leave her tepee, his intentions and feelings clear. Nothing more needed to be said.

"Lone Wolf," Ghost Dancer's soft voice stopped him. "I am sorry about your grandfather, I had no choice but to banish him."

Lone Wolf never even turned around. "He defied you. It had to be."

"You are generous," she whispered.

"No." He turned darkened eyes to her for only the briefest of seconds. "I am loyal to my Ghost Dancer."

Chapter 12

The two riders emerged from the giant shadow that cast its darkness over the side of the hill, keeping the sun's light and warmth from them. The scent of pine and dampness clung to the air. Sounds common to the dense, black forest combined with the steady clomp of their horses' hooves striking dirt and rock.

Cameron stopped, and Ghost Dancer pulled up her mount beside him. They both turned to look at the valley through which they had just traveled. Its simple beauty left an unforgettable impression on them both. For Ghost Dancer, it was just one of many times, and each time she experienced a greater feeling of awe.

"Are you sure you want to leave?" Cameron pulled his gaze away from the scene before him and concentrated on the fair face looking up at him. He found himself waiting for her answer, fearing she would turn back.

Once they had reached the fort she would be happy there and never want to return to the Sioux. He was convinced of that. But he also wanted her to leave the hills of her own will. Suddenly, it became important that this was her decision. It would make his leaving her easier in the end.

She nodded. "I know I must make this journey, Cameron Wade."

Reaching out, he brushed his fingertips down the satin curve of her cheek. "Are you afraid?"

"A man who does not know fear is a fool." She gave him a confident smile. "But the man who conquers his fear is brave."

Cameron's laughter drifted across the hills and echoed off the rock walls over and over again until it was a murmur in the distance. Her smile faded and a tiny frown curved her lips down.

"Did I say something foolish?"

Her look of dismay caused him to curb his amusement. "No, Angel. You didn't say anything wrong. I just find you delightful, that's all."

This seemed to ease the trouble in her mind, but questions still came. "In what way am I a delight?"

"In every way."

Cameron's smile warmed Ghost Dancer. She still wasn't certain what he meant, but it didn't matter anymore. All that mattered was the tender look in his eyes. "I am very glad," she breathed, terribly aware of the man who had claimed both her heart and her body.

"Well," started Cameron, reluctant to turn away, "I guess we should move on. We have a long ride ahead, Angel."

"Yes," she agreed sadly. "I have never been away from the hills before."

"Just remember, I'll be with you. And, if you get homesick, I'll kiss your tears away."

Heat stained her cheeks. "Do . . . do you promise?"

He nodded but it was the fire in his eyes that said it all. "Cross my heart," he said, doing just that.

"Cameron Wade," she began as a thought came to mind, "where is your home?"

"I live at Fort Laramie, Angel. You know that."

"No. I mean, where was your home, before you came here?"

Cameron's dark head turned to the east. "My family lived in Boston. On the coast."

Ghost Dancer followed his gaze. "Where the great waters gather?"

"That's right. Where the great waters gather." The smile that had curved his mouth disappeared. "I'm the only one left now, my mother died a few years back, and my father and two older brothers were killed in the war."

"I am sorry for your losses, Cameron. Did you, too, fight in this war between your northern and southern tribes?"

"I fought—and was lucky enough to survive."

"How is it you have come here? So far from your home?"

He shrugged. "I don't really know. I guess. . . ."

When he didn't go on, she prodded a bit further. "You guess what?"

"It's like . . ." A faraway look drifted across his face. "It's like something drew me here."

As soon as the words were out, Cameron realized what he had said. Had Angelique brought him here? Was there truly such a thing as fate?

A shock wave tumbled through Cameron. "It isn't what you're thinking," he mumbled. "It can't be."

Ghost Dancer said nothing.

Cameron leaned forward, stretching his arm out and sliding his hand behind her neck to draw her closer. "Tell me."

"You must decide for yourself." Ghost Dancer allowed her horse to move closer. Cameron's nearness made her blood run hot and wild. "Your heart will tell you the truth."

"Damn, I hate it when you do that."

"Do what?" she asked innocently, her voice growing deep with emotion. His lips were so close.

"You know." He brushed his mouth against hers.

Ghost Dancer could feel the warmth of his breath on her face, but most of the heat came from within. "I know what?"

"Never mind."

When Cameron took her in his arms, she went willingly. It almost seemed as if he drank of her, so complete was his kiss. He pulled her from her horse and onto his own, his muscled arms swallowing her within their strength. With seeming reluctance, he finally pulled his lips from hers.

"Do you think we can continue this later tonight? When the stars are out? We'll let the moon be our candlelight."

"That will be a promise I will gladly keep," she

agreed with a smile. Then she marked an "X" over her heart. "Cross my heart."

"What is it that troubles you?"

Her voice drew Cameron's look to her. She sat up and laid a hand upon his shoulder. The heat of his skin fused with her own. Only moments before, she had fulfilled her promise. Her body still tingled from his loving touch.

"I don't know, Angel. I just have a feeling we're being watched." He paused, his eyes turning back to search the blackness, intent and alert. "Someone's out there."

"They have been following us for hours."

He turned back to her. "You've known they were there all along?"

"Of course."

"Damn." He rubbed a hand over his stubbled chin in obvious concern. "Why didn't you tell me?"

She shrugged. "I did not think it was necessary."

"Good God, woman!" His hands clenched into fists. "Just when did you think it *would* be necessary?"

Ghost Dancer blinked at his sudden outburst, uncertain why he was yelling. "There was no need. We are in no danger from the Cheyenne."

"The Cheyenne! This is getting better by the minute." Cameron started to stand, but she pulled him back, her arm hooked in his.

"Cameron," she began firmly, "you are bellowing like a sick buffalo, and it would be best if you stopped."

His mouth settled into a straight line, his eyes flashing daggers that said more than his words. "And what would *you* suggest we do?"

By now Ghost Dancer had begun to understand Cameron's knack for sarcasm. She decided to let it pass. This time. "I would suggest that we do nothing. Except perhaps get some sleep." With studied calmness, she lay back down and pulled the blanket over her bare shoulder, her back turned to Cameron.

"Sleep?" he demanded, pulling her around to face him again. "Sleep!" The last came out in a hushed holler.

"Of course." She reached up to touch his cheek. The tender motion eased some of the hard lines etching his face. "They will not cause trouble."

"How can you be so sure?"

She smiled in an all-knowing way. "Trust me."

"I . . ." His face revealed his hesitation. "I can't. I just can't."

Ghost Dancer turned away to hide her hurt.

His hand cupped her chin to pull her face back to him again. This time a bit more gently. "I'm a soldier. I'm here to protect you, and it goes against my nature to ignore a possible threat."

She laid her hand on his. "I understand." It was strange, but she did know what he was feeling. "I will sleep, you may stand guard."

There was a strained silence between them the next day. Neither interrupted the other's thoughts as they covered the miles that took them closer to Fort Laramie. Their Cheyenne shadows kept pace with them, always within sight.

Cameron used the time to study the woman who rode quietly beside him. Wasn't he becoming too involved with Ghost Dancer? A resounding yes echoed through his mind and fear followed that echo. What of his vow never to marry? No, it still held firm, of that he was certain.

Conflicting memories bombarded him. The arguments of his parents every time his father came home, and his mother's tears when her husband left again pulled at his heart. Shaking his head, Cameron freed himself of that painful remembrance only to recall Angelique as she lay sleeping in his arms, warm from their lovemaking, to pull him once again the other way.

No, he could never marry. Then why couldn't he stay out of her loving arms? One touch and he was lost to her sweet seductiveness.

It was like his mind had declared one thing and his heart another. He certainly wasn't making things better by being so damned weak. What about the time he would have to say good-bye to Angelique? Could he?

Of course! She was a kind of brief madness. That was it! Now that Cameron had named his weakness, he felt certain it would pass.

It was just after midday when the Cheyenne made an appearance. Cameron and Ghost Dancer halted their horses and waited.

One warrior rode forward, then stopped.

"What do they want?" Cameron asked, turning to Angelique. A hardness claimed her eyes that he had not seen before. The strength and power he saw told him he was looking at Ghost Dancer—not his Angel.

"Cameron, I beg of you, say nothing, do nothing. You *are* a soldier and I understand this, but *I* am the Ghost Dancer. You must not question what I do."

On some level deep inside him, he knew she spoke the truth and said nothing.

Ghost Dancer moved forward to face the single Cheyenne.

The painted warrior lifted his war lance to her, the eagle feathers shifting in the breeze. It was then that she recognized him, remembering the day she had found Cameron. In response to his greeting, she raised open palms to him. He nodded, and, seemingly satisfied by this, turned to ride back to his men.

The small party of warriors rode off, never giving them a second look. The dust settled, and the noise of their departure faded into the distance.

"Why are they going?"

Cameron's voice brought Ghost Dancer's gaze back to him. Gone was the coldness he had witnessed only a few brief moments before, making him wonder if he had imagined it in the first place.

"We are getting closer to the fort, they can come no farther."

"Then why bother following us if they weren't going to cause trouble?"

Ghost Dancer wasn't certain which area in

which to delve first. "The reasons they followed us are their own, I can only guess at them. The Cheyenne who came forward did so to show me he did not fear me. And he also showed that he respected who I am. The raising of his lance was a salute in reverence to my power."

Cameron just couldn't leave that one be. "Power?"

"Yes," she said, her chin lifting with pride. "I am the Ghost Dancer, and my powers are great. You, Cameron Wade, do not believe the legend. Neither did the Cheyenne, until the day I came upon you."

"What are you getting at?"

"I am only trying to answer your questions." Her delicate brows drew together in confusion. So often Ghost Dancer did not understand his anger, let alone his questions.

"All right." He removed his hat and ran his hand through his sweat-dampened hair. "Just tell me, who are you? What are you?"

"A woman. I am a gift from the Gods Above."

Once again, Cameron felt a strange sensation raise the hairs on the back of his neck, followed by an immediate uneasiness he did not like. "Don't give me all that hocus-pocus, Angel. I just don't believe it."

Cameron placed his hat back on his head. "We'd best get going." Spurring his stallion into a gallop, he ended their discussion.

Ghost Dancer urged her own mount forward. She felt happy. "Whatever you say, Cameron Wade, you are beginning to believe."

Chapter 13

"Where did ya get the squaw, Captain?"

Cameron pulled his horse to a halt and turned in the saddle to look at the man who had spoken. The mount he led stopped and all eyes turned to its rider. Ghost Dancer slumped a bit more and pulled the blanket that covered her head tighter.

"Found her a mile or so back. She's sick and needs medical attention."

The soldier took a couple steps toward Ghost Dancer, his hand reaching out to pull the blanket from her head.

"Best not get too close, Ed," Cameron warned.

Just then she let out a loud, nasty-sounding cough and Ed backed off, almost stumbling in his hurry.

"Ain't no telling what she's got." Cameron smiled and nudged his chestnut forward, pulling Ghost Dancer's great white behind him. "Could be contagious." This caused Ed's eyes to widen even more.

Ghost Dancer had to bite her lower lip to keep from laughing at the look on Ed's face and was certain he was imagining all the horrible things she could be spreading around. She was also certain she heard Cameron chuckling.

"You will worry that poor man to death, Cameron." She spoke just loud enough for him to hear. "You are like a child."

He didn't have to see her face to know she was smiling, it was in her voice.

"Me? I wasn't the one who let out such a whopper of a cough. Sounded kind of like the hacking of some old buffalo."

This time she couldn't restrain a giggle. "I suppose sometimes I am also like a child."

"No, Angel. You are nothing like a child. Nothing at all."

He turned back around; his glance had only touched her for a second. But it left its mark, leaving her shaken and flushed. They passed building after building, but it all went unnoticed by Ghost Dancer, her mind occupied by Cameron's sizzling look.

"Angelique."

Ghost Dancer looked up. "Yes."

"This is the post surgeon's quarters. Get off here, just as we planned, and go around back. Follow me to Colonel Dawson's house. Stay hidden in back until I call for you."

She nodded and slid off her horse, quickly disappearing between the buildings. Satisfied that no one had seen her, Cameron moved on.

When he reached the two-story, white-washed building, he dismounted and tied his horse. He stepped onto the veranda that stretched along its front, not only on the first floor, but the second as well.

Cameron's boots clamped loudly on the wooden boards as he made his way to his commanding officer's living quarters. He couldn't help but smile as he thought of how easy it was going to be to keep an eye on Ghost Dancer. The bachelor officers' quarters occupied the right side of Old Bedlam, just across from the colonel's apartment.

That is, he hoped it would be simple. Would the colonel and his wife be willing to help them? Cameron knocked on their door. It was late, and Cameron was counting on the colonel being home with his wife. Luck was with him. The colonel himself answered.

"Captain," he said, relief showing on his face. "Come in, come in."

He ushered Cameron inside and closed the door behind him. The colonel's wife, Wilma, appeared in the doorway to the kitchen, wiping her hands on her apron.

"Captain Wade." Her smile was warm and welcoming. "It's good to see you back safe and sound."

Cameron had always sensed that within the short, silvery-haired woman lay a tough inner strength. Her soft gray eyes often sparked with fire and he liked that.

"Please, sit," Colonel Dawson offered. "You must be beat."

Cameron wanted to get right to the point. "Colonel. I have a favor to ask of you both, and . . ." Cameron hesitated, suddenly realizing how strange this was going to sound.

"What is it, son?" Wilma asked, sitting down beside him and laying her hand on his.

Cameron could not help but smile, overwhelmed by the strong feeling of family that he experienced whenever he was with this kindhearted woman.

"Yes," the colonel prodded. "What have you found at the Sioux camp?"

Cameron decided the direct approach was best. "I'm convinced that the Ghost Sioux are in no way involved. My question is, how far are you two willing to go to help me prove it?"

It was Wilma who answered. "If they are innocent, Captain, as far as need be."

And right on her heels came the colonel's next question. "What does this have to do with anything?"

Cameron felt uncomfortable trying to explain something he wasn't even certain he understood himself, but for Angelique's sake, he told them the story of her dreams. When he had finished, he gave them a moment to digest all that he'd said, then added. "We need your help."

"Have you lost your mind, Captain?"

Colonel Dawson's reaction was not unexpected, but the look on his superior officer's face told Cameron he had gambled and lost. "Angelique believes that the man responsible is here, at the fort. That's the reason she returned with me. She has a strange loyalty to these people, so I thought I'd play along. That's the only way she would come willingly."

The colonel threw up his hands and stood. "You have lost your mind!" he shouted, then stomped across the room.

"Now, William, we can at least hear Cameron out. You're always jumping to conclusions before the end of the story." Wilma cast a shut-up-and-be-silent look to her husband, soothing it by an I-love-you-anyway smile.

"Now, Cameron, what exactly do you need us to do?"

"Ghost Dancer needs someone to stay with. I don't think anyone should know she's been living with the Sioux. It would make things more difficult for her."

Colonel Dawson's stony face kept him from going on. "You brought this Angelique here?" His look was incredulous.

"I didn't know what else to do. I thought, with time and Mrs. Dawson's help, Angelique would see that this is where she belongs. She's a white woman, and it just isn't right that she's living with the Sioux. But she's too stubborn to see it."

"Well," the Colonel conceded, "you're right there. But what's all this nonsense got to do with our immediate problem?"

"The way I see it, someone's trying to frame the Ghost Sioux with these murders."

"And what makes you so sure they're being framed? All the evidence points to the Indians."

Cameron fought his frustration but failed. "I don't *have* any proof, I just have a gut feeling! I'd bet my life on it, Colonel."

A stout finger pointed in his direction. "You have, boy. Your life and your damn career."

"They are innocent, and we've got to find out the truth."

"If they aren't responsible, dear, you could be causing a war over a grave injustice," Wilma pointed out softly.

"I gave you two weeks, and you've got one left. You'd better make the best of it, Captain."

"Does that mean you'll help Angelique?"

"Yes, dear," Wilma answered for her husband. "We'll do whatever we can."

Again, Cameron met the colonel's hard look. "My wife is overly generous, but I don't see any way out of this. And," he stressed the word, "don't expect me to believe in all this dream malarkey."

"Your not alone there, Colonel," confessed Cameron. "I have problems believing an awful lot about Angelique."

The carriage rolled down the dirt lane and around the parade grounds, the sounds of stamping feet and drilling sergeants growing faint as they passed by. The smell of baking bread drifted to their noses just before they left the fort and its collage of buildings, its visage lost in a cloud of dust. The carriage wheels rattled across the bridge that spanned the Laramie River, then the horses headed toward the small town of Laramie, about three miles out. Colonel William Dawson and his wife were on their way to pick up their niece coming in on the morning stage.

Cameron and Ghost Dancer left well before daylight and rode to meet the stage on the road. Luckily, there were few people on it, no one seeming very curious about the new passenger that climbed aboard. They were tired and didn't care that she was boarding only a few miles from the next stop. Nor did they notice the dress that hung on her, several sizes too big, as were her shoes.

Ghost Dancer looked out the window at Cameron's face.

"Are you going to be all right, Angel?" His voice mirrored the emotion on his face.

"Of course." She smiled, relieving some of his concern. "I will see you soon."

Cameron shook his head as if to free it of his sudden somber mood. "I'm being foolish. I'll see you at the fort later."

Ghost Dancer watched him ride away. He paused, his horse rearing slightly on its haunches, and Cameron turned back to her.

She waved as the coach started on its way again, watching until he was out of sight. Ghost Dancer settled into the wooden seat, trying to get more comfortable, grateful they only had a short distance to travel. Then her mind turned to the day ahead and the new challenges it would bring. She felt a bit frightened but also exhilarated at the same time. Silently, she asked *Wakan Tanka* to give her courage and strength.

"Angelique," Wilma cried, waving her delicate handkerchief in the air to catch her eye.

Ghost Dancer found herself being hugged, squeezed, and patted. The older woman made her feel as if she truly were a family member.

"It's so good to see you, dear." Wilma pulled her into her plump arms again.

"And it is good to see you both," Ghost Dancer said, a feeling of strangeness overwhelming her.

"Come now." Wilma hooked her arm through Ghost Dancer's and led her away. "We really must get you some clothes to wear, child. That old dress Cameron found is just hanging on you like a flour sack."

"Now, Wilma, how are you going to explain buying the girl a whole new wardrobe?"

Wilma's eyes sparkled, and she gave her husband a don't-you-worry pat. "William, you just run along and do whatever it is you men do when we women do our shopping. I'll think of something. Angelique's got to have clothes to wear during her visit."

Colonel William Dawson knew better than to stand in his wife's way when she had clothes on her mind. "You know where to find me when you're done, dear. Angelique, don't let her tire you your first time out." He gave his wife a quick peck on the cheek, then started off down the street, his chuckle of laughter filtering back to them over the street noise.

The older woman smiled. "Now let's go shopping."

Ghost Dancer followed obediently. "Shopping?"

"Yes, dear. We are going to buy you some new dresses and all the trappings."

It was still unclear to Ghost Dancer what they were going to do. But she felt a tingling of excitement, catching it from Wilma's exuberance. "Yes, let us find all the *trappings*." Another thought disturbed Ghost Dancer. "In order to buy these clothes, is it not necessary to have money?"

"Of course, but you needn't worry, Angelique. Cameron has provided for your needs. He said to get you anything and everything you need. He was very generous."

"Yes," Ghost Dancer agreed, having no real concept of the value of money. "Cameron Wade is a generous man."

As they entered the door to the shop, a small bell tinkled above them. Ghost Dancer jumped.

"Relax, dear," soothed Wilma.

It seemed to be a woman's place, filled with soft and delicate items. Ghost Dancer's eyes grew big with delight as she drank in the loveliness that surrounded her. It was small, but the shelves brimmed with neatly wrapped bundles of fabric. Exotic textures of materials in all colors caught her eye. Even the smell seemed special, giving her a wonderful feeling of anticipation. She longed to touch and experience the pleasure of "shopping." Such a wonderful custom her white sisters enjoyed.

Wilma saw the awe on Ghost Dancer's face and was reminded of a child in a candy store. When the middle-aged woman came out to help them, Wilma took command, knowing that her charge wouldn't know where to begin.

"Good day, Wilma."

"Hello, Pauline. How are you today?"

The proprietor didn't have a chance to answer.

"Mrs. Dawson," Lillian Thomas cooed as she swished in the door, her full skirts, lace, and perfume filling the small room with her dominant presence. "It's so very nice to see you."

"Lillian, Mary Beth. How are you two?" Wilma smiled at the plain young woman who stood behind the striking vision in green. "My, Lillian, you look striking today. As a matter of fact, you both are as pretty as a picture."

Lillian seemed to grow under Wilma's praise, like a flower reaching toward the sunlight. Mary Beth blushed and looked down at the polished wooden floor.

The two girls were like day and night. Mary Beth was painfully shy, what prettiness she possessed generally unnoticed by those around her. Her hazel eyes were downcast, her light brown hair neatly tucked into a bun, and her slender figure was disguised beneath an unobtrusive dress.

Then there was Lillian, a beautiful woman—and one who knew it. Her attitude showed in everything she did, confidence at every turn, every look, every subtle, but well-played, movement. Her sharp green eyes were alert and she was keenly aware of what was going on around her, always hearing what was, as well as what was not said.

"Ladies, this is my niece, Angelique." She turned her motherly gaze back to Ghost Dancer. "Angelique, this is Lillian and Mary Beth."

Lillian's cool look was quick to appraise Ghost Dancer, flicking over the ill-fitting dress and loose, unkept hair. "Charmed . . . I'm sure."

Ghost Dancer didn't get the feeling that the white girl was sure, but Mary Beth's look was pure friendliness.

"Why, Mrs. Dawson," Mary Beth cried, revealing

a very toothy grin. "I didn't know you were going to have company. You never mentioned a word of it the last time we saw you."

"I know, dear. But I didn't get her letter until just a few days ago. I barely had time to meet the stage this morning."

Mary Beth nodded in agreement, even though there really was nothing to agree with. "Well, we all know how reliable the mail is. Anyhow"—she turned to Ghost Dancer—"it's a pleasure to meet you."

"Charmed, I'm sure," Ghost Dancer mimicked in the same tone Lillian had used, bringing a blush to the redhead's face and a giggle from Mary Beth as she looked away.

Lillian pulled her chin up in defiance, casting a scathing glance at Ghost Dancer, then at her friend, but Mary Beth refused to acknowledge the scowl. "What brings you here, Mrs. Dawson? I thought you had your dress for the dance Saturday night."

Wilma was already picking through the bolts of cloth on display. "Yes, I have my gown, Lillian. We're here to find some things for Angelique."

Lillian once again assessed Ghost Dancer's dress, making it obvious the distaste she felt. "Yes, I can see the need."

"You know," Wilma rattled on, ignoring the rudeness of her remark, "the strangest thing happened. The wheel broke on the stage coach and *all* of Angelique's trunks were thrown off the top and lost in a deep canyon. Come near to tossing the poor girl out the door."

Mary Beth's eyes grew wide. "Oh, my. That's a horrible thing to happen." She turned to Ghost Dancer. "They lost everything?"

"Yes, everything." Ghost Dancer nodded, trying to keep her face serious.

"A woman was kind enough to give Angelique a dress to change into." Wilma was tossing colors this way and that. "But it is quite worn. So we are going to buy her a few things to make do." She turned to Pauline. "Do you have anything already made? I know it's dreadfully short notice. But the girl will have nothing to wear to the dance."

Pauline smiled at Wilma's obvious mission to reclothe her niece. "I have a dress I've been working on for myself, but heaven knows, I could do without it. I think it would fit Angelique, with a tuck here and there."

"Oh my!" Wilma was moved. "That would be so good of you, Pauline. What color is it? Would it be good with her pale hair?"

"It's blue and will look lovely." Pauline disappeared into the back room to get it.

Lillian watched Wilma cut a path through the store like a tornado hitting a town. "You know, Wilma," she raised her voice and pointed to Ghost Dancer, "with such a slender, even boyish figure"—her cold eyes met amused ones, then moved back to Wilma—"you'll have to make sure Pauline pays close attention to those tucks."

Wilma stopped abruptly and turned to Lillian. "You *are* so sharp, child. But I'm confident that Pauline will see that it fits properly."

Fingering a piece of delicate lace, Lillian agreed.

"Yes, sometimes I think Pauline can work miracles. So, are you planning on having Pauline make your new wardrobe, Angelique?"

"No, I see no need," Ghost Dancer answered, leveling her gaze at Lillian again.

Lillian smiled wickedly. "But you have no clothes."

"Clothes do not matter to me."

With the definite purpose of belittling Ghost Dancer, Lillian's eyes lowered. "I can see that."

Mary Beth was quick to step in, embarrassed by her friend's cattiness. "I think blue would be a good color on you. It would set off your eyes and hair beautifully. And I would be happy to loan you a few things while you are here."

Ghost Dancer felt her distress. "That is very kind of you, Mary Beth. Would you like to help us with our shopping today?"

"I would love to." Mary Beth smiled shyly.

Lillian turned to leave, her full lower lip pouting in a childish manner. Ghost Dancer stopped her. "I had hoped you might stay as well, Lillian."

Wilma was impressed by Ghost Dancer's generosity and patience. "Yes, Lillian. You have such good taste when it comes to clothes and things." It was true, the girl dressed to perfection, and Wilma couldn't really believe she meant most of what she said.

Lillian puffed up and moved back to Mary Beth's side. "Very well. I suppose I really don't have any other plans this afternoon."

Ghost Dancer met Wilma's look, a twinkle

alight in them. "I am so pleased, Lillian, Mary Beth."

Wilma turned to enter the back room. "Now, let's see that dress."

Chapter 14

"Wilma," Ghost Dancer interjected between the ladies gossip and chit-chat, "I will not possibly need all of these things."

"Of course you will, dear." Wilma's warm eyes sparkled with the energy of a woman who loved taking care of someone. "We may even need to buy more."

Her laughter was contagious, and the other women joined in. Ghost Dancer wasn't even certain why they laughed, only that it felt nice.

"Good day, ladies. Your laughter has certainly made it a good one for me."

Major Jack Bender tipped his hat to Wilma and then to the other familiar faces, but paused when his eyes met Ghost Dancer's. "I don't believe I have had the pleasure."

"Mr. Bender, I would like you to meet my niece, Angelique. She is going to be staying with William and me for a while."

"The pleasure is all mine." Bender reached out to accept her hand, but she made no move, her eyes rudely glued to his disfigured hand.

Ghost Dancer had never felt such paralyzing fear in all her life. His appearance had caught her so off guard she could not think, she could not even move. Mary Beth casually pushed her elbow out so that Ghost Dancer's hand met his. The contact of their flesh instantly drew Ghost Dancer from her stupor.

"I'm so p–ple . . ." She could not say it. She wasn't pleased to meet him. She wasn't charmed. And certainly the feelings weren't mutual. Weren't those the three choices Wilma had so kindly explained while she was trying on the blue dress?

She felt only repulsion. The urge to withdraw her hand was hard to control. But when he turned her hand over, palm up, and placed his other hand over hers to hold her one in his two, she could not keep from pulling away.

A slight flash of anger appeared in his eyes, but was expertly stilled. "What an unusual mark on your hand, Miss . . ." He didn't know how to finish, Wilma had not given her last name.

Before Wilma could speak, Ghost Dancer replied, "Miss Dancer." Just then, she noticed the young Sioux woman behind Bender's tall form, her brown eyes growing overly large when she recognized the marking on Angelique's palm. Trying to see better, she accidentally bumped into him.

Bender spun around so quickly he almost caused the Indian to fall, but did make her drop the packages she held. "You ignorant savage," he muttered between clenched teeth, his hand ready to strike. "How many times must I tell you to keep your distance?"

His hand came down to slap her, but Ghost Dancer interfered, her own arm deflecting his blow. He was astounded at first, then overcome with fury.

"I would suggest, Miss Dancer, that in the future, you do not interfere in my business."

Ghost Dancer returned his blackened look without hesitation. "Then I would suggest, Mr. Bender, that you do not strike women."

With a sudden outburst, he laughed and turned a brilliantly evil smile to Mrs. Dawson. "She's a spitfire, your niece. I think I am quite taken by her. Might I be permitted to call?"

Wilma had paled at the whole scene and wanted only to be on their way. "That's up to my niece, Mr. Bender." Her glance was nervous as she watched Ghost Dancer help the Sioux woman up and then collect what had been dropped for her. "And to be honest, I don't think she was taken by you."

A sparkle lightened the hooded eyes that also studied Ghost Dancer. "I have always welcomed a good challenge."

Ghost Dancer could tell the Sioux knew who she was, and when she touched the symbols on her palms, she was certain. Shyly, she closed Ghost Dancer's hands, hiding the sun and the moon from Bender's eyes as he took a step toward them.

"Come, we must be going." He clamped a possessive hand on the Sioux's elbow and led her away. His dark head nodded in Ghost Dancer's direction. "Again, the pleasure was all mine."

When he was well out of hearing, Mary Beth breathed a sigh of relief. "Angelique, that was certainly a brave thing to do. He has always frightened me."

Lillian sniffed loudly. "I say it was a very stupid thing to do. Major Bender's the most eligible man in town. Well, almost. Cameron Wade has more money. Though you certainly wouldn't know it."

Ghost Dancer's eyes were drawn from the busy street that Bender had disappeared down to Lillian as she rattled on and on. "Is it so important to have money?"

Lillian's laughter was her answer, but she elaborated any way. "Important? Goodness gracious me. Mrs. Dawson, where has this girl been? She almost sounds like Captain Wade himself. I swear, leaving Boston and all his money and influence . . . It's insane! Well, I can tell you. When Cameron and I are married, we will most certainly return to Boston."

Wilma came near to choking on her gasp, and Ghost Dancer's own shock went unnoticed as she tended to the older woman. When she turned back to Lillian, her eyes were hard and cold, but were unnoticed as Lillian was absorbed in her single-minded thoughts. "I did not know that you were to be married."

Lillian had the decency to blush at her own blundering. "Well, if the truth be known, Cameron and I are not to be married. At least, not yet." Her hand carefully smoothed back her hair, though not a single strand was out of place. "Let's just say, *I* have decided he is the man I want to marry and, surely, he will come around to my thinking soon enough."

"Why would you think that?" asked Ghost Dancer, curiosity eating away at her.

"Why?" Her look was genuinely confused. "I have never had a man deny me anything."

Mary Beth agreed. "It's true."

Ghost Dancer felt sudden pity for Lillian. "Sometimes our futures do not hold what we wish for."

Lillian's eyes narrowed and her voice grew deep with anger. "I suppose your future does include Cameron Wade. A man you haven't even met." She was being facetious and never expected the answer she got.

"Yes. I believe that it does."

It was the look of honest certainty in Ghost Dancer's eyes that disarmed Lillian. "I see." Then jealousy claimed her, strong and fierce. "Well, we know were we stand, don't we? I don't give up what I consider to be mine. Do you understand, Miss Dancer?"

Ghost Dancer nodded. "Yes, Miss Thomas, I do."

Cameron knocked, but no answer came. He knew that the colonel and his wife had returned with Ghost Dancer and a carriage full of packages. He knocked again.

He needed to reassure himself that everything had gone all right and he needed to see Ghost Dancer. When no one answered, he entered.

"Angelique," he called, "are you here?"

He heard some rattling of paper and moved to the back bedroom, easing open the door that stood ajar. The four-poster bed was piled high with wrapping and boxes.

It was not an overly large room, but everything within it was perfectly done in blue and white. A feminine attitude was evidenced in the atmosphere of frilly, white eyelet lace so crisp and light against the dark cherry wood furniture that adorned the sunny bedroom. Ghost Dancer stood in front of a full-length, oval mirror, scantily dressed in a chemise and pantalets. She was deeply concentrating on a piece of clothing in her hands.

"Angel," Cameron said, his voice whisper-soft.

Whirling about, she squealed happily and ran to him. "Look at all my new things. Wilma took me shopping."

A smile curved his lips, and he was pleased by her childish delight. "Did you have a good time?"

"Yes, I did. Look, Cameron Wade." She pointed to the bed then bounced upon it playfully. "It is for sleeping."

This made Cameron laugh.

"And later, Wilma said she would heat my bath water. Then she will fill a large tub and I will wash in it. I cannot imagine such a thing, but she says that is how it is done."

"Yes, that is exactly how we do it." Cameron picked up a small bottle of perfume and smelled it. "I see Wilma even thought of a scent for your bath."

A giggle from Ghost Dancer brought a twinkle to her own eyes. "It is flowers in a bottle."

"Roses," he whispered, his gaze never leaving her as she continued to flit about in delight.

"But I must confess I do not know what I will do with so many things. And I do not even know what most of these things are." She handed him the item she held. "What is this?"

Cameron lifted the piece of lacy cloth to examine it. "It's a corset. It's to wear about your waist. See." He held it up to show her. "You tighten these strings to make your waist smaller."

"Why would I want to do that?"

Lifting his shoulders in a shrug, he smiled again. "I don't know. Women just want tiny waistlines. It's the fashion."

Ghost Dancer seemed to consider this and took the satin corset back to examine it better. "What is stitched into it?"

"Whale bones."

"A whale"—she continued to study the item—"is a giant fish that swims in the oceans."

"Yes."

She tossed it aside, her nose wrinkling up in disgust. "Women wear fish bones about them and tie themselves in to make them smaller."

"That's about it." Cameron grinned, thinking it quite absurd when she put it that way.

"It is silly."

"I agree. I kind of like you just the way you are, Angel." Cameron pulled her into his arms, all too aware of her thinly clad body.

"White women wear too many clothes."

"I couldn't agree with you more."

Cameron's lips sought the smooth line of her neck as it curved into her shoulder, trailing a path of kisses along the smooth expanse of her skin. His tongue darted out to taste her creamy flesh.

"Where is Wilma?" he mumbled, his face lost in her thick mane of hair that fell in loose tangles on her shoulders.

"She is taking care of a few important things," Ghost Dancer said, repeating exactly what she had been told. "She has mentioned a dance."

"Oh, yeah," Cameron moaned, his mind on the silk of Angelique's skin. His hands moved up to cup the full roundness of her breasts. "She's hosting a dance Saturday night."

"Cameron," Ghost Dancer whispered, "what is a dance? Is it like the Sun Dance or the Ghost Dance?"

Cameron pulled his mouth away from her sweetly scented neck, wishing for the briefest of seconds that she was not quite so inquisitive. "No. Our dances are purely for fun and enjoyment. We have a band, and everyone dances to the music."

"Is it difficult?" she questioned, a serious mood descending on her.

"Is what difficult?"

"To dance." She smiled shyly. "I do not know how to. Not as you would. I know only the dances of the Sioux. I would guess that your dancing is very different."

Cameron saw how important this was to Angelique and tamped down his hunger for her.

"Different, but not hard." He took her hand in his. "Here, I'll show you."

Her eyes lit up with excitement.

Cameron pulled Ghost Dancer into his arms. He hummed a tune and moved her about the room in time to his tempo. His dangerous eyes claimed Ghost Dancer, drawing her inside. She was unaware of his steps. Only Cameron filled her mind. She melted to him. His movements became her own. His hard, muscled body molded hers close to his, as Cameron's arms tightened about her with each step he took. His lips were near her ear, his breath tickling and warm, creating bumps on her bare skin.

"I wouldn't mind you modeling your unmentionables more often, Angel. It certainly does something to me."

Being so close to him, she didn't need to ask what that was, she could feel his hardness against her. But she had a question. "What are unmentionables?"

His deep laughter vibrated inside his chest. "It is the undergarments you are so barely clothed in, my darling."

She smiled mischievously. "Then I shall have to remember that. Later, when we are alone."

Cameron's own eyes were aglow from desire. "We are alone."

Looking about her, she nodded. "You are right. We are alone."

His lips stole away her smile, then as his kiss deepened, it drew the strength from her, leaving her weak. His hand moved from her waist and caressed the supple curve beneath her bosom. The tips of his fingers traced the circle of her nipple covered only by the sheer, cotton fabric. His lips left hers and kissed her neck, then moved lower to the silken valley between her breasts. His fingers, nimble and quick, undid the ties to her chemise, freeing her fullness to his scorching gaze. His mouth tasted first one breast, then the other, causing her to groan in tortured ecstacy.

Ghost Dancer's head fell back weakly, her hair hanging past her buttocks, tickling the back of her calves. She heard the fast pacing of her heart. Cameron's mouth was creating havoc inside her body, the heat pulsating through her with each strong beat. His teeth now pulled at the strings of her pantalets as he knelt before her. His tongue tasted of the tender flesh of her belly, making it quiver beneath his wet touch.

"Angelique."

At first, Ghost Dancer thought it was Cameron calling her name, but slowly, it dawned on her who it was.

"Wilma," she whimpered, pulling Cameron's head up to stop him.

"Angelique." Wilma walked into the room and found Cameron on his knees, his head between Ghost Dancer's hands, looking up at her. "Oh, my," she breathed in shock, then turned and left the room. "Oh, my."

"Hell!" Cameron quickly jumped to his feet. Even faster than he had loosened Angelique's clothes, he fixed them. He took a minute longer to cover her in a robe he found among the clothes on the bed, then pulled Angelique into the parlor where Mrs. Dawson sat in rigid silence.

Cameron felt awkward and cleared his throat. "Mrs. Dawson, I'm afraid I owe you an apology. I—"

"Cameron," Ghost Dancer interrupted, "what is it that you are sorry for?"

He raised his hand as if to keep her from going on. "You don't fully understand our ways, Angel. Please, just let me explain to Mrs. Dawson."

Ghost Dancer smiled, calm and collected. "There is nothing to explain. We are lovers. It is no secret."

A sob tore from Wilma at Ghost Dancer's blunt statement.

"You did not know this?" Ghost Dancer asked in total innocence. "It is not something to cry over."

This caused even greater tears.

"Angelique"—Cameron turned her to look at him—"we are not married. In our world, you do not make love to a man unless you are man and wife."

"Cameron," she whispered to him, her eyes full of love, "in my world, we are man and wife."

The dark tanned skin on his face paled in an alarming manner. "What do you mean?"

Wilma perked up. "Yes, dear. What do you mean?"

"I am the Ghost Dancer. I am free to choose my own mate. It has always been so."

Cameron backed off a few steps, feeling a sudden terror claim him. "I don't remember any ceremony. Hell! I don't even remember being asked."

"The question was asked the night when I came to you, offering myself. You said yes when you accepted my womanhood."

"Oh, no!" he bellowed. "Did you really expect me to send you away? My, God! You are the most beautiful creature I ever laid eyes on. I'm only a man, not a saint."

Wilma broke in. "The boy's right, Angelique."

Ghost Dancer and Cameron turned amazed looks at her.

"I am?" he echoed at the very moment Ghost Dancer cried, "He is?"

"Yes." She turned sympathetic eyes to the younger woman. "Dear, a man can only control his needs to a certain extent. To give yourself to him does not make you his wife. It must be done properly, in front of a man of God."

"Hold on. I still have something to say about all this." Cameron felt as if he were being trapped, with no way out.

"The man always has a say in a marriage. Should you not wish to be married, you are free to choose another."

This stopped him cold. "I am?"

"It is our way." Ghost Dancer smiled bravely.

"It certainly isn't ours," claimed Wilma, her look disapproving.

Ghost Dancer turned understanding eyes to Wilma's worried gray ones. "Cameron, perhaps you had better go."

He didn't need to be asked twice. "Yes, I think you're right."

"Can we continue what we started, later, in the privacy of your room?" she asked in a tone low enough for his ears only.

A sudden stab of guilt urged him to say no, to end it now. The weight of his self-imposed promises moved to stand guard. Things were getting too complicated. He knew that. But, defying all common sense, he whispered, "You've got a date."

After Cameron had left, Wilma drummed her fingers on the arm of the chair. Her posture was ramrod straight and unbending. "It's just not proper, Angelique."

There was that word again, "proper." Ghost Dancer was beginning to dislike the sound of it. "Wilma, you have been so kind. I do not wish to see you upset with me."

"Oh, dear child," she said, taking her hand into her own. "I am not upset with you. You only know the way of the Sioux. On the other hand, Cameron does know better."

Ghost Dancer sat on the floor beside her chair. "You need not concern yourself with this."

"It is hard not to."

"Please, try to understand. I love him and all will be right."

Wilma placed her hand on Ghost Dancer's cheek. "You believe this?"

"Yes," she said, her heartfelt words reaching out to the other woman. "Our souls have been united. That is better than marriage."

Wilma sighed, resigned for the moment. "If you say so, dear. If you say so." But, somehow, she did not believe what she was saying.

* * *

Ghost Dancer stood at her window, watching the activity below. It was all so new and strange—the fort, the soldiers, the ways of the white man. She wanted to understand, but found only confusion and underneath it a great fear.

She had found the man of her visions, the four-fingered man with evil black eyes. Major Jack Bender, a soldier like Cameron, yet a vicious murderer of women and children. How could it be? And why?

Her first instinct had been to tell Cameron, but another emotion made her keep silent. Ghost Dancer still struggled with the hurt of Cameron's denials, of who she was and the truth of her visions. He had laughed and he did not try to understand. Sadly, she knew he would not believe her if she told him about Bender.

No, he had said they needed proof, something to show his guilt. It was the way of the whites, and she must do it their way—hers was not acceptable. Questions still remained. How was she to do this? Could it be done in such a short time?

I must, she resolved with great determination. Her people were depending upon her, and she would not fail them.

Chapter 15

"Good day, Miss Dancer."

Ghost Dancer turned her attention to the voice, her heart pounding when she met dark, black eyes. "Good day, Major Bender."

"It's a nice day, wouldn't you say?"

His attempts at polite chatter irritated her, but she did not show it. Instead, she quickly came up with the *proper* response from the many that both Wilma and Cameron had schooled her in. "Yes, it is." Trapped between the confining dress and layers of white, lacy petticoats and other *unmentionables* beneath it and the rush of heat she felt in Bender's presence, she felt as if she were suffocating.

"Are you all right? You look a bit flushed." He took a step toward her, in case she might faint. The normally creamy color of her skin was tinted with pink and her cheeks were marked with a much darker rosy hue.

"I am fine, thank you." She wished he would turn those damnable eyes away from her. "I am not used to the damp heat." It was a lie, she had never seemed to mind the warm days of October just before the rains. It was the clothes she minded.

"Yes." He smiled, white teeth flashing in his evil good looks. But the smile quickly disappeared when the woman he smiled at made no attempt to return it. "It can be overwhelming."

Ghost Dancer could find nothing else to say and there was silence.

"Is there something I can help you find, Miss Dancer? You obviously came in for something." Again, he gave her a charming smile, his intense black eyes watching her.

Her eyebrows raised in surprise. "I would not want to bother you."

"It's no bother, I assure you." Actually, he had seen her enter the post trading store and intentionally followed her in.

"How is it you came by the Sioux woman, Major Bender? None of the other officers seem to have servants."

The question was unexpected, but everything about her seemed to be unexpected. "I won her in a card game." Then he added, almost making an excuse for himself, "I also have a hired lady who tends to my house."

"You have a house?"

"Yes, at the edge of the compound. And none of the other bachelor officers have houses."

"Oh." It was all she said, but the small word carried much more punch than she had intended. It seemed to say, *I hadn't really cared to know all this.*

His disappointment showed for a brief second,

then he brought it under control. "I believe in the finer things in life, Miss Dancer."

Lillian's face reared in her mind. "It seems to be of great importance to many people. Why is that so?"

Bender was truly shocked. "Why?"

"Yes," she asked in earnest. "Why is it that people place such value on money?"

"Money is everything." His look changed, a fierceness replacing the handsomeness from his features. "It is all that life has to give, and without it, there is no reason to go on."

Ghost Dancer felt his immense greed, his twisted mind only knowing one thing—money. Gold. The word struck her with horror. "How far would you go for money, Major?"

Like a mannequin, Bender moved every feature into the right mold, presenting, once again, the dashing image of an officer. "I am a man who knows what he wants and I am also a man who lets no one stand in his way." He flashed a smile that never quite reached his devil eyes. "And you, Miss Dancer, seem to be a woman of mystery. I do not believe for a moment that you have no need for money and what it can do for you."

Finally, she smiled, but it was a sad one. "Believe what you will." She turned to leave.

"Miss Dancer." He stopped her. "You have not gotten what you came in for."

"I only came in to look around. I was curious."

Again, he stopped her departure. "Are you by chance attending the dance tomorrow night?"

She turned back to face him. "Yes, I am."

"Would you save a dance for me?"

Ghost Dancer's mind was filled with visions of Cameron Wade, his body molded against hers as he taught her to dance. She shivered as his image was replaced by Bender's. "I am not sure I wish to do that."

The slightest flash of anger touched his mouth, then with skilled theatrics, disappeared. "I guarantee that it is quite proper."

She felt confused. Everything seemed to navigate around what was proper and what was not. And she didn't know which was which. Ghost Dancer only knew that the thought of being close to Bender did not appeal to her in the least. As a matter of fact, it turned her stomach inside out and twisted everything into a painful knot inside her. Again, she shivered despite her warmth.

"I really must go."

Jack Bender watched Angelique leave, a strange concoction of anger and intrigue barraging him. It was a rare experience for a woman to show such indifference toward him, and he was angry. Yet, on the other hand, this same indifference intrigued him. And what of this strange notion she had of money?

Quickly, he surmised it to be a ploy. A woman's game, he was sure of it. After all, he couldn't believe anyone wouldn't want or need money.

Uncomfortable memories haunted him, childhood grievances worked firmly into his adult mind. The humiliation of being poor, the sadness of his mother's eyes, the shame of what she did to feed her child. . . .

Bender pushed away the melancholy and reconfirmed his view on the subject—money was everything in life.

Cameron Wade saw Ghost Dancer enter the post trading store from across the compound. By the time he finished his task and got there, she was leaving.

"Angel," he called, catching her attention.

A smile immediately claimed her, lighting up her whole face. "Cameron," she called out, and waved in acknowledgment. A new, welcome warmth trickled through her, and she waited for him to catch up to her.

She was unaware of Bender's watchful eyes, or of his clenched fists that shook at his side. She was unaware of the jealousy that rattled through him as he witnessed the loving smile she gave to Cameron Wade. To him, she had given nothing, nothing at all, even the simplest of polite smiles.

"Are you all right?" Cameron asked in concern, noting the flushed coloring of her face.

"Why is it that everyone is so interested in my welfare?"

A scowl wrinkled Cameron's smooth forehead as a tiny alarm sounded in his head. "Everyone?"

She caught the edge of apprehension in his voice. "Yes. Major Bender asked the same thing."

Again, he repeated her words. "Major Bender?"

"Yes, he was in the store."

"Wilma told me that you ran into him in town yesterday. Why didn't *you* tell me?"

His tone was sharp, a note of something unusual in it. Something Ghost Dancer had not heard before, and this added to her confusion. "I did not run into him, Cameron. I saw him, but I did not *run* into him."

The jealousy slipped from him with ease, her innocence once again like a salve upon a sore wound. Instead of a growl, he chuckled. "I didn't mean it literally, Angel."

"Oh," she whispered, her color deepening even further. "I seem to misunderstand a lot."

His smile told her that it was all right.

As they walked along, she worked her lower lip, wondering about her conservation with Bender. "If a man asks you to save a dance for him, is it proper?"

Ghost Dancer made an obvious effort to use some of the words Cameron was fond of, but her attempt was lost on him as the green-eyed monster slithered into his thoughts again. "Who asked you that?"

"Bender," she answered, uncertain of what was changing Cameron's mood so quickly, so easily. "He is the only man I have seen since I arrived. Except, of course, for you and the colonel."

"Of course." The terse edge came back to his voice.

She misunderstood his look. "It is not proper? He told me that it was."

"No, Angel," he gave in to her confusion. "It is quite proper to dance with him. If that's what you want."

She stopped and turned hurt eyes to him. "It

would be proper to dance with him, just as we danced last night?"

"Well, not quite the way we danced. A bit less friendly maybe."

Another question immediately followed. "You can dance with a man in a different way?"

"Yes." He took her elbow and started walking again. "Remind me to show you *exactly* how to dance with other men, later, tonight."

"Perhaps we're missing something."

Cameron was thinking and he just stared at the colonel a long moment, as if dazed, before he spoke. "The Cheyenne."

"What about the Cheyenne?" Obviously, William Dawson didn't have the foggiest notion what Cameron was getting at.

"Yes," he declared, as if stumbling upon something important. "They followed us all the way here. Maybe, just maybe, they have something to do with all this."

The colonel still did not know the reasons for the young man's thoughts, and asked, "Why the Cheyenne, boy?"

"The same warriors who had me pinned down followed us here, but they rode off after a very strange confrontation with Angelique, or Ghost Dancer I mean." He thought harder on this new twist. "Something happened after I passed out. Something she won't tell me about."

"Do you think they're out for revenge?"

Cameron gave this consideration. "Could be. She got me away from them and it beat's the hell out of me just how, but she did."

"She's certainly a strange one, Captain."

It was an honest statement, even Cameron thought that same thing many times. "I certainly haven't figured her out, Colonel. And I'm beginning to wonder if I ever will."

Ghost Dancer turned back without being noticed and returned to the kitchen where Wilma was puttering around.

"Wilma," she asked, "what does a woman do to encourage a man's advances?"

Wilma turned to look at Ghost Dancer, her eyebrows raising in amazement. "Looks to me like you've done enough encouraging and not enough discouraging."

Confusion reigned free. "I have encouraged Major Bender? In what way?"

"Oh, no, child. Of course not the major. I was referring to Cameron." Wilma couldn't help but wonder. "Why on earth would you want to encourage that scoundrel?"

"I heard Lillian say that if you were to encourage a man, it might benefit your cause. I am not certain I understand how this could be?"

Wilma didn't answer directly, but took time to pour them each a cup of coffee and sit at the small table covered with a starched, white linen. "Well, it could be she's right. Sometimes a man who's smitten will do a lot of talking to impress a girl."

"Smitten?" Ghost Dancer asked, smelling the brew before taking a sip. It was pleasing.

"Attracted. You know." Wilma smiled and rolled her eyes.

"Yes." Ghost Dancer laughed. "I believe I am beginning to understand."

"But," continued Wilma, "that doesn't explain your sudden interest in Major Bender."

Ghost Dancer did not want to go into detail, but did explain just a little. "I saw him again today, at the post trading store. I do not think that I like him."

Wilma snorted. "I can't say that I do either. But why encourage him if you feel that way?"

"He may know something of importance. That is what I am here for."

"Yes, I suppose you are."

"Wilma," asked Ghost Dancer, "who is Jack Bender?"

"Well, none of us know much about him"—a gleam snuck into her eyes—"but I know the basics."

She took a moment to begin her story. "He came west, after the war, with his mother." Her eyebrow lifted, its meaning lost on Ghost Dancer. "She was certainly an odd sort and she died a few years ago. Seems their family lost everything in the war. Jack was at West Point when the war broke out, and with his mother's encouragement, he joined the Union army. She was from the north."

"And this war put father against son?"

"Exactly. Some say that Jack was with Sherman's army and he marched right through his own home territory, fighting against his family and friends . . . even destroying his own home."

Wilma paused. "He was quite taken by you, Angelique."

"Good. Perhaps, if encouraged, he will talk too much."

The women worked steadily, their labor happily performed in anticipation of the upcoming dance. Laughter interrupted the steady drone of feminine voices. It was a warm, comfortable scene, and Ghost Dancer hummed a soft tune as she meticulously created the decorations Wilma had given her. Fold once, twice, three times. Ghost Dancer felt proud at her accomplishment, even though it was unclear what it was.

"That's a beautiful tune," Mary Beth said. "I can't place it, though. Is it something new?"

Ghost Dancer smiled. "It is very old. Perhaps too old for you to know." She didn't feel the need to explain that it was a song of the Sioux. Somehow, it made her feel closer to her people when she filled her mind with their music; it made her miss them just a little less.

"You look sad, Angelique," Mary Beth ventured.

"Do I?" Ghost Dancer was surprised at the girl's astuteness.

"If you want to talk," she began shyly, "I'm a good listener."

"I will remember your kindness."

A commotion across the room drew both women's attention to the small group who gathered in the corner. Screams erupted and women scattered in panic.

Ghost Dancer stood and moved toward them.

"Nasty critters," Wilma cried, her hands clutching a broom like a weapon. In seconds, she was after the unseen creature with a vengeance. The straw bristles rapped the floor with a loud thump. "I'll get you!"

At that moment Ghost Dancer saw the tiny brown creature scampering from the blows that befell it, its size infinitely small compared to Wilma's well-rounded figure.

"Wilma," Ghost Dancer called. The older woman did not seem to hear her. Ghost Dancer stepped to her side and grabbed the handle of her deadly broom. "Wilma. It is only a mouse. It cannot harm you."

Wilma opened her mouth to speak, but the look on Ghost Dancer's face stopped her. "I guess you're . . . you're right. I don't know what came over me."

The other women had calmed some, and the mouse cowered in a corner under their horrified stares. Ghost Dancer moved past them and knelt down to pick up the animal. "It must have been brought in with the things from outside. I will remove it."

Obviously amazed, Wilma nodded. "Yes, you go right ahead. I'm sure that the poor thing's just scared to death." When Ghost Dancer moved past her, Wilma shuddered. "Come now, girls. There's work to be done."

Ghost Dancer held out her palm and the mouse sat up, its nose twitching in the air. Gently, she stroked its small, fur-covered head.

"It is so strange that one so small could create such confusion."

"What's strange," Cameron observed, leaning casually against the white porch column, "is a woman petting a mouse, and even stranger yet, the mouse seeming to enjoy it."

Ghost Dancer let the creature down so that it could scurry off to safety. "Why is it strange?"

"I don't know." He shrugged. "I guess I just never saw anyone do that. I thought they would bite."

"It is fear they sense." She smiled tolerantly. "I do not fear the animals. They will not harm me."

Cameron moved closer to her. "And why is that?"

Ghost Dancer felt the heat of his body, his masculine scent arousing. "They are messengers of the Gods Above. I, too, am a servant. We are kindred spirits."

Cameron's cool gaze chilled Ghost Dancer. "You talk nonsense, Angel."

"I speak the truth, Cameron Wade. It is your own heart that plays you false, not me."

"Maybe you're right. Maybe you are everything you say. All I know is that I cannot believe as you do."

Ghost Dancer reached out and pushed back a stray lock of hair that had fallen across his forehead. "One day, your mind will understand, and the war will no longer rage within you. Then you will be at peace and you will know in what direction your future lies."

A mixture of seriousness and playfulness radiated from him. "Tell me, my mystic, does my future include you?"

"My heart tells me this is so. But I do not know for certain. I have had no dreams of us."

Cameron grinned mischievously. "So, we are on our own. No cards or tea leaves to tell us if we're right for each other?"

"Yes, Cameron Wade." Ghost Dancer could not help laughing aloud. "We are on our own."

Chapter 16

"You look beautiful tonight, Miss Dancer."

Those same words, only moments before, had sent a wonderful tingle down her spine and brought a flush to her face. But it had been Cameron who had spoken them and now it was Bender saying the words. When his lips touched the back of her hand, a wave of nausea churned her stomach. Still, when he lifted his dark eyes to hers, she offered a smile. She knew it was a lie. He read it as a promise.

"Thank you, Major Bender. You are too kind." Ghost Dancer repeated the words which she had practiced. She hoped her downcast eyes added to the picture of coyness she wished to portray.

With obvious reluctance, Bender let go of her hand. "On the contrary, I'm certain there isn't a man here who wouldn't agree that you are the most beautiful woman in the room."

"On that point, I wholeheartedly agree." Cameron's deep voice drew Ghost Dancer's gaze.

His smile caused her heart to tighten, and she missed the black scowl that shadowed Bender's face.

The music started again, the beat strong and steady, and the wooden floor vibrated to the rhythm. Cameron's smile widened. "I believe this dance is ours."

Ghost Dancer glanced back to Bender. "If you will excuse me, I do believe that he is correct."

Bender nodded in acquiescence. "Perhaps you will save the next one for me?"

It took all her concentration to give him the smallest of smiles. His look of pleasure proved that her effort was successful. "Perhaps, Major."

Cameron pulled Ghost Dancer into his arms and swept her onto the crowded dance floor. The swish of whirling skirts and the stomp of moving feet kept time with the music. Laughing, talking men and women gathered to share a good time. Yet all the noise and clamor drifted into the distance, leaving Ghost Dancer feeling that she and Cameron were alone.

Ghost Dancer noticed that Cameron kept her at arm's length. Still, the slightest contact of their bodies created havoc within her.

"God, Angel. You *are* beautiful."

His whispered words tickled her ear, but it was their meaning and the deep huskiness of his voice that sent tremors through her.

"Yet you do not hold me close," Ghost Dancer pointed out.

"As delightful as that sounds," he sighed, "I can't. We *are* supposed to be strangers . . . not lovers."

Ghost Dancer raised sad eyes to him. "I know you speak wisely but I still wish we could dance as we did before."

Cameron swirled her about so fast, her feet barely touched the floor. "You are a little minx," he said as around and around they spun. "And I love it."

Bender's gaze followed the couple moving about the floor, and as every second ticked by, the heat within him grew until his grip tightened about the delicate hand he held.

"Major Bender," Lillian objected, "you're hurting me, sir." She lowered her eyes demurely, her lashes fluttering in feigned despair.

Bender flashed a brilliant smile, as well rehearsed as any of her coy looks. "My humble apologizes, Miss Thomas. My mind must have been elsewhere."

A warmth stained Lillian's snowy cheeks as he so rudely announced what she had already ascertained. Unused to a man's attention wandering, she pulled her shoulders back in a haughty manner. She then stiffened her spine to push her full breasts even tighter against the straining fabric and lace of her dress. As she had planned, the pink flesh rose with each deep breath and the delicate mounds quivered to be free of the confining mint-green satin.

Bender gazed freely at what she offered so willingly, and a lascivious grin curled his lips.

"Major . . ." Her voice drew his black steel gaze to hers. What she had meant to say was forgotten, and Lillian withdrew her eyes in sudden cowardice, a feeling that was new to her.

The corners of his mouth twitched, and Bender

lifted a hand to brush his thumb over the curve of her cheek. "You are a very lovely woman, Miss Thomas."

"Why, tha–thank you, Major Bender." The hammering of her heart was replaced with warning tremors of fear. "If I might be so bold to say, you look quite dashing yourself." He flashed her a brilliant smile, but Lillian couldn't quell the uneasiness that rioted inside her.

Bender saw the fear written so clearly on her face, and he felt strength pump through him with each beat of his heart. His power to create terror was a drug that ran like red heat in his veins. She was afraid, and he grew strong from it.

Suddenly, he recalled another pair of eyes, eyes the color of a cloudless sky, eyes that held no fear. Once again, he searched the crowded room for Angelique. It didn't even matter that Lillian sighed in relief that his attention was no longer on her.

Ghost Dancer felt his eyes on her, like a foreboding omen touching her soul with its chill. When she lifted her gaze from the small crystal cup she held, she met the evil intensity of ebony eyes. The song had ended, and she knew from the look he gave her, that he would be coming to ask for that promised dance.

Lillian sashayed across the floor on Bender's arm, her eyes flashing dangerously at Ghost Dancer. The layers of Lillian's starched petticoats crinkled with each step, ending with an elegant swish by Ghost Dancer's side, the soft green catching the sparkle of light with every exaggerated movement.

"Why, Angelique, that dress does look much better on you than I thought it would."

Actually, Lillian thought the pale blue crepe-de-chine gown was lovely, its white intricate applique embroidery enhancing Angelique's delicate beauty. The dusty color brought out the brightness of her eyes and the honey-peach tone of her skin. In fact, the cut of the dress was so attractive that even Lillian was reluctantly impressed.

Lillian's voice held a sweetness that bespoke falseness. Cameron lifted an eyebrow in amazement and Bender chuckled at the woman's open cattiness.

"It is so nice to see you again, Lillian." Ghost Dancer's words were as smooth as doeskin, no anger or annoyance in the tone. "Your dress is very lovely. Did you buy it at the shop where we met?"

Lillian's laughter tinkled in the air, the high notes rising above the clamor. "Oh, dear, of course not. The styles here are much too out of date. Years, in fact. I had this designed especially for me just before I left school in New York City. Even the ladies in Paris haven't anything better."

"I would certainly think not," Ghost Dancer agreed, restraining the smile that wanted to erupt into a giggle. "I envy your taste in clothes, Lillian. I must admit that I have little experience in such matters."

Lillian looked genuinely horrified. "Oh, my.

How very dreadful. I cannot think of anything more important than how a woman looks. And clothes, Angelique, can make or break a woman."

"I am sure that they can," Ghost Dancer again agreed in mock interest.

The music was beginning again, and Bender turned to Ghost Dancer. "Might I have the pleasure of this dance, Miss Dancer?"

Ghost Dancer felt something akin to relief at being rescued from Lillian's innate chatter, but dread squelched it readily at the prospect of dancing with Bender. Then she reminded herself of her reasons for being at Fort Laramie.

"Of course," was all she could say, accompanied by a weak attempt at a smile.

As he guided her onto the dance floor, she caught Cameron's look of anger cast her way. But in the next turnabout, she saw Lillian attach herself to him and move onto the crowded floor, a look of immense satisfaction on her face.

"You have a lot of patience, Miss Dancer. I admire that."

His voice was soft, almost caressive, leaving a trail of bumps down her arms. But not the same sort as Cameron created and it took all of her self-control not to pull away from him in horror. "Patience?" she questioned, uncertain of his meaning.

"Yes, with Lillian Thomas. Most women would have scratched her eyes out for what she said. But not you. Instead, you flattered her." His admiration was sincere.

"I saw nothing to be angry about. Clothes are of no consequence."

"You are certainly the strangest woman I have ever met," he confessed.

This statement brought her head up. Why did everyone think she was so strange?

"What I mean to say, is that you are different than other women. You've told me that money holds little value to you, and now you say that clothes mean nothing. Most women are like Lillian, money and clothes mean everything. Why are you so unlike them?"

"I do not mean to be unlike the others," Ghost Dancer offered, uneasy under his close scrutiny.

Curious now, Bender questioned her further. "What is important to you?"

"Many things," Ghost Dancer said, as she recalled the image of her home and family. "But I do not wish to bore you with them."

"I don't think, Angelique," he nearly whispered the words, "that you could ever bore me."

The look on his face and tone of his voice made his statement seem intimate and personal, causing Ghost Dancer to be uncomfortably aware of his closeness. She could feel the hardened muscles beneath the finely tailored jacket, and she understood his strength and power. This made her even more nervous.

Thankfully, the dance ended. Then, with only a slight bow, Bender left her.

"Oh, Cameron."

Lillian's shrill laughter cut through Ghost Dancer like a knife, edging her nerves closer to the breaking point. She turned to watch Cameron and Lillian cross the few feet that separated them, Ghost Dancer's look darkening with a sudden, unpredictable anger.

Lillian swirled about as she turned to look at Ghost Dancer, a circle of petticoats and lace frosted with the glimmer of mint. Her eyes sparkled with challenge as she clung to Cameron's arm in a possessive way, her smile almost too pretty. "Angelique, dear," she cooed sweetly. "Aren't you having a good time?"

"Of course I am, Lillian . . . dear." The last word came out very hard. "Why do you ask?"

"You just looked odd, that's all." Lillian patted a stray curl back into place as her gaze immediately traveled back to Cameron.

Cameron, too, had noticed the look on Ghost Dancer's face. "Are you sure you're all right?"

"I said that I was," Ghost Dancer snapped, causing Cameron's brow to shoot up in surprise for the second time that evening. In turn, she cast him a scathing look.

"Cameron," Lillian gushed, her arm weaving even tighter through his muscled arm. "You are a marvelous dancer. It's such a pleasure not having my toes trod upon as most of these clods do. Sometimes I can barely walk by the time the evening is over."

Ghost Dancer had to bite her lower lip to keep back her instinctive retort, and clasped her hands tightly in front of her to keep from tearing the redhead off Cameron's arm. "Yes," she almost whispered to herself, "he is a wonderful dancer."

Remembrances of Cameron holding her close and their bodies swaying to the music that only their hearts had heard made the heat within her rise even higher. An unfamiliar pain twisted inside her belly and she felt the sudden need to cry.

"Miss Dancer."

All eyes were drawn to the young man who took a shy step forward. Feeling awkward under their stares, he cleared his throat, and straightened his jacket.

"I was wondering if I might have this dance?"

Jerked from her world of jealous pain, Ghost Dancer could not reply.

Cameron felt her distress and came to her rescue. "I'm afraid the lady just accepted my offer to dance." He turned a polite look to Lillian. "If you will excuse us."

Lillian was quick to recover from her disappointment with trained expertise, and smiled becomingly. "Of course." Then like a chameleon, she cast a fiery glance at Ghost Dancer which said much more than words.

With grace, Cameron danced her away from the crowd, his arms guiding her with natural ease. "Are you feeling better, Angel?"

She looked up into the face that studied her so closely. "I"—Ghost Dancer felt the tears choke her—"I am not sure I know what way I am feeling. It is so strange but I am hurting deep inside. And I am also angry."

A wonderful smile lit his face and he wiped away the tears that now slid down her cheeks. "I do believe you are jealous. Perhaps of Lillian?"

The tears stopped and the roundness of her eyes narrowed into slits. "Jealous? I am not . . ." Ghost Dancer stopped herself, aware of the denial she was about to give him. Was it the truth or a lie? Was she jealous? "Lillian thinks that she will marry you."

Again, up went both his eyebrows, and he laughed. "And what if I don't wish to marry Lillian?"

"She is very beautiful, Cameron." Self-doubt washed over her again, leaving her shaken.

"Not more beautiful than you, my Angel."

His voice turned soft and loving, his words leaving a trail of shivers over her. "You don't care for Lillian?"

"Not in the least. You have captured my heart, Angel. How can I even notice another?"

Tears filled her eyes again, but for a different reason this time. "I love you, Cameron Wade."

Cameron's eyes closed for the briefest of moments, and when they opened, his own feelings were shining within them. "Stay with me, Angelique. You belong here with me. You . . ."

"Please, no." She put her fingers to his lips to stop whatever he had been about to say. "I cannot bear to have you ask me this, for I must give you an answer you do not want to hear."

"Why? Why must you?"

She heard and felt his hurt, causing her own to burst forward, wrapping its strong unbreakable grip about her heart. "You know that I cannot stay. I will return to my people when we are done. You know this."

"Your people!" His voice rose, but he quieted down when people began to stare. "Look at you. You belong with me, here, among your own people. Can't you see that?"

"I see much more than you will admit."

A muscle in Cameron's jaw twitched, but he did not reply. The music ended, and he led her off the floor. Stiff and unsmiling, he turned to Ghost Dancer. "As always, it was a pleasure."

He turned and walked away, not waiting for her response. "Cameron," she called, but he only paused a brief second, then disappeared into the crowd of onlookers, his ramrod back unyielding.

"I say we should teach them savage sons of bitches a lesson."

Ghost Dancer felt a chill and turned toward the angry voice. A group of men had gathered around the colonel, his own look one of barely controlled fury.

"And I say, you'd best keep out of this matter, Ted. It's for the Army to handle." The colonel's voice shook with suppressed tension.

"It seems"—Bender picked a tiny piece of lint from his immaculate dress blue jacket—"that the Army has not been doing its job."

The colonel's face darkened to a deep, ruddy red. "As I said," he stressed even more, "the Army is in charge and will continue to be so."

Bender held the older man's look, and replied more evenly than his look implied. "I think that if the Army doesn't do its job soon, those redskinned bastards will do some more killing."

The men echoed his sentiment, their clamor of

comments rising above the music. Terrible words of prejudice and hatred drifted to Ghost Dancer, and her mind was filled with the visions of her nightmare, the cries of the dying adding to the confusion within her. She turned away and leaned upon the long banquet table for support, sickened by the sight she witnessed.

"Damn, Bill!" one man yelled. "Ain't no time to be sweet on those godless heathens."

"Yes," Bender agreed, a thread of distaste so obvious in his tone. "This isn't the time to take their side. There isn't a one worth defending. The only good Indian's a dead Indian."

Their chorus of agreement blasted through Ghost Dancer's numbness. That sentiment seemed to run strong in the crowd. She straightened and her hand clamped about the smooth, wooden handle of the butcher knife that lay on the table by the ham it had carved. She felt the intense heat of fury surge through her and she whirled about, weapon in hand, her instincts guiding her.

"That isn't the way, Angelique."

Cameron stood before her, between her vengeance and the man she had grown to hate with all her soul.

"Your way has taken us nowhere," she hissed, her voice shaking as much as her body.

Cameron sighed. "But if you kill him there will be another to take his place. Then another and another. We will never remove the guilt already placed on your tribe. It is not the solution we seek."

Ghost Dancer raised her eyes to look directly

into his serious face. "You think you can stop me?"

"If I must, Angel, I will."

A shadow of a smile came to her lips, almost a challenge lifting the corners. "Cameron Wade. One day you will learn."

She twisted about and buried the knife deep into the table, piercing the white linen and hard wood with its sharp edge. Then, this time, she walked away, leaving Cameron to stand alone.

The snap of the rope brought Cameron's gaze from Ghost Dancer to the iron chandelier that hung above Bender, the many flames of the candles flickering from the sudden movement. Without thought, Cameron all but flew through the air to knock Bender aside, just as the iron beast crashed to the floor. The quick actions of some of the other men doused the flames before they could spread, and within seconds, it was over. Slowly, the two men picked themselves up from the floor.

"It seems, Captain Wade," Bender spoke as he brushed his clothes free of dust and wrinkles, "that you saved my life. I am in your debt."

Cameron was barely listening, his eyes already studying the chandelier. "You owe me nothing, nothing at all." He lifted the end of the rope and examined it. It wasn't frayed, the fibers had been cut clean, as if a knife had sliced through it. If it had been partially cut, then hung, some frazzled ends would still be evident. But it was clean, as if cut in one, swift chop.

All the blood drained from his face and he

looked up to find Ghost Dancer. She was nowhere in sight. Quickly, he made his way to the front veranda and was surprised to find it was pouring rain, but even more surprised to find the woman he sought, standing in the night storm.

"Angelique," he called as he stepped into the downpour.

She did not move.

"Angel." This time he was right behind her and she turned to him.

"Yes, Cameron."

"Why are you standing out here? Look at you, you're soaked to the skin." He pushed a wet strand of hair off her face. "And turning quite blue."

Her blank eyes just continued to look at him, all emotion gone. "I was much too warm."

Cameron ran a hand through his hair, slinging water in all directions. His sigh was heard above the hard driving rain and he lifted his face to let the wetness fall on it, the coolness clearing his muddled mind. His confused eyes moved back down to her.

"Did you do it?"

Ghost Dancer could barely hear his question it was spoken so softly. "Did I do what?"

This time her innocent rhetoric was unwelcome, and it did not bring a smile. "You know damn well what I want to know!"

"Yes, I suppose I do," she said, but made no attempt to continue.

"Was it you?" he repeated, a bit louder, more desperate than before.

This time, Ghost Dancer sighed. "If I say yes,

you will not believe me, for you are afraid to. If I say no, you still will not believe me, for the doubt has been placed within your mind. Either way, I lose."

"Hell." He threw up his hands in frustration. "I hate this."

Her tears mixed with the rain, and Ghost Dancer reached out to touch his face tenderly. "What do you want me to say?"

"I don't know, Angel." He smiled weakly. "I just don't know."

Chapter 17

The glass shattered, splaying about Bender's feet. Very slowly, drops of blood squeezed to the surface of his skin then dripped onto the white-washed boards of the veranda. On his face was written dark anger and jealousy twisted his guts into a painful knot, like a lead weight deep inside his stomach. He hadn't heard any of the words they had exchanged, he had only witnessed them from afar. Still, every look Cameron and Ghost Dancer exchanged the entire evening had been noticed. They pretended to be strangers, but he suspected differently.

The cuts on his hand only distracted him a brief second as he withdrew a clean handkerchief to wrap around it to soak up the blood. The blackest of eyes returned to the couple who still stood in the rain, watching them intently. Sweat beaded his upper lip, and the muscles in his jaw worked furiously as his teeth ground together.

"No man takes what I want," he muttered to himself. "Not even you, Cameron Wade."

* * *

The old man's mouth was lost in his deeply wrinkled face, but when he smiled, a snaggle-toothed grin split it in two. Lackluster eyes of brown observed Ghost Dancer and Cameron but also stopped to rest on Bender, who hid in the dark shadows of the building.

Broken Arrow was delighted at his good fortune. The game being played was still an unfamiliar one, but he made his plans to become a participant.

"Ghost Dancer," he called to her, knowing she was too far to hear. "You have not defeated me yet."

Ghost Dancer felt a sudden chill, and she turned her gaze to the darkness that surrounded them. Searching the shadows, she saw nothing, but still shuddered as an ill wind touched her.

"You're trembling," Cameron said. "Here, let's get out of this cold rain."

He took her elbow, but she didn't move. "What is it, Angel?"

Finally, she turned back to him, her eyes wide with an unknown fear. "I do not know."

Concerned, he lifted her into his arms and carried her toward his quarters.

Ghost Dancer felt secure, snuggled in the circle of his arms, and laid her head upon his muscled chest. She let the troubled moment slip from her mind. Somehow, everything was always better when he held her.

The beat of his heart soothed her. A powerful feeling of love came to her, drawing the breath from her body, and with it, her own strength. She knew that if she had been standing, her legs would not have supported her.

Cameron edged open his door and entered the room, quietly closing it behind him.

"You're still shivering," he whispered as he sat her down on his bed. Crossing the small room, he added some wood to the cast-iron stove in the corner.

Cameron returned to Ghost Dancer, his eyes filled with concern. "Here." He pulled her to her feet. "You need to get those wet things off."

Ghost Dancer's teeth chattered and her body shook. Why had she wandered into the rain? She couldn't remember. The myriad of emotions she'd experienced in such a short time left her spent. Like a child, she allowed Cameron to undo the many buttons that ran down the back of her dress, content to be taken care of so tenderly.

One by one, Cameron worked his way through the looped pearls, the first few giving way to reveal the honey-colored skin of her back, then the delicate lace of her chemise. Unable to resist the temptation of her flesh, he brushed his lips over the satiny contour, following the graceful shape of her neck.

This time Ghost Dancer's shiver was from the sensation of his warm lips. Deep inside smoldered her love, a flame that was easily brought to life. Its intensity grew steadily, a new warmth spreading through her as passion's fire dispelled the chills with its heat.

When the last button was freed, Cameron ran

his hands up her back and over her shoulders, sliding the clinging, damp gown down. It fell free into a forgotten heap about her feet. Ghost Dancer felt the finely woven cotton of her wet undergarments cling to her.

Slowly, Cameron turned her to face him. She heard the quickening of his breath and her own caught in her throat at the look she read in his darkened eyes.

"Are you warmer, love?"

His whispered words sent a heated flush through her, turning his question to fact. "I am beginning to feel the fire."

Cameron smiled. "I'm glad to hear that."

"Well," Ghost Dancer returned, "perhaps I am not so terribly warm, after all."

"Well," he mimicked, "perhaps I should do something about that."

"What can you do?"

"I'm not sure. We'll just have to think of something." Cameron caressed her cheek, then slid his hand behind her neck and began to massage away her tension.

Ghost Dancer closed her eyes, content to enjoy the relaxed moment. She could smell the dampness on him, the man scent of him mingling with the rain water. He was close, their bodies almost touching, yet so enticingly far, and she imagined the moment when they would melt together. He brushed his lips over the fullness of her earlobe. Her lips parted in wanting. She heard his uneven breathing, as he sought the special place where her neck curved into her shoulder. His other hand found the roundness of her hip and followed the curve of her waist. Then he explored the swell of her breast.

Cameron stepped back and untied her chemise, his fingertips pulling away the lacy fabric to bare her to his gaze. The look in his eyes, the raggedness of his breath, told Ghost Dancer how she affected him. It made her feel weak to know the power she possessed. She reached for Cameron, and he came to her, his lips seeking hers. Ghost Dancer felt dizzy from anticipation and breathless from the building desire that stirred inside her. Yet, her feeling went much deeper than passion, even deeper than love. This man had become her life's blood, her red power.

Cameron's lips wandered down her throat, leaving a trail of fire and kisses. Slow and deliberate, each kiss deviously enticed her as his mouth moved from the sensitive slope of her shoulder to her slender arm, then to the softness of her breast. His tongue teased her nipple into hardness, the warmth of his mouth raising goose bumps on her skin. Her hands cradled the back of his head, her fingers entwining in the dark hair that brushed the collar of his uniform.

Unable to bear the delightful torture he administered, Ghost Dancer pulled his head away. She needed his mouth on hers. The feel of his tongue sliding over her bottom lip made her part her lips, inviting him in. Their tongues touched, tip to tip, before twisting together in a wet dance. The heat that now possessed Ghost Dancer coursed through her, out of control.

Cameron drew back, his green gaze piercing her very soul. He drained her of everything except the passion that churned inside her.

Her hands moved to his chest and began to unfasten his buttons, the wet fabric making it difficult.

"Here." His hand stilled hers. "Let me. I can't wait all night."

When he pulled the jacket and shirt off, she couldn't resist touching the bronzed skin that stretched across the muscles of his chest. She leaned closer, to taste of his dark flesh, to explore him with her lips. He tasted good, he smelled good, he felt good. She laid her ear above the place she knew his heart lay. And the sound was good.

Cameron's hands worked into the dampness of her hair, pulling the heavy lengths free of the many pins that had been so carefully placed into it earlier. He worked the tangles free with his long fingers, the sensation soothing in its movement. Unable to deny the urge, he buried his face into her golden curls, filling his senses with the sweet smell that was so much a part of her.

A low moan escaped Cameron. "You are so beautiful, Angel."

He lifted her and lay her gently on the bed, then carefully stretched out beside her. Again, he kissed her, long and hard.

Ghost Dancer felt her toes curl and the heat wave intensified tenfold. Their hearts moved in unison, the rhythm strong, the sensation of two hearts beating as one, an unbreakable bond. She drew him to her and within her, her sense of loving him overpowering.

Now they were truly one.

Cameron held her close, his arms cradling her against his chest. Over and over his thoughts rattled about, running headlong into emotions. Deep-seeded emotions. He thought of his family, the years of separation, the heartbreak of his mother . . . of his promise. His promise . . . his resolution never to marry. And where did that leave Angelique?

Guilt created a painful knot. He'd sworn to stay away from her, but he constantly took her to him. Why couldn't he walk away from her? Plain and simple.

Or was it? In all honesty, he couldn't walk away and he probably never would. It was no longer his duty to rescue her from the Indians that kept him involved, nor the desire to find the truth in this urgent matter. It was the woman herself. It was Angelique.

He loved her!

Suddenly, he was filled with an overwhelming feeling, an honest feeling of love. A love he was only beginning to understand, a love he had only just discovered in that very moment. His promise paled in comparison to this new, exciting feeling that surged through him with each strong beat of his heart. He lifted her chin so he could see the emotions that shone plainly upon her face, and found her love for him returned so openly, so honestly, that it frightened him.

"Marry me." He felt her stiffen, then her eyes filled with tears. "I love you. I want you to marry me. I want to share my life with you."

She remained silent.

"I believe my heartfelt confession requires a response."

"I . . ." Ghost Dancer's voice broke, a sadness taking away the happiness that had been in her eyes. "We are married, Cameron. I have told you that."

"Yes, but I don't *feel* married. You see, it's our custom for the man to ask first, then a preacher marries the man and woman. That's the way I want it. The right way."

"I have already placed my heart within your care, never to be mine again."

Cameron grinned weakly. Would she ever cease to surprise him? "Is that a yes?"

"I do not know, my love." The tears ran down her rose-stained cheeks.

"Well, I know. I want you to be my wife, all legal and done up right."

"I am honored, but . . ." She stopped, unable to go on, her words too difficult to speak.

He felt a rush of blood crowd into his skull, a red haze filtering in. "But what?"

"If I marry you the right way, you would expect me to stay here with you."

"Of course I would. My work, my life, is here. And your place would be with your husband."

A sob tore from her before she could reply. "Cameron, we have gone over this before. Why must we continue to hurt each other this way?"

"Is that a no?" he asked abruptly.

Her lower lip trembled. "I have no choice."

Cameron pushed her away, the hurt in his eyes. "You always have a choice."

Ghost Dancer reached out to touch his face. "I know you do not understand, but for me there is no freedom."

"Damn if there isn't," he growled, drawing back from her touch. Throwing the covers aside, he stomped across the room. "You're really going to go back to the Sioux?" He was in shock, never thinking she would really go back. Not now, not after. . . .

Ghost Dancer moved her head in confirmation. "I *must* go back. I was brought into this world for one purpose, to serve the Ghost Sioux. I cannot deny *who* I am and *what* I am."

Anger jolted him like a violent slap in the face, the intense emotion causing color to flood it. "You've known this all along, haven't you?"

"Known what?"

"You know damn well what!" He felt close to being out of control. "You always planned to go back, letting me think otherwise. Letting me hope! You deceived me."

"I have never deceived you, Cameron Wade. Your hopes were born of your own creation, not from any false words from me."

It was true, he realized with a clarity that sickened him. His own foolishness had given him hope, not Angelique. Not *Ghost Dancer.* "Now what?"

"I do not know."

Slowly, Ghost Dancer crawled from the bed, a sudden tiredness draining her strength. She gathered her wrinkled clothes from the various spots on the floor, and donned them. When she was ready, she could not make herself leave. Sniffing, she used the back of her hand to wipe the tears that wouldn't stop falling.

Their eyes met and Cameron felt pain rip him open. "Perhaps you and I aren't meant to be."

For the longest time, she stood in the middle of the room, staring at him.

When Ghost Dancer did speak, the words were barely audible, the emotion whispered with true regret. "You are right. Perhaps the reason I had no visions of you, Cameron Wade, is because we have no future."

He wanted to tell her no, that was not the reason, yet he didn't. He let her go. The sound of the door shutting was the most dismal sound he had ever heard.

By the time she reached her room, Ghost Dancer felt as if one more step would have been too much. She sank on her bed, her tears falling as fast as the rain outside. The pain in her heart was so severe she couldn't breathe.

It was true. There had been no visions of Cameron as part of her future, and the only forecast for her was one of loneliness. She had given her heart to him; there would be no other man for her. That's why there had been no dreams, there was no one to dream about.

A sob shook her, then there were no more tears,

only a great emptiness. He believed she had a choice, to stay or to go. If only he understood that it was not a matter of choice. To stay was never a thought to be considered. She was the Ghost Dancer and her place was with her people. That was understood. That was the only way it could be.

She curled up on her bed, hugging her knees to her chest, her chin resting on them.

"Oh, Grandfather," she whispered, lifting her gaze above to *Wakan Tanka*. "Why have You chosen to give me such pain? Have I not been worthy of the Spirit that You placed within me?"

Ghost Dancer closed her eyes, the strangeness of her bed making her feel even more forlorn. Nothing felt right this night. Even her skin, tender from Cameron's touch, felt as if it belonged to another woman. She knew there would be no rest and wished for morning.

Chapter 18

Ghost Dancer crossed the sitting room to answer the knock, stifling another yawn. Her hand touched the doorknob, and she felt a wave of apprehension. The knock sounded again and, taking a calming breath, she opened the door.

Before her stood Jack Bender dressed splendidly in blue.

"Major Bender. . . ."

"Miss Dancer. I was hoping to find you home."

Ghost Dancer stirred uneasily beneath his dark gaze. "What can I do for you?"

Stepping back, she allowed Bender to enter and offered him a seat, just as she had seen Wilma do. Having heard the door, Wilma bustled into the room, missing a step when she saw who her visitor was.

"Major. How very nice," she said coolly.

"I hope I have not come at a bad time, Mrs. Dawson."

Wilma waved a hand in the air. "Of course not. No such thing as a bad time for visitors."

Ghost Dancer sat in a chair across from Bender, wondering why everyone had to bother with such politeness. In fact, she had to squelch the urge to scream at him to get out, to leave her alone. Instead, she smoothed the wrinkles from her skirt.

"As always you are a generous hostess."

Bender's smile was practiced, yet Ghost Dancer felt chilled.

"Would you care for some coffee?" Wilma asked, unable to shirk her duties.

"I must confess, I had hoped that Miss Dancer would join me for an afternoon ride." He turned to Ghost Dancer. "It's a beautiful fall day. We may not have another chance. We're already into our rainy season."

"A . . . a ride?"

"I am not a man who takes no for an answer."

No was exactly what she was about to answer. Then, quite distinctly, her mind recalled Lillian's words, "If you encourage a man in the right way, it could very well benefit your cause." That idea ran headlong into the urge to take a knife to his black heart, followed immediately by Cameron's words, "It is not the solution we seek."

"Then I see that I have no choice." Ghost Dancer heard Wilma's gasp of surprise and did not need to see her to know her lips were pursed in a very disapproving manner.

"Shall we go then?" Bender stood, offering her his arm. "We won't be late, Mrs. Dawson."

The buggy bumped over the road that followed the river. Ghost Dancer swallowed a squeal, fearing the white man's strange contraption was going to tip over. She grasped the side and the seat until her knuckles were white. As the winding road sped by in a blur, she closed her eyes to still the dizziness she suddenly experienced. Bender was watching her, and she dared not let him suspect how disquieting she found his carriage.

"It's a beautiful day," Bender commented, making an awkward attempt at conversation.

"Yes." Ghost Dancer opened her eyes and turned her gaze to him. "You did mention that."

The color rose to his neck and he cleared his throat. "Yes, I suppose I did."

Ghost Dancer looked around, really noticing how splendid an afternoon it was. "But then perhaps it is worth stating a truth twice."

Bender could not know that Ghost Dancer's comments were made in total honesty. Her way was not an easy one to understand. He did not try to engage her in any more conversation.

His silence suited her mood, and she said nothing in turn. She still wasn't certain why she was with him or to what end. Only that it was . . . was what?

Ghost Dancer put her fingers to her temples and massaged the pain that throbbed inside her head, her eyes closing. It was not a good day for thinking. Everything was mixed up and confused.

The carriage rolled to a stop, and her eyes opened to the most pleasant of sites. A grassy bank hugged a bend in the river. Nearby a grove of trees spread an umbrella of red, brown, and gold over the water's edge. The cool bite of a breeze stirred the dying leaves, sending showers of color onto the ground.

The leaves that lit on the blue-brown water drifted with the current and disappeared into the distance. Suddenly she wanted to drift away, to forget about the man who was waiting to help her down, to forget the burdens she bore, to forget she was the Ghost Dancer.

"May I help you down, Angelique?"

His voice broke into her thoughts, drawing her eyes down to his.

"It is all right if I call you Angelique?"

She hesitated, then held out her arms to him. "I see no harm in it."

His strong arms lifted her easily to the ground, and he paused briefly before stepping aside. Silence once again fell between them, so they began to walk down to the river's edge.

Ghost Dancer emptied her mind of her troubling thoughts, willing only the peaceful beauty to exist. She gave no mind to the man who stood by her side, nor the man who was forever in her heart. Only the river and its soft sounds were heard, only the colorful scenery did she see.

Bender's thoughts were focused solely on his companion. Never had a woman made him feel this way. There were moments he felt like a lovesick boy, uncertain and inadequate.

His eyes narrowed in distaste. For the first time in his life, he was not in control of his feelings. His four fingers curled into a fist as he mulled over his chaotic thoughts.

Her aloofness drove him mad, still, he seemed

to crave it. Somehow, Bender knew she was an honest women. If he had discovered one thing about Angelique Dancer, it was that all she said and all the things she did, were truthful. He had not thought any woman could be that way, since the women he had known were artful in deceptions and coy lies. Even his mother could not be trusted.

Memories intruded into his mind, remembrances he put from him just as quickly as they had come. They left a bitterness inside him, a small monster to gnaw at his reserve.

Bender reached out to capture a lock of her hair which the light wind tossed about. He rubbed the softness between his thumb and finger, the feel of it tempting him further. He stroked the long length of spun gold.

"You have beautiful hair," he whispered, not even aware that he had spoken aloud.

She stepped away from him but did not speak.

He allowed her to walk away, but inside Bender wanted only to pull her to him. To crush her to him. To . . . He would not allow himself to think on it further.

"You seem quiet today, Angelique. Even more than usual."

Her eyes finally turned to acknowledge him. "I am tired, that is all."

Heat spread through him in a flash, hot and dangerous. With sudden clarity, he recalled Wade lifting her into his arms and carrying her to his quarters. His own night had been spent in hell, his imagination running rampant with visions of the two lovers. She should be his—not Wade's!

"You left the dance early," he started, then watched her face carefully for a reaction, but none appeared. Disappointed that she could hide so easily behind her cool facade, he finished. "I saw you leave with Captain Wade."

He wanted so much to get a response, even if it was anger. But he saw no change in her expression. "I could not help but notice that he is attracted to you. Not that I can blame him. I find myself also quite taken with you, Angelique. I'm even beginning to think I'm in love with you."

Ghost Dancer heard Jack Bender's confession and didn't know what to say. She was playing a dangerous game with an evil man whom she knew killed with no conscious thought. What did she really hope to accomplish by this? It had *seemed* the right thing to do, yet nothing the white man did seemed to have any logic behind it. And, at that very moment, she thought herself a fool a thousand times over. She did not fear him anymore, she merely loathed hearing him speak words of love to her. It turned her stomach. She could not bear his touch. She had no heart for playing this scene out.

"I am sorry Major . . . Jack. You and I are of two different worlds. We can never be." She turned away from his unsmiling black eyes, but not soon enough to miss the anger that twisted his face into a scowl of pure evil.

"You haven't given me a chance." Words came from him in a hurried jumble. "I have so much to offer. I could make you happy."

Ghost Dance felt a twinge of sadness at hearing the pleading in his voice. She knew he was not the type of man to beg. "You have nothing I want, and I have nothing to give." She turned back to face him. "I would like to go home now."

She took a step toward the road, but was stopped as he moved in her path. His look was forbidding. "I am not a man to be denied, Angelique, especially when you give to others so freely."

Ghost Dancer understood the look that was so clearly written on his face and she was sickened.

"Dearest Angelique"—his tone became hard and cutting—"I will enjoy what Wade did last night."

Ghost Dancer assumed he knew about her and Cameron and did not play at innocence. "I do not think that will be possible." Again, she tried to step past him.

And again, he moved to stop her. "Why not?" he demanded harshly.

"Because"—she tried to keep calm—"what Cameron Wade *enjoyed* was given willingly. It was of my choosing. To you, I give nothing."

Her last statement was laced with the contempt she felt, her emotions winning out over calm control.

Bender drew a deep breath, the sound making her think of a snake drawing back to strike. Only this serpent's poisonous venom was in his evil words.

"Oh, my sweet. It doesn't matter what you choose. I take what I want."

His hand clamped around her wrist, keeping her from getting past him. She tried to twist free, but he pulled her to him and his arm captured her tightly, crushing her to his body with a fierceness and strength that frightened her. He pulled her head back cruelly with a handful of her hair, and stifled her angry cry with his mouth.

Ghost Dancer felt a wave of disgust as he invaded her mouth, and she bit down on his lip. When he pulled back, she shoved away, but not in time to dodge the back of his hand as he struck out at her in fury. The force of the blow sent her reeling, and she felt herself falling. His hands grabbed for her and she heard her dress tear. She hit the ground, then he fell on top of her, knocking the air from her.

"Bitch," he growled, laying his full weight on her shaking body. "It's time you learned I am not a man to be toyed with."

Ghost Dancer kicked and struck out as he pulled her skirts up. She felt the coldness of his hand sliding up her leg and over her hip.

"Ahteh," she cried out. "Father!"

She heard the bird screech before she saw the black hawk dropping from the sky, like an arrow sent to earth from the heavens. He dove at Bender, his razor-sharp talons digging into his unprotected back. Then the messenger of the Gods rose high above, only to swoop down again to slash at her attacker. The second attack produced deep cuts on his cheek and neck.

Bender picked up a stick and swung it through the air in an attempt to fend off the vicious creature of flight. Surprise and confusion tempered his burst of angry lust, which was quickly replaced by irrational fury. Where this feathered advocate of the devil had come from, he didn't know, and at that moment, didn't much care. Only one thing became clear: He had to get away from its ripping talons.

He used his coat sleeve to wipe at the blood on his face, all the while, dodging the bird's sweeping attacks. Bender didn't need a mirror to know that the hawk had done permanent damage to his face. This realization held a horror all its own.

Slowly, he made his way back to his carriage. Once he was within a few feet of it, he dropped the piece of wood and jumped inside, wasting no time in making his escape.

Ghost Dancer watched him disappear down the road, abandoning her. She felt safer now. Again, she heard the bird's cry and looked up to watch him soaring overhead. She smiled and held her hand out. When the bird landed on her outstretched arm, she stroked its regal head.

"Thank you, my father."

Cameron knew a sudden wave of fear.

"What's the matter, Captain? You look as white as a sheet."

"Where's Angelique?" he questioned.

The colonel sensed something was wrong. "Why, I left her at home with Wilma this morning."

Cameron's hand brushed his hair back from his eyes before putting his hat back in place. "I had better go see if everything is okay."

Without even waiting for a reply, he was off,

leaving his commanding officer to wonder at his sudden departure. He was running before he reached the colonel's house. The fear that choked him grew with each step he took. Just as he reached the colonel's porch, he stopped. A sound called to him. Looking up at the sky, he heard the sharp, clear cry of a hawk. Yet he saw none. When he turned to go up the stairs, he even wondered if he had heard it at all.

He came to a halt in front of the door and immediately began to pound on it.

"Heavens," he heard through the barrier. "I'm coming. I'm coming."

Wilma threw open the door before he could resume his barrage. "Why, Cameron, what in heavens is the matter with you?"

"Where's Angelique?" he demanded, already stepping past her to look about the sitting room. "Is she all right, Wilma?"

The tone of his voice frightened her, and she held her hand up to her face. "She was fine when she left."

"Left," he whispered. "Where did she go?"

Wilma was afraid to tell him, but she knew she must. "She left with Major Bender."

The silence that followed nearly caused Wilma to faint. "Lordy, my boy. What has happened?"

Seeing the fright he had given her, Cameron held out a supporting arm and led her to the settee. "I'm so sorry, Wilma. I shouldn't have come charging in here like this. It was damn foolish of me."

He sat her down then took a seat by her side.

"I'm not even certain I know something's wrong."

"Perhaps you had best explain."

Cameron felt a bit foolish. "I can't. I mean, I don't know what got into me. I was working. My mind wasn't even on Angelique. All of a sudden, I was filled with fear. I thought my heart would burst inside my chest."

Wilma worried her lower lip as she thought it all out. "She's in trouble. You have felt her fear."

"That's ridiculous," he objected, while wondering if it was true. "Where did they go?"

"I don't know. For a ride somewhere."

Cameron stood and paced the floor. "I've got to do something!"

Wilma felt her heart go out to the boy. "There is nothing to do but wait."

"Blast it all. I hate being helpless."

"I understand, but we've no choice. Sit. I'll get us some coffee."

"Thanks, but no thanks," he declined. "I'm going to find her."

By the time Ghost Dancer climbed up the last step, she felt exhausted to her bones. She thought she might sleep a week. Her head ached from last night's sleeplessness, her face ached from Bender's cruel hand, and her mind was weary beyond thought. But, most of all, her feet hurt.

"Damnable shoes," she grumbled, repeating one of Cameron's expressions. She paused long enough to rub the bottom of her feet. Ugly blisters marred her soft skin, and bruises discolored her flesh.

She limped up the last few steps and reached for the door. It flew open and two pairs of eyes locked onto each other.

"Angelique." Cameron stood, blocking her way. "Where have you been?"

His next question seemed to freeze in his throat, and slowly, anger inched up his neck to flush his face, replacing his initial shock. She could see him quickly appraise her appearance, taking in her stained and ripped dress. When he reached out to touch the bruise on her face, his hand shook.

"He hit you?" It was more an amazed statement than a question. "That son of a bitch! I'll kill him."

Ghost Dancer believed his threat. "I am all right, Cameron. He did not hurt me."

Cameron seemed to explode. "Hurt you! My God, he . . . he . . ." Suddenly, he realized what Bender *had* been about. His red coloring drained to white.

"Oh, my dear. I should never have let you go with him."

Wilma's whimper brought both of their eyes to her. Ghost Dancer moved past Cameron, and wrapped her arms about her friend's shaking shoulders. "Wilma. Listen to me." She looked back at Cameron. "Both of you. Major Bender did me no harm. I promise you. The worst is that he struck me."

The older woman sniffled. "I shouldn't have let that happen."

"Wilma, you have been wonderful, allowing me to stay with you and the colonel. But I must make something very clear. I make my own decisions. What happened between Bender and myself was my own doing. Not any concern of yours."

"And is it any concern of mine?"

Cameron's voice was a mixture of hurt and anger, but it was the look in his eyes that caused Ghost Dancer pain. "No, it is not."

His fist hit the doorjamb, causing the women to jump. "Damn if it isn't!" he yelled, making them flinch. "I'll kill him for doing what he did."

Heat surged inside Ghost Dancer, giving her the strength she had lacked moments before. "And what exactly was it that he did?"

"Don't play your games with me." His finger pointed at her accusingly. "I'll not stand for it. And . . . we both know what it is he did!"

Ghost Dancer stood and faced him, her hands placed firmly on her hips. "Yes, I guess we do. Bender was only wanting me to give him a little of what you were getting last night."

The look that came to Cameron's eyes stopped her from going on. "He's a dead man."

"I see," Ghost Dancer whispered, feeling the anger leave her as fast as it had come. "You would kill him for striking me, yet you stopped me from taking a knife to him last night for inciting your people against mine. Your white man's justice is wrong."

"No, you just don't understand."

"Yes"—her eyes showed her disgust for their ways—"yes, I do." Ghost Dancer turned away and disappeared into her room.

"She's right, son."

Cameron turned to Wilma. As the rage seeped from him, he knew Wilma was right, and so was Ghost Dancer.

"I *want* to kill him."

"Well, now, maybe you can understand a little better how she feels. But we're civilized people and we do not kill someone just because we want to."

"I should have let that chandelier fall on him."

"But you didn't." Wilma patted him on the arm. "Water under the bridge, Cameron. Now, maybe you'd best go settle things between you two." Her eyes moved to Ghost Dancer's closed door.

Weary of fighting with Angelique, Cameron saw no purpose in seeking her out. "Wilma, it's more than just what happened today. It also has to do with last night."

A crimson blush flooded the older woman's face and she muttered, "That's none of my concern, dear boy."

"I asked her to marry me, and she flat turned me down."

Wilma showed surprise, both at his asking and Angelique's refusal. "What on earth did you do to make her say no?"

Cameron glowered at Wilma. "What makes you think *I* did something?"

"I'm sorry, Cameron. It's just I know how much the girl loves you. There isn't anything she wouldn't do for you."

"Except stay here with me as my wife. She says she has no choice and must go back to the Sioux."

"I know it's hard to understand, I'm not so sure that I do, but something tells me she truly belongs with them."

"She's a white woman. She belongs among her own." Cameron was tired of having this argument. Had the whole world lost its mind?

"Her skin's white, Cameron, but her heart . . . it's pure Indian. Believe me, I didn't think I'd ever say that, but it's the truth, plain and simple. Take her away from her people and she'd die."

He shook his head, unable to accept any of what she was saying. "You're talking nonsense."

Wilma shrugged. "Think what you will, young man. But, mark my words, you'll lose her if you don't think on this a bit more."

"Well, I can be stubborn and mule-headed myself. I can't just give up my own life, my career, everything, for her. It's not the way things are done." Suddenly, Cameron thought of his parents and of the years that they had spent apart. Wasn't he expecting the same thing his father had? Wasn't he doing the very thing he had promised himself not to? Then he considered the colonel and Wilma. They were obviously happy, and she had no regrets in marrying him. Hadn't she given up everything to be with her husband?

"Exactly what do you have here that would be so hard to leave?"

Wilma's question caught him off guard, and though Cameron gave it thought, he had no answer.

"Seems to me that Angelique has more to give up than you do."

Annoyed, Cameron started for the door. "Damn women. You stick together, don't you?" He took his anger out on the door, slamming it shut behind him.

Chapter 19

Bender pushed the Sioux squaw from him. "Go on, get out of my sight." He turned a shoulder to her, giving her no more thought. His lustful needs had been eased momentarily, but the heat within his mind could find no release.

The young girl quietly moved across the room, anxious to get out of his cruel reach. Freshly marked bruises overlaid old scars—scars of the mind as well as the body. His anger had once again lashed out at her, and she bore it in silence.

Seeing his back to her, she allowed herself the comfort of tears and lay on her mat. At one time, she had been pretty, but her youth had been spent at the hands of this diabolical man. She hid her small, round face beneath her arms, her sobs making no noise. He had made certain her cries were forever silent.

"Bitch!" he yelled, bringing her woeful eyes back to him. Bender's hand moved to the swollen, red welts that marred the perfection of his face. He winced, not only from pain, but from pure, unleashed fury. "You'll pay for this, Angelique."

He stood and crossed to the mirror, once again examining the damage. It would scar, and this did not settle well with his ego. Fury also seared a scar upon his mind, like an invisible brand. A mark he would not and could not forget.

"She's a fool!" Bender smashed the mirror with his fist, cracking his image into small pieces.

"They are all fools," he growled, turning away to pour himself another drink. "I'll show that idiot colonel for not retaliating immediately. And, Wade, you will pay for your interference. I'll have the gold and Angelique Dancer."

He continued to rant and rave, finally coming to the conclusion that it was time to act with a vengeance. To hell with caution. To hell with everyone!

"Here you go, darling." Wilma bustled into the bedroom, a tray overloaded with food and drink in her hands. She set it on the bed next to Ghost Dancer.

"You spoil me, Wilma."

A loving smile rounded her face. "Nonsense. Now you eat, then you can rest."

Ghost Dancer took a bite of a warm biscuit. The butter was sweet, the jelly tart. She gave Wilma an appreciative grin. "I shall miss your cooking and your kind ways."

"Cameron said you were planning on returning to the Ghost Sioux. He was hoping you would change your mind."

"I have never led him to believe otherwise."

Wilma patted her hand, the sadness in Ghost Dancer's heart showing in her eyes. "I know, child. Sometimes men are slow in understanding. I can't say I understand it all either, but I just feel you belong with the Indians. God forgive me, I do."

"You need not ask for God's forgiveness, Wilma. It is the Great One Who leads me down the path I have chosen."

"It'll be lonely without you, Angelique. I guess it's more proper to call you by your Indian name, but I don't know it."

"I am Ghost Dancer."

Wilma seemed to think about something a long moment. "Ghost Dancer," she repeated carefully. "You're something real special, aren't you, dear?"

Ghost Dancer saw the seriousness on her face and understood what she was asking. There was no fear or doubt, only admiration and pride. "Being the Ghost Dancer is a gift from *Wakan Tanka.*"

This, too, she seemed to consider. "Cameron will come to understand that. I know he will."

Ghost Dancer's own eyes brimmed with tears. "He fears believing."

She could see that Wilma wanted to say something, to ease her worry. But nothing came. Instead, Wilma pulled her into her arms and hugged her, giving her love instead of words.

"There now," Wilma mumbled as she cradled her. "There now."

Ghost Dancer allowed the tears to come, and she allowed the woman she had grown so fond of to give her the motherly comfort her broken heart ached for. When the crying stopped, she felt drained and completely emotionless.

Gently, Wilma tucked Ghost Dancer into the bed. "You'll feel better in the morning, dear." She started to leave, but paused at the door when Ghost Dancer called to her.

"Wilma. Thank you."

The arrow cut its path through the night air in silence, an unheard assassin of death. With only the lightest of thuds, it buried its sharpened head into flesh, slicing deep, stopping only when striking bone.

The man's unfinished step faltered, then he stumbled and fell, his look of surprise frozen in death. He never felt the cold, damp earth against his cheek and, blessedly, his unseeing eyes never witnessed the destruction that swarmed about his home. Nor did his deafened ears hear the screams of his wife. He was touched only by a strange peacefulness.

The quiet of night was broken as an orchestra of violence erupted, strong and powerful notes of destruction. The steady drum of the horses, riding fast to their master's bidding. The riders' cries of doom and their laughter blended with those of terror and pain. Animals bellowed out in fear as flames touched to old wood instantly roared into life. The chaotic song of death sung.

Bender surveyed his men's work, a smile of pleasure pulling at the corners of his tight-lipped mouth. This group of lawless vagabonds had proven their loyalty once again. Either that or the promise of gold prompted them to do his bidding. Most likely, it was the gold. Yes, this was bound to get everyone riled up, and in turn, they would set a fire under the Army. Especially with a bit of prompting from him.

A full smile flashed in the blackness of night. It was amazing how easy people were to manipulate. But the grin disappeared as quickly as it had come. A vision of a blond-haired beauty flashed through his mind. A powerful heat surged through him.

Except for Angelique Dancer.

The child's cry pierced deeply into her tender heart, drawing her from the cruel visions of sleep. Ghost Dancer's own scream broke the silence, chilling all within hearing distance with its note of terror and pain.

Within seconds, Wilma and the colonel were knocking at her door, drawing her mind from the horror she had witnessed.

Wilma rushed in, not waiting for a reply. "Angelique, what on earth is the matter?"

"We must go."

Just then, Cameron burst into the room, his own concern showing clearly on his face. In three long strides he was by her side, drawing her into the protection of his arms.

She pulled away, struggling to get out of bed. "We must go."

The urgency in her voice alarmed Cameron. "Go where, Angel? Where must we go?"

"I fear it is too late." She started pulling clothes on over her gown, mumbling. "Too late . . . too late."

Cameron swallowed hard, his own apprehension growing. "Stop it." She paused and turned to him. "Too late for what?"

He stood and moved to stand in front of her, grasping her shoulders, his voice and grip firm. "What have you seen?"

Tears filled her eyes, then fell in a steady stream down her pale cheeks. "We must go," was all she said, then moved to leave.

Cameron asked no more questions, but followed, motioning for the colonel to do the same. "You tell Sarge we're going and I'll get the horses."

The night had turned out violent, much like the atmosphere that clung to Ghost Dancer's memories. Icy rain drenched the earth and the three riders, but it did not slow them. Cameron and the colonel struggled to keep up with her as she rode like a demon possessed, unheedful of any danger. The cry of a babe rang in her head, obliterating all other thought.

When they came upon the homestead, they sensed the presence of death. They could feel it, they could smell it, they could taste it in the damp, smoke-filled air. The downpour had stopped the flames from consuming everything, and half of the charred cabin remained untouched, as if all were well.

Ghost Dancer slid from her horse, following the noises of her mind. She walked directly to the dead man, and stood staring at his still body. Hesitantly, she reached out and touched the quill of the arrow that protruded from his back. Cameron came up behind her, resting his hands on her shoulders.

"It speaks of lies," she cried, twisting around to see his face. "Lies!"

Cameron tried to pull her from the grisly scene. She struggled against him, unseen forces drawing her to the cabin. "It is too late," she whimpered, stepping away from him. "Too late."

Cameron grabbed her arm. "Don't, Angel. I'll go inside. It might not be . . ." He couldn't find the right words to explain his fears of what he might find.

"I have already seen it, Cameron."

From the look on her face, Cameron believed her and let her go. Together they stepped into the partially burned shell. The husband's wife lay on the floor, her life over at a very young age. But Ghost Dancer gave her little mind, her eyes searching the room.

"What are you looking for?" Cameron asked, a strange feeling brushing the hair on the back of his neck.

"You do not hear it?"

His forehead wrinkled in doubt. "Hear what? I only hear the rain."

Annoyance overwhelmed her. "You cannot hear the baby crying?" She covered her ears as if to block out the sound. "I hear the cries of a babe."

Desperately, she began to search the disarrayed room. She threw things aside in her mad search and Cameron watched helplessly. He did not know what to do.

She was sobbing quite hysterically now. "I must find the baby. I will not let his evil kill the child. I will not let his lies touch another innocent!"

Cameron felt his heart twist painfully in his chest, and he went to her. "Angelique, please, we must go."

She turned fierce eyes to him. "Not until I have found him. I can still hear him."

"There is no crying baby." His voice became hard in his own desperation. He feared this craziness. It frightened him to see that look in her eyes. "There is no baby."

She heard his words and felt angry, her determination setting her chin at a firm angle. "I will not go." Again, she searched.

Unable to bear her madness any longer, Cameron swept her into his arms and forcibly carried her from the cabin.

"No," she cried, fighting his superior strength. "No!"

Her screams tore at his heart, piercing straight to his soul with their sharpness. He felt near tears of his own. "Colonel."

The colonel appeared from around the corner. "Yes, Captain?"

"We've got to get her out of here!" Cameron yelled, struggling to keep her in his arms.

The older man's tired gaze widened in surprise. "What's the matter with her?"

"The baby!" she shrieked, her arms reaching out to the darkness. "I cannot go."

"Heavens," the colonel muttered. Suddenly, the

sky dried up and silence smothered the earth.

Ghost Dancer stilled.

A small cry fell like a whisper on the air, chilling them with its meaning. Cameron set Ghost Dancer on the muddy ground and was only one step behind her as she ran back into the cabin. This time she found the child, carefully hidden by his mother when she had known there was danger.

Ghost Dancer cradled the child to her breast. She had no strength left and needed Cameron's help to walk.

Cameron touched her face lovingly with his hand. "I'll take you home, Angel. I'll take you both home."

Cameron brushed the tangled strands of blond hair from her flushed face, her eyes closed in exhausted sleep. Wilma had immediately taken possession of the baby and left Angelique in his care. Even the colonel insisted he stay with her the rest of the night, the strangeness of the evening still clear in both their minds.

Walking to the window, Cameron pulled the curtain aside to look out into the stormy night. His thoughts tumbled one into another.

Skepticism had made him ignore her pleas, almost forcing her to leave.

"Dear God," he called to the darkness. "Why can't I trust her dreams? Hasn't she proven herself to me?"

Finding no answers, Cameron returned to the chair by the bed, finally closing his eyes in weariness. He knew he needed to rest, all hell was going to break loose in just a few brief hours.

Lord, what were they going to do?

Sleep had evened his breathing, the easy rise and fall of his chest stirring the silence softly. An uneasy whimper cut through the scene of slumber, followed on its note by another more desperate one. Her cry cut through him, and Cameron jerked awake in tense alertness.

Ghost Dancer sat straight up in bed, her eyes open yet unseeing. Only the nightmare clearly recalled within the recesses of her mind could be seen, the terror of it written clearly on her face.

Cameron was by her side, but something kept him from touching her. Never had he felt fear grab him with such fierceness as it did at that moment. For the first time, he knew what she must hold in her heart.

"Zee inyon."

Ghost Dancer's broken voice cut through his numbness and he pulled her to him, holding her close.

Again, she muttered in Sioux, "Yellow stone."

The words had no meaning to Cameron, only the sadness in her tone. He wasn't even sure if she had fully awakened before she drifted back off into a fitful sleep. He sat for the longest time, watching her fight against her dreams. He wanted more than anything to take them away. He wanted to give her peace.

For the first time, it occurred to him how terrible it must be for her, unable to stop what was already done. Twice now, she had dreamed of the massacres, the bits and pieces of her visions too late to prevent them.

It was like a bolt of lightning reaching down from the sky, its jagged fingers enclosing him with a realization that jolted through him with such force it took away his breath. He was no longer a disbeliever. He could no longer deny her dreams and their meaning.

"I've been selfish, my Angel," he muttered, gently laying her down on the bed. "Perhaps it is time I rethink a few things."

"Murderin' savages!"

The ugly words snuck into Ghost Dancer's sleep, prying her from the dark world of the oblivious. She didn't want to wake up, not yet.

She turned over onto her side and pulled the quilt over her head. Yes, she preferred the quietness of slumber.

"I say we show em' that we're not t' be messed with."

"Kill them. Kill them like they did our own!" came another deep-throated yell.

Stirring, she pulled a little closer to wakefulness.

"The only good Indian's a dead Indian," went up the cry.

This brought her awake, her heart pounding inside her chest with fear. She eased out of bed and followed the noise.

"I say we should be acting, not talking."

Cameron's voice cut through the crowd's noise. "You seem to have a lot to say."

His sarcasm hit hard and the men roused in anger.

"Settle down!" the colonel yelled. "The only say that means diddly squat round here's mine! Now, all of you go on home. This is for the Army to deal with, and I'll not tolerate your nonsense any longer."

Dawson's commanding voice quieted many of the men. He was a man of authority, and not many had the nerve to go against him. So, slowly, the crowd dispersed.

"Damn troublemakers," the colonel mumbled under his breath.

Cameron turned an alert look to him. "It's a good thing Major Bender isn't around. He'd have them ready to wipe out the entire village, guilty or not."

Now it was Dawson's turn to worry, a short-fingered hand running over his thick, white mustache. "What are we going to do? So far we've gotten nowhere with this."

"They've got to trip up sometime," Cameron replied, his voice mirroring a bit of his own uncertainty.

"I sure as hell hope so, time's running out."

A deep sigh drifted on the humid air to where Ghost Dancer stood, the colonel's mood bringing a worried frown of her own. She closed the window against the cold wind, and turned her back to it. The colonel was right. They had gotten nowhere. Her people would suffer greatly if they did not prove their innocence. And soon. What was she to do?

That, she didn't know. All she knew was a great tiredness of body and soul. Her eyes drooped, and she could no longer fight the sleep her body cried out for. Once again, she found the warmth and comfort of her bed.

She was holding something in her hand, a map of some sort, and in her other, she held a broken arrow. It was dark, like ink on paper. Ghost Dancer threw the rolled parchment from her and it was lost in the wind, lost to the blackness that surrounded her. It began to rain, hard and driving. She felt it pounding her down, and the thick mud dragged her deeper into its mire. The huge, heavy drops blinded her, they choked her, stealing away her breath. She couldn't breathe . . . She couldn't. . . .

Ghost Dancer awoke with a start, her breathing labored and strained, her gown soaked in sweat. An inexplicable urge drew her from her bed and forced her to put her clothes on. Something guided her and she followed.

Chapter 20

"Now." Bender smiled, more from amusement than friendliness. His teeth clamped down on the thin, brown cheroot he smoked. "Let me get this straight."

Lounging casually, he took a long, even draw, blowing rings of smoke into the air. "You're saying that Angelique Dancer is really this legend you call Ghost Dancer."

Broken Arrow sat across from Bender and shook his head up and down, long grayed hair shifting with his stilted movements. "Yes. It is so."

"Why are you telling me this?"

His question was expected. "Because I hate her. The Spirit should not have been passed on to a woman, especially not a woman of the white man. She is too powerful among the Ghost Sioux and they foolishly follow her, blind to her false blood."

"And you're jealous of this *power*?" Bender grinned, enjoying it all a bit too much.

Broken Arrow scrunched his lips into a wrinkled pout. "What man would not envy a woman who is greater than himself?"

"Tell me, old man. Why is she here?"

Aged eyes studied Bender quite astutely. "I do not know."

Bender drew in a deep, calming breath. "I find that hard to believe."

"I do not know her reasons for her deceptions." His pucker deepened. "Ghost Dancer has banished me from my own people. She has shamed me before my family. I know only that I wish to see her fail in her purpose, whatever it may be."

Leaning closer, almost nose to nose, Bender stated, "She has deceived me, played me for a fool. I will see that she does more than fail."

Broken Arrow seemed unaffected by his threat of death. "If I were young again, I would see her dead by my own hand. I would see that the Spirit is driven from her traitorous body and blessed upon a warrior of the Nahhe Lahkota. But, I am old and not strong enough to battle her powers."

"Power," Bender barked, almost laughing. "That's twice now you've mentioned this. What the hell do you mean?"

"White men do not believe in the power of the Ghost Dancer, but be warned, she should not be taken lightly. It would mean your end."

A smile lifted one corner of his mouth and Bender drawled, "Don't you worry, old man." He puffed on his cigar once again, unconcerned. "I'll watch my step."

Bender rubbed the festering cuts that marked him, a frightening look coming into the blackness of his eyes. "I'll not be caught unaware by that witch."

It was dark again. Somehow, she had missed another day. And for all her sleep, Ghost Dancer still felt tired, a mental exhaustion having overcome her. She gave little thought to where she walked. She only knew the unknown that called to her, guiding her footsteps.

The wind whistled over the buildings, their windows dark and silent. It would rain again. The air seemed heavy with the dampness, and blackened thunderclouds rolled across the night sky, blocking the quarter moon from view, dousing its feeble yellow light. Ghost Dancer pulled the heavy cloak around her shoulders more snugly, the chill sneaking in past its warmth.

When she did stop, she found herself standing in front of Bender's home, its darkness silent, if not ominous. She grasped the front gate with her hands, her cold fingers wrapping around the white-painted steel. For the longest time, she just stood there, staring. Then, she opened the gate, the slight squeak of hinges loud in the silence. She walked inside the small yard and up to the front door.

Ghost Dancer lifted her hand to knock, but hesitated, an unaccountable fear disturbing her. But the urge to go on was stronger, more insistent. Taking a deep breath, she pounded loudly on the wooden door with the brass knocker. She waited. No answer came. She knocked again. Still, no one answered.

Before she even gave thought to what she would do, she tried the doorknob. It opened. Darkness greeted her and an unnerving silence. Taking courage, Ghost Dancer pushed the door farther open and walked inside, the slam of the door behind her making her jump. She had never been in this house, but found her way easily. When she walked to the door of the library that same strange feeling drew her inside. Her dream began to flash through her mind's eye, mixing reality with her visions. She searched the room, looking for something, but what she didn't know. She saw the map flapping in the wind, hen-scratched markings drawn across the aged parchment.

Ghost Dancer moved to Bender's desk, the contents of the neatly arranged tabletop proving of no interest. She sat behind it, the feeling shooting through her with greater intensity. She closed her eyes, confusion rambling wild inside her, her heart beating strong and fast, keeping pace with her short shallow breathing. She took in a deep, calming breath to ease her laboring lungs and to quiet the fluttering in her chest.

"What am I doing here?" she questioned the darkness, knowing she would get no answer. At that moment, she did not understand her motives or reasons. Only her hands seemed to know as they began to search the drawers and their contents. She found nothing out of the ordinary and, frustrated, she dropped her head into her hands.

Wakan Tanka. She lifted her head to look up to the heavens. "Why have you brought me here?"

A renewed determination made her search the large desk again. This time, when she tried to close the center drawer, it jammed. She pulled it all the way out and reached back into the hole to feel around. Her hand touched paper. She grasped it and pulled it out, her heart pushing at her ribs with each resounding beat.

With trembling fingers, she unrolled it. It was the map she had seen in her dreams. Carefully, she studied it, and finally, it all began to form some logic within her mind. It was old man Smith's map. She had seen it many times at his shack as he had painstakingly marked each tunnel and shaft of his mine. There was something she had not seen before, a place distinctly marked, bolder and more defined than the others.

Ghost Dancer looked away, her tears making it difficult to see. Samuel Smith had found his dream. He had discovered a rich vein of gold.

"*Mahzaskaze,*" she whispered sadly. "It all had to do with gold."

A hand suddenly touched her arm and Ghost Dancer nearly fell backwards in the chair she was so startled. Almost frightened to death, she found herself eye to eye with Bender's Sioux woman.

Frantic, the Sioux was motioning for her to leave, pulling her arm to emphasis her meaning.

"Yes," nodded Ghost Dancer in total agreement. "I had better go."

"I believe it's a little late for that, my sweet."

Bender's deep voice reverberated in her head, much like a canyon echo. Fear clamped about her throat, making it difficult to speak, her breathing already irregular and labored. Flashes of a broken arrow pounded through her mind, making her composure flee altogether.

"Broken Arrow," she cried.

A shadow behind Bender moved, turning to flee, but the major grabbed the feeble old man and forced him into the light. Broken Arrow covered his face in fear but to no avail.

Ghost Dancer moved forward, her eyes filled with hot anger. She spit at his feet in disgust. "You are even more despicable than I ever imagined."

Broken Arrow pulled free of Bender's strong grip and straightened as best his humped back would allow. "I should have known that you would see me in your visions. Your powers are too great."

His head bowed in final submission. "Your eyes have been cast upon me and I shall die. It is as you said."

"And because of your foolish play, our people will suffer. You deserve what shall befall you."

Her words were hard, even in his defeat. He had done a grave wrong with no forgiveness in his future. It was his final payment for the petty jealousy he had allowed to grow into a dangerous obsession.

"Well," Bender mused sarcastically, "this is a touching reunion, but we have some important business to take care of."

Ghost Dancer had never hated anyone so much, and she experienced a loss of composure. "And you," she choked out with vehemence. "You are the most evil of all. You killed the old man for his map and you have killed innocent people so that we would be driven from our land. And for what? A yellow stone of the earth."

His laughter caused everyone to wince, the sound so vile. "Yellow stones. God, you are an innocent!" Bender moved to stand in front of Ghost Dancer. "It's hard to understand why this old man is so frightened of you." His hand brushed the softness of her cheek, and a frown wrinkled his forehead when she pulled away. He then touched his own face and the ugly red marks left by the hawk's talons.

"And you"—he turned to the Sioux woman who cowered in the corner, his long finger pointing at her—"you are a betraying little bitch."

He walked toward her and his hand snapped up, clamping viciously about her neck. "I can no longer trust you, so what use are you to me?"

"Leave her be," Ghost Dancer cried, moving to interfere.

Bender whirled about, his face a mask of fury. "And you . . . What shall I do with you, Angelique? Or . . . is it Ghost Dancer?"

Again, his laughter filled the room, keeping Ghost Dancer's eyes glued to him and therefore unaware of the men who moved behind her.

"Tell me, sweetness. What are these powers this crazy redskin's been telling me about? He thinks I should be afraid of you, like he is."

His thumb pointed to Broken Arrow who now sat cross-legged on the floor, lost in his own world, mumbling indiscernible words as he prayed.

"He thinks he's going to die now."

Bender turned his cold, hard eyes back to Ghost Dancer. "I think perhaps he's right."

Ghost Dancer felt the blood drain from her face and a chilling numbness settled over her. She had never faced such evil before.

"Haven't you anything to say?" he prompted, seemingly pleased with himself.

"What would you have me say?" she whispered.

"Perhaps, I would like to hear you beg for my mercy. Yes . . . that would be nice to hear."

"I have no need of your mercy."

That was not what he wanted to hear, and a red haze engulfed him, bringing a horrid wickedness to his eyes. He grabbed the Sioux woman once again about her slender neck, with one strong hand choking the life from her. "If you will not beg for yourself, then maybe you will beg for her miserable life!"

Ghost Dancer stepped forward in fear as the young girl sagged under his powerful hold. "Bender"—she brought his devil eyes back to her and saw the unbridled hate in them—"please. . . ."

His gaze paralyzed her, and she tasted the bitterness of his malevolence. Had his hand been about her own throat, she could have called upon her *protectors*, but she was powerless to help the Sioux woman. "Please, I am begging you. Leave her be."

Something akin to an animalistic cry growled from deep within him, and he snapped the woman's neck as easily as a twig. When he let go, she sank to the floor, her eyes still open in fright.

Ghost Dancer felt her knees weaken, and she fell. Her own anger surfaced, mixing its potency with fear and pain. She screamed out her agony in one long, woeful cry. All the mirrors shattered and the glass windows broke, allowing the wind and rain to enter. As her wail grew, so did the storm, its violence much like what she felt in her sorrowing heart.

Bender shifted, suddenly nervous. He looked at the old Indian whose prayers became more frantic. But it was Ghost Dancer who caused a sliver of panic to rise within him. He motioned for his men to take her.

Mac and Jim were prepared and clamped a cloth doused liberally with ether over her nose, sending her quickly into a world of blackness.

Bender stood over her still form and snickered. "Even your magic cannot help you now."

Again, he motioned to his men, and they took her from the room. Then his attention turned to Broken Arrow. The old Indian's chanting grated on his nerves. A slow, diabolical grin came to his face, and he moved toward him.

"You were right, old man. You are going to die."

The grin turned into a laugh as he pulled his knife from its sheath hidden inside his coat. Bender stepped up behind the Indian, the aged medicine man, who was completely lost to his own fear and horror.

Cameron came awake, instantly alert. Yet he heard only the silence of the night and the fast pace of his heart. Once again, he felt a stirring of panic come from nowhere, for no reason. His thoughts turned to Ghost Dancer.

Sliding from the warmth of his bed, Cameron put on his pants and shirt. Without giving thought to the lateness of the hour, he went to the colonel's apartment. By the second round of fierce pounding, the door was opened to his demands by a sleepy-eyed Dawson.

"Christ, Cameron? What the hell's the matter now?"

It had been a difficult few days and his commanding officer's worried eyes showed it. "Sorry, Colonel," Cameron apologized, suddenly feeling foolish. He had purposely avoided Ghost Dancer all day and now he was breaking doors down in the middle of the night to see her. It made no sense. "I'm acting the fool, that's all. I'll see you in the morning."

Cameron walked away from the door, a strong feeling cutting through his gut. "You're turning into a mother," he grumbled, running his hand through his tousled hair. "A damn mother."

He returned to his room, the small apartment oppressive and cramped. The short space of wooden floor was polished by his bare feet as he paced back and forth the rest of the night. A few times he tried to lie down but sleep evaded him with a vengeance. The insistent feeling of doom grew inside him as the hours ticked by in agonizing slowness. By the time the sun began to inch up into the eastern sky, he was nearly crazy with undefined worry.

Cameron stood by the window, watching the golden sphere burn its way into the black night, turning the darkness to a gray hue, hinged with pink-tipped orange. As they had during the entire night, his thoughts clamored, the subject always the same. *Angelique . . . No, Ghost Dancer.*

He was totally confused. He didn't even know what to call her anymore. From the first, he had preferred Angelique, more comfortable with the white man's name. But now it was beginning to feel strange on his tongue and Ghost Dancer more familiar. Never before had he known such agony of not understanding, of not believing, or trying to. He needed to find the answers, and soon, or he would most certainly go mad.

Unable to contain himself any longer, Cameron left his room and retraced the same steps he had made only a few hours earlier. This time, he made himself remain in control, his emotions now under a tight, yet strained, rein. Just as he started to knock, the door flew open, and he came face to face with Wilma. This time he felt like someone had kicked him in the stomach.

"Cameron," Wilma sniffed, quick to turn away from his worried gaze. "Come in."

Cameron entered. "What's wrong?" His eyes fell to her wringing hands, then moved back up to her stricken face. He swallowed hard to ease the sudden dryness of his throat. He wanted to ask again, but was too afraid.

"She's not in her room, Cameron. We had hoped she had gone to you."

The colonel's voice drew his eyes back to him, the look on Cameron's face stating clearly that she hadn't. "Where is she?" he asked a bit foolishly. He knew that they had no answer, either.

"I knew it," Cameron cried out in anger. "I knew something was wrong, but I ignored it. I'm the biggest kind of fool!"

Wilma placed a comforting hand on his slumped shoulders. "You couldn't have known. She must have gotten up in the night and left. Now where on earth would she go?"

Cameron sunk into a nearby chair, his posture showing his beaten mood. "I *did* know, Wilma. I'm beginning to feel when she is in danger. Somehow, someway, I know."

He held his head in his hands. "And I did everything to deny it."

The colonel sat across from Cameron. "Do you have any idea where she might have gone?"

Cameron's head shook in a negative answer.

"Maybe she went back to her tribe," Wilma offered with false enthusiasm.

"Maybe, but we should start looking here, in town," her husband added.

Cameron's voice turned to pure steel and his eyes held a dangerous look as his jaw took on a hard edge. "Yes. Let's start with Bender's place."

Chapter 21

"I'm sorry, Major Bender is not here today, sir."

Cameron had to fight hard to maintain control over his anger. "And where would Major Bender be?"

The servant's nose raised even higher into the air at the undercurrent of sarcasm in his words. "I believe he is tending to business in Laramie. If it's any business of yours, Captain."

He gritted his teeth at her disdainful sniff. "When do you expect him back?"

"I certainly don't know."

Unable to stand her unsmiling face any longer, Cameron turned and walked down the steps and out the gate.

"Captain Wade," Mary Beth called, waving her gloved hand delicately in the air to catch his attention.

Cameron stopped and turned to the soft voice that called to him. He waited patiently for her to catch up to him before speaking. "What can I do for you today?"

Mary Beth drew a deep breath, her face flushed from her hurried walking. "I just wanted to tell you how sorry I am that Angelique had to leave so suddenly. What a pity her stay was cut short."

Cameron's face drained of color and the slightest tremor sounded in his voice. "What do you know of Angelique's leaving?"

"I just saw Wilma and she said Angelique's parents were ill and that she had to return home. I believe she mentioned catching the stage that left early this morning." Suddenly, she became embarrassingly aware of his stricken look. "You . . . you didn't know?"

Cameron was quick to pull his thoughts together. "Of course I did," he lied. "I just didn't think she would have to leave so suddenly, without saying good-bye."

"Yes," she agreed. "I will miss her, we were just beginning to get to know each other better. I do hope she can come back soon."

Cameron could only nod, his thoughts already running in another direction.

"I must be keeping you from your duties." Mary Beth looked down at her feet shyly. "It was good to see you again, Captain."

"The pleasure was mine." Cameron tipped his hat and moved on down the lane, his step quickening with each passing second.

The darkness was like a heavy blanket laid over her head to steal away the light, to steal away the sound and to thin the air. Ghost Dancer knew only pain, jolting through her in a steady rhythm. Over and over, a great throb moved inside her head.

Suddenly, the smallest of lights appeared in the distance. Time passed, marked by the steady, dull ache that came with each movement. The light grew larger with agonizing slowness, enlarging into a tiny window of hope. She saw a hand reach out of the darkness, a helping hand to pull her from the pain.

Ghost Dancer stretched her hand out, reaching out in desperation. She was almost there. The hand was so close, so close.

The light went out and the hand slipped from hers.

"She's waking up, Mac. Best give her another snort of that ether stuff."

Mac looked over his shoulder to the mount he led. Ghost Dancer lay over the horse, face down, her long hair dangling as limply as she did. A low moan escaped her as the horse trotted along, bouncing her like a rag doll on its bony back.

"Yeah," he agreed, pulling on his horse's reins. "Let's rest here a bit. Damn rain's miserable cold."

Jim, in full agreement with his partner, sniffed loudly. "You can say that again. We're out here freezin' our asses off. I sure hope the boss man knows what he's doing."

Mac slid from his horse and hollered back to Jim. "He's never led us wrong, pal. Seems t' think no onen'll ever find her there. Even that Injun-lovin' captin won't think t' look there."

"Yeah, I know. But to haul this"—he pointed toward Ghost Dancer—"this Indian witch woman all the way to the mines seems a bit unnecessary to me. We should just kill her and be done with it."

He walked his horse over to tie up next to Mac's. "Instead, we're out here in this damnable rain, keeping her drugged just to leave her to die in a cave."

"Well," mused Mac after thinking it over, "I'm not so sure I would want t' be the one t' kill her. She's a strange one, and I don't want to take any chances."

"Hah!" Jim cackled like a chicken. "What's got you so spooked, Mac, old boy?"

Mac riled instantly. "Damn right, I'm spooked, Jimmy boy. Didn't you hear what that old medicine man said?"

Jim laughed a short, loud snort and recklessly jerked Ghost Dancer off the horse, catching her like a sack of flour. "Ain't nothin' to be scared of. She's just like any other woman. Ain't nothin' to this hocus-pocus stuff, Mac."

A wide grin spread across the older man's sun-wrinkled face. "If she's *just* like any other woman, why haven't you had your way with her?"

"Jesus, Mac," he objected too loudly, "she's unconscious."

This time it was Mac who snorted a laugh. "Ain't never mattered much before. To you, a warm body's always been good enough. N' sometimes, I've wondered if you'd take 'em dead."

Jim shifted, uneasy at his friend's accuracy. "Don't have no taste for this one. Imagine, Mac. A white woman living with a bunch of red savages.

Ain't right, I say." He emphasized his distaste by dumping her on the muddy ground.

"You're just as scared of her as I am, and you damn well know it," Mac gloated, handing his companion the bag that held the ether and cloth. Another moan brought their attention to the subject in question. "Give her a good dose, Jimmy boy. I don't want t' take a chance of her waking up on us."

Jim took it and nodded. "Yeah. I gotta admit, I don't want to deal with her should that happen."

The storm made the early evening seem late, premature darkness reflecting the black mood of the two men who approached Bender's door. For the second time that day, they pounded on it, bringing the somber woman to answer. The day was nearly gone, and Cameron was no closer to finding Ghost Dancer. The lines on his face showed all he felt.

"Is Bender back from town?" His words were curt, even rude. Cameron knew it but cared little about etiquette and manners.

"Major Bender is not receiving this evening, Captain. I will tell him that you called."

It was the colonel who interfered. "This isn't a social call, madame. And the major *will* see us. So be good enough to tell him that we are here."

The old woman was loyal to Jack Bender, but she also knew when to back down. Resigned to do as they asked, she disappeared, only to reappear within a couple seconds to show them to the drawing room. "Major Bender will be right with you."

Cameron had time to pace the floor only twice before Bender appeared.

"Colonel Dawson." His voice was deceitfully smooth and unconcerned. "Captain Wade. To what do I owe the pleasure of this visit?"

Cameron felt control of his temper sliding from him, but remained quiet, allowing the colonel with his trained diplomacy to handle the situation.

"We were wondering if you might know anything about Miss Dancer's departure earlier today?" Colonel Dawson's question was direct, but contained none of the anger that showed in Cameron's eyes.

Both the colonel and Cameron knew the futility of asking such a question; obviously Bender was not about to confess any participation. It was merely for the sake of asking.

It was like a game. Some sort of bizarre game. Calculated movements, courageous bluffs, and devious planning. Cameron knew the irony of it all. Ghost Dancer had come here to find evidence to prove her people's innocence. Now, the game was taking a strange turn, and the rules were no longer within reason. Somehow, he knew that her very life was at stake, but why and who was responsible evaded him. And this galled Cameron to the core.

"I was not aware that Miss Dancer had left."

Cameron wondered at how cool Bender always remained.

The colonel's face showed genuine despair. He was getting too old for this. "She left sometime last night."

Bender's face, in turn, showed nothing. "I'm sorry to hear that, Colonel Dawson. As you know, I found Miss Dancer quite interesting. A woman of her character is so rare."

Unconsciously, he touched the red marks on his face and a flash of uncontrolled hatred touched the dark recesses of his black eyes. Hot and potent.

Cameron watched him closely and read the lie of his words and the truth that sparked in his eyes. At that moment, Cameron wanted to beat that truth from him. But his loyalty to the colonel was strong and his direct orders kept him in line. They were here to observe, not to threaten.

"We appreciate your time." The colonel cleared his throat. "We'll not bother you further."

Cameron fell into step behind him as they made to leave, but couldn't resist a question. "What happened to the place, Major?"

Black eyes met steady green ones. "Such a strange thing. Must have been a freak wind during the storm last night. Broke all the windows, every one of them."

The hair on the back of Cameron's neck prickled and stood on end. "Does seem a strange thing to happen." His gaze moved back to Bender's. "Quite a wicked mark on your face. Too bad, it looks like it will scar."

The slightest of quivers broke Bender's rock-hard expression, telling Cameron the affect his words had had, hitting nerves deep in the steel armor Bender always presented.

"Another strange occurrence, Captain."

Cameron stopped directly in front of him. "Looks like your having a bit of bad luck."

Their eyes clashed in dark anger, each man casting a heated challenge to the other. Each man understanding the hatred that ran thick in their veins.

Cameron pulled the buckle tight, then dropped the stirrup down. "I can't sit around here just waiting, Colonel."

The colonel had to agree. "I suppose not. It's just that such a nasty storm's brewing. Wilma will worry about you both now."

"Maybe Ghost Dancer did go back to the village. We need to know for sure."

"Well, you be careful, Captain. Come back as soon as you know anything. We're sitting smack dab in the middle of a pack of trouble."

Cameron turned to his commanding officer, but felt like he was facing a friend. "I will. Tell Wilma I'll be careful. I promise. This whole thing . . ." Cameron paused, then went on, "it's a bit more than we bargained for. Isn't it, Colonel?"

Dawson nodded, his mind recalling that rainy night and Ghost Dancer's urgent pleas to find the baby. "Yes." He couldn't hold down the shiver. "A bit more than we bargained for."

Cameron stepped up into the saddle and nudged his mount forward, then he looked back at the colonel. "Ask Wilma to say a little prayer, will you?"

* * *

The rain came down in icy sheets, unending in its torrent. Cameron had been forced to stop, darkness and the nasty weather making it impossible to see. Fearing his horse might stumble and get hurt, he stopped for the night. He huddled beneath an old tree, its sparse, bare branches providing little protection, the cold dampness seeping through the wool blanket he used as a crude shelter.

"God," Cameron prayed as his eyes swivelled up to look out into the blackness, "I could use some help here."

His stiff, cold fingers raked his wet hair from his forehead, a deep tiredness robbing him of coherent thought. Where was she?

He raised his hands high, reaching to an unknown entity in the black rain and cried out in fear, frustration, and pain. "Where is she?"

Yellow-gold eyes blinked, disappearing for the briefest of seconds in the inky blanket of night. Wolfdog laid his wet head on his paws, never taking his gaze from Ghost Dancer who lay only a few feet from him. In the distance, a low howl sounded, answered by another, then another as his brothers settled in around the three people.

"Sounds like a whole damn pack of them devils," muttered Jim, looking about nervously as his hand tightened about his gun.

Mac's eyes rolled up in his head. "Keep your britches on, Jimmy boy. Those wolves are a long ways off and they'll be keepin' their distance."

Jim took another swig from the bottle of whiskey he held, then mopped the wetness from his bristled face. "I'll be damn glad to get rid of that witch." He took another generous swallow. "Ghost Dancer or not. Tomorrow's her last day on this earth."

Reaching out for the bottle, Mac's head bobbed up and down in agreement. "You could say that again."

With great patience and love, Wolfdog waited out the night near his mistress.

Chapter 22

Something pulled her drugged mind from the bleak abyss she had fallen into. Ghost Dancer struggled against the monster darkness, its harsh, ugly hands gripped so tight about her, keeping the air from rushing in freely. Again, the small light appeared. So close yet so far. The smallest part in the far recesses of her mind came alive; the smallest glow began to warm the evil chill that enveloped her.

"She's coming out of it again," Mac grumbled.

"Ain't no never mind." Jim grinned wickedly. "This is the end of the line for the little Injun' lover."

Mac looked down the eerie mine shaft and swallowed hard, a low howl touching his ears as the cold wind swept into its long passageways. "Well, let's get it over with. You got that map?"

"I'll read it, you carry her."

Jim lifted a blazing torch to see the parchment better, then pointed the way as Mac struggled behind with his burden hefted over his shoulder.

The two men moved deep into the mine, a place that had never seen the light of day. Streams of water ran down the rocky pathway, a small river, washing into the earth's secret center. As they went deeper, the walls grew thicker, the air thinner, the dampness heavier.

"This is it," Jim said, almost too quietly.

Both men looked into the small boarded-up shaft with caution, a low whistle sounding from one. As Jim poked the torch into the cavern opening, bats rushed out, their squeals of anger echoing off the damp rock walls, creating a chamber of noise and clamor.

"Jeeeesusss!" Mac cried in disgust as he dodged the ugly creatures, the flapping of their wings mixing with their horrendous screeches.

"Let's get this over with, Mac," Jim called, already tearing at the decayed planks that had been nailed across the entry's beams. "Looks like it's already fillin' with water. Won't take it long for it to fill right on up. 'Specially when we cover this hole here."

Mac nodded, suddenly feeling a touch guilty. "Seems t' me, we could do her in a bit kinder. Leaving her trapped in there t' drown seems a bit cruel, even for the boss man."

Jim stopped, throwing a slivered piece of worm-eaten wood aside, his look impatient. "It's what he wanted. We always do it his way. Cruel or not, that's what we are goin' to do."

Again, Mac nodded. "I know. I know. Just seems a bit much is all." He adjusted her slight weight on his shoulder, his uncomfortableness more from the deed they were about, than the burden he carried.

His friend knew that look. "She's some sort of witch woman, old man. Now dump her down the shaft and let's be done with it."

Mac, as always, did as he was told and moved forward to the gaping hole. From the dim light of the torch, he could see it went in a few feet then dropped almost straight down into a black abyss. The walls seemed to be crying, dampness running off the cold stone in excess. Where they stood was now several inches under water, a small stream flowing into the manmade pit. The shaft had obviously been too dangerous and had been boarded up.

Now this was to become Ghost Dancer's tomb. Mac shivered at the thought. She was still drugged, only a low moan had come from her of late. Maybe she would never waken to know her fate.

Jim helped Mac lift her from his shoulder and together they committed the foul deed, sending her down into her watery grave.

Then, in silence, they finished the job. The dampness had rotted the timbers framing the hole, and it took little to work them free. The heavy rock and mud quickly covered the opening, sealing Ghost Dancer within.

"What is it, Cameron Wade?"

Cameron stared at Black Hawk. "I don't know. I just feel something. Like a dreadful fear."

Black Hawk nodded in a knowing way. "In time, you will come to understand better."

"You think she's trying to tell me something?" They didn't have time, he needed to understand now.

"Perhaps."

Cameron rubbed his bristled jaw, frustration showing through his weariness. "You don't seem very worried."

A patient smile touched the older man's face. "My daughter will call to you. You must wait."

"Wait! How can I wait? She's in danger, that much I do know. I feel it!"

"Until she talks to you, you will not know where to go. You must wait."

Cameron tried to settle his voice and manner. "What if she can't *talk* to me?"

Black Hawk considered this. "Ghost Dancer has the protective eye of *Wakan Tanka*. A way will be found."

"I wish I had your faith, Black Hawk. I really do."

"That, too, will come with time."

Ghost Dancer lifted her head only to drop it down again. She tried to open her heavy eyelids. The immense blackness that greeted her made her doubt she had opened them. Slowly, she moved her hand to feel her face. Her eyes were open.

She wondered then if perhaps she had no sight. The terrible pain in her head contributed to that idea. Finally, the trickle of water filtered past the haze that clogged her mind, and she realized the tremendous numbness that claimed her. Ghost Dancer tried to move her legs, but felt nothing.

As the drug wore off, she became more and more aware of her surroundings, and fear began to creep in as a dominant thought. She had no idea where she was or why.

With slow regret, she remembered her encounter with Bender. Then she knew the why, but still did not know where.

Great chills overtook her, and her teeth chattered. She tried to think, but the pain and grogginess kept her incapacitated. The longest time passed before she could move, and then, she merely rolled onto her belly. That made her dizzy, the complete darkness making it difficult to determine up from down. She managed to crawl, using her arms to drag her legs behind her. That was when she discovered the growing pool; the numbness in her legs had been caused by the icy water. She moved away from it, only to find her exit blocked, the stone weeping rivers of its own. Carefully, she examined the walls with her fingers, her only way to see. Inch after inch of cold, hard rock was her only discovery.

Discouragement moved into her weary, aching mind. Ghost Dancer propped her back against the wall and rubbed the numbness from her legs. They began to ache terribly, but that was better than no feeling at all. She pulled up her knees to hug them close, chills still shaking her, draining her of any remaining strength. She laid her head on her knees, closing her eyes against the unbearable darkness that crowded her. Many minutes had passed before she realized the water was once again covering her feet.

She swallowed hard, her throat dry and raw. The water was rising, and Ghost Dancer struggled to keep the terror from claiming control of her and the pure panic from overcoming her. In spite of her efforts, tears came to her eyes. She felt lost and terribly alone. She tried to pray, but only one thought came to her shaken mind.

"Cameron," she whispered, her voice hoarse and trembling. "Cameron."

Cameron awoke. He listened but only heard the normal night noises. Still, he knew she had called his name. He heard it. He was sure of it.

Within seconds, he was dressed and ready to go. But where?

"Damn it," he swore, clenching his hands into fists at his helplessness. "Where are you?"

He looked up, his eyes catching the golden flash of another pair of eyes. Wolfdog moved forward and let out a low howl, his head tilting as he spoke to Cameron in his eerie yelps.

"You know where she is," Cameron spoke as he watched the wolf move to the tepee's flap. The animal stopped and looked back, as if waiting for him to follow.

"I'll be damned," he whispered. "You do know where she is."

Cameron followed Wolfdog into the storm, taking only a few minutes to get his horse. It took most of the night to reach the mine, Cameron riding like a madman through the rain-drenched darkness. He was off his mount before he had brought the horse to a full halt. He never missed a step and followed the animal into the tunnel, lighting a torch as he went. Several times Wolfdog stopped to wait for Cameron, his eyes catching the light of the fire. For the first time, hope surged within Cameron. He knew her pet was taking him to her.

When the animal came to the wall of stone and rubble, he stopped. Wolfdog let out another low howl, his cry echoing in the long shafts that crisscrossed the vast mine.

Cameron stood in front of a pile of timbers and rock, despairing at the problem at hand. Wolfdog started digging, his feet clawing at the mud and gravel frantically.

"Angelique," called out Cameron. "Angel, are you in there?"

There was no answer.

"Oh God," Cameron prayed, "I've never been much of a church-going man, but I've never doubted my faith. Should You be inclined, I could use a bit of help. Looks like a lot of rock to move and some of its pretty damn big."

He jumped right into it, throwing the debris aside as he worked like a man possessed. Every so often he stopped to call to her.

Ghost Dancer roused from her fevered sleep, choking on the rising water. She had crawled as far up the hole as she could to escape the rising water line. She had nowhere else to go.

"Angel."

She wondered if she were dreaming, while she was awake. Then she heard it again.

"Cameron," she tried to speak, but it came out a croaked whisper. Her tears came again, but this time she felt a glimmer of hope.

She tried again. "Cameron."

The weak cry hit a nerve in his mind and tore at his heart. "Angelique! Are you all right?"

Panic made him dig faster. "Angel!"

Ghost Dancer struggled to stay above the water. "Cameron, help me."

It was so slight a sound, so soft a plea. "Hold on, I'll get you out."

Her face was pressed against the cold stone, the water threatening her with every passing second. "The w–wa–wat . . ." she tried to call out, but took in a mouthful of water.

Wolfdog was yelping, a strange cry of panic. In turn, it prompted sheer terror in Cameron. He tore at the blocked passage with renewed vigor, fear giving him strength. Still, two very large beams blocked the way and he could not budge them. As hard as he tried, he couldn't move them a single inch.

"Angelique!" he yelled to her. "I can't move the timbers. I'll have to go and get help."

"N–nooo . . ." cried Ghost Dancer weakly in horror.

He felt his throat tighten and tears filled his eyes. "I can't move them. I've got to have help." In spite of the chill, he was sweating from exertion, his tears mingling with the beads that rolled down his face. "I've got to go."

He started to turn away, but the soft cry clung to him, and he could not force another step. What was he to do?

Ghost Dancer was coughing up water, as there was very little air left. Blindly, she reached out, touching the black rock that kept the air and light from her.

"Chinyeh," she whimpered. "Red Bear, my brother."

Unable to go, Cameron put his shoulder once again to the timber and gave it all he had. He groaned in rage, his muscles strained to their limit.

"God!" he yelled, standing back. "I can't move it alone!"

Just then, his attention was drawn to the appearance of a giant bear, its red fur aglow in the dim light of the torch. Cameron froze in sheer amazement and in fear. His rifle was still on his saddle and he had not brought his pistol with him in his haste. The animal rose onto his hind feet, his huge paws clawing the air, an ominous sight to behold. He let out a deafening growl, then dropped back down onto all fours.

When the bear moved toward him, Cameron slowly moved aside for the lumbering creature of might. The beast reached the blocked opening into the shaft and put his paws on the very timber Cameron had been struggling with only seconds before. With great strength, the animal pushed against the wooden beam. In an unheard rhythm, he bounced, each time a grunt marking his tremendous effort. Soon, it began to move, then gave way under his persistence, mud and stone falling free with it.

Cameron was stunned, but only for a second. He started pulling the loose debris away. The animal moved to the other structure and began to work it free, too. When it gave way, so did the confining wall and the water behind it. Cameron was thrown back by the rush of water. Gaining his footing, he began to look for Ghost Dancer, giving no further thought to the great red bear.

"Angelique," he called, searching the muddy water for her. "Angelique."

Wolfdog found her, lying face down in the mire, and set up a howl. In two long steps Cameron was there, pulling her up from the mud that strangled her. A swift slap on her back started Ghost Dancer coughing and ridding herself of the water she had swallowed.

Cameron took her into his arms, his tears flowing freely. He was shaking, as was she. She trembled from illness, he from the end of a terror such as he had never known. It left him drained emotionally and physically. For many moments, he just held her, the fear of never doing so again still too familiar, making him cling to her.

"Oh, Angel. I thought I had lost you for good," he whispered into her ear, holding her even closer. "I thought I had lost you."

"What's he doing?"

Black Hawk turned his even gaze to Cameron's tired, haggard face. "He is praying."

Cameron rubbed his jaw, several days of growth darkening his face. "Praying?" He looked like he was about to burst. "Shouldn't he be doing a bit more than that?"

"He is our medicine man, Cameron. Our ways are old and he will tend to Ghost Dancer as we have always done."

The steady beat of the drum nearly drove Cameron crazy. "She looks so damn pale."

As always, Black Hawk was patient. "She has been given a drug to make her sleep. Her coughing and shivering were taking all her strength."

"Is she . . ." Cameron didn't finish what he started to say. He could not voice his greatest fear.

"You must rest," said Black Hawk as he led him away. "It will do you no good to grow ill yourself."

"Sleep." The word sounded as doubtful as his look. "I could not possibly sleep."

"Then I will have my wife fix you something that will help."

That night, he slept the sleep of the dead.

When he woke, Cameron felt a wave of panic wash over him. How much time had passed? He tried to clear his mind, slumber still invading his thoughts, creating slow, cumbersome images.

"Angelique," he mumbled, fear sweeping through him in the wake of his panic.

He listened. There was no sound. There was no beat of the medicine man's drum. No sound at all.

Cameron jumped from his pallet, pulling his pants on as he went. Why had the drum stopped?

Visions rushed into his mind, bringing back the terror he had known in the mine. It was still too fresh, too tender, too painful. His breathing became labored and fast. As hard as he tried to gain control of his fear, he could not. To lose her now would be unbearable.

Too vividly he recalled her mud-streaked face, a face so deathly pale. All the way back to the village she shivered, the chills taking all her strength, leaving her delirious with fever.

Why had the drums stopped?

Cameron pushed back the tepee cover and slipped inside. It was dark and much too quiet. It took several seconds for his eyes to adjust to the blackness, then he saw her, lying on her pallet, still and unmoving. Too still.

Kneeling beside her, Cameron took her hand into his. It felt cold in the warmth of his own larger one. So very cold.

"Angel," he whispered, his voice strained and cracking.

Ghost Dancer's eyes fluttered, slowly focusing on the pain-filled face above her. She tried to speak, but her throat was too dry. So she smiled.

Cameron brought her hand to his lips and kissed it. "Oh, God," he cried. "You scared the hell out of me."

He closed his eyes to bring the rush of emotion under control. Her palm touched his cheek.

"I . . ." She swallowed and tried again. "I love you, Cameron Wade."

This time he smiled, his own love softening the lines of his face. "I love you, too, Angelique."

Tears came to her, a mixture of happiness and sadness. "I am Ghost Dancer. That is the way it must be."

He nodded. "You are right. You are,"—he caressed her cheek lovingly in turn—"the Ghost Dancer."

Chapter 23

The fire crackled loudly, spewing bits of charred wood out of its stone ring, while the meager light of the flames created shadowed images on the hide walls of the tepee. Cameron lay on the pallet, Ghost Dancer snuggled into the curve of his arm, her head on his chest.

Each languished in the joy of being together, the simplest of acts most precious. The love that existed between them was understood. Words were unnecessary.

Cameron stroked her long silken hair, the feel of it like satin beneath his fingertips. He had been unable to leave her for more than a few minutes at a time, the fear of her brush with death too new and tender. Every so often, he would hold her even closer, hugging her to him in silent desperation. Finally, he spoke, "Are you still awake?"

Her head moved, and he knew she was. "I was wondering about something, Ghost Dancer."

This brought her eyes up to meet his, each caressing the other with their look. "What is that?"

"Well," he started, then stopped, a look of uncertainty on his face. He didn't seem to know what he wanted to say.

Ghost Dancer moved up onto one elbow and laid her hand on his chest, the feel of his flesh warm beneath hers. "What is troubling you?"

The look of love on her face prompted him to go on. "In the mine, something strange happened. Something I don't understand. I . . . uhhh . . ." He stopped again, seemingly searching for the right words. "I saw a bear. A giant red bear." His hands moved through the air to emphasize just how big. "He came out of nowhere and pushed the beams aside that I couldn't move. He . . . he saved your life."

A knowing look gleamed in Ghost Dancer's eyes. "It was my brother's protective spirit, the red bear. I called him when death was near. I feared you would leave, and I had no air."

Cameron felt a surge of skepticism, but squelched it immediately and quite thoroughly. "You have protective spirits?" He was careful to keep all doubt from his voice.

A feeling of proud warmth touched her heart and she felt good at his fight for understanding. "Yes. A gift from the Ones Above, and my father and brother. They offered of themselves to provide me with protectors, one in the image of a red bear, the other a black hawk."

"And they are your protectors? A kind of bodyguard?"

"Yes, for when I truly need help. Such as when Jack Bender attacked me. I called to my father and the black hawk came."

This prompted Cameron's eyes to round. "The marks on his face," he whispered as he remembered the deep scratches Bender bore, forever scarred for his wickedness.

"Yes," she said again, also recalling that day. "The hawk's talons were vicious."

His surprised eyes moved across the room to where Wolfdog lay, sleeping by the warm fire. "And the wolf, is he a protector?"

Ghost Dancer laughed this time, a soft sweetness in the notes. "He is of a sort, but not from the spirit world. He is flesh and blood, just as you and I."

"But he knew where you were."

"He did. Wolfdog is the most faithful of pets."

Cameron all of a sudden turned quite serious, his eyes mirroring remorse. "So much has happened, I . . ." He didn't know how to finish.

"In time you will come to understand all that has happened. Be patient, Cameron." She smiled, truly feeling that way.

"I love you, my Ghost Dancer," was all he could say in answer to her loving graciousness.

Her smile broadened even further. "I love you, too, Cameron Wade." Then she also became serious. "I must ask something of you."

Cameron reached out and brushed the soft pink of her cheek, then followed the delicate line of her jaw. "What is it?"

Ghost Dancer nibbled at her lower lip as she considered the best way to approach the subject that rolled about in her mind and lay heavy in her heart. "Jack Bender has yet to be dealt with, and, in truth, we are no closer to proving his guilt than when you first came to us."

Anger clenched Cameron's jaws and fire spewed from the dark centers of his eyes. "He's going to pay, that I promise."

Slender fingers wrapped about larger, calloused ones and Ghost Dancer gave his hand an understanding squeeze. "Yes. He will pay for what he has done to my people."

"He . . ." Cameron's voice rose, taking on the steely edge she had heard before. "He will pay for what he did to you."

"Cameron, please, you must not allow your anger to control you. It will come to no good."

Cameron felt the heat within him rise to the danger level. "No good is what that son of a—"

Ghost Dancer laid a finger on his mouth, stopping his hate-filled words. "You must listen to me."

Somehow, he managed to control his fury. "All right." He calmed down, letting his breath out, slow and easy. "What do you have in mind?"

"Cameron, there is so much you do not understand, and I know the struggle that goes on in your heart as you try. So I must ask that you trust me."

"I do trust you," he whispered. "I do."

"I nearly failed my people, Cameron Wade." She raised her head to meet his gaze head on, and her voice told of her determination. "This time, it will be done my way, the way of the Ghost Dancer. With the power I hold, vindication will be ours, and vengeance shall be yours."

The smallest shadow of doubt trickled over his face before he could squelch it. "You could do this?"

"That, I promise."

Cameron looked over to where Ghost Dancer slept. But her pallet was empty. A surge of panic immediately roused him from sleep. He searched the darkened tepee and found her sitting by the fire, her thoughts obviously lost to the flames that played before her with renewed vigor as she fed it more wood.

"Angel," he said, drawing her shadowed eyes to him. "Weren't you warm enough?"

She smiled. "I was plenty warm, Cameron."

"Then come back to bed, you must rest."

Like an overbearing mother, Cameron stood to help Ghost Dancer to her bed. He tucked the furs around her, then sat beside her. Pushing back a stray lock from her forehead, he asked, "Is something bothering you?"

As hard as she tried, she could not keep the slight tremble from her voice. "It is nothing."

"It seems to me," Cameron encouraged, his voice soothing, "that if it were nothing, you would have been asleep rather than sitting by the fire."

Cameron's perceptiveness caused a small twinge of pleasure. "It is the Ghost Dance."

"What is the Ghost Dance?"

For a long moment Ghost Dancer merely stared into the fire, searching for the words to make it clear. "It is what I must do to defeat Jack Bender.

The Ghost Dance is what I am here for. It has been so since the First."

"Then what has you worried? The Ghost Dancer performs the Ghost Dance."

Woeful eyes turned to face him. "I am afraid."

This took Cameron by surprise. "Why? You seem to fear so little, why would you fear this?"

"I have never done the Ghost Dance before," she confessed.

Cameron's mouth opened in a silent oh. "Never?"

She shook her head. "There has not been a need to dance for over one hundred years. It is done only when absolutely necessary. It is powerful. It must not be used lightly."

This prompted something akin to fear of his own, but her seriousness about the dance made him even more curious. "What exactly is the power it possesses?"

Ghost Dancer realized it was time he learned of certain things. "I possess the power, the dance merely channels it to where I want. I will use the dance to gain control of Jack Bender. I will use the dance to control his mind, his will, his soul. Like a puppet, I will guide him, then we will know victory as I play him into a trap of his own doing."

Cameron had to grapple to find the right words, intelligent thoughts evading him altogether. "You can do this?"

She nodded. "I can do this." Ghost Dancer's mind seemed to drift. "I remember the last time the dance was performed."

Confusion made him ask, "But it was over one hundred years ago. How can you remember?"

She continued to stare into nowhere, the visions of her mind taking her away. "Important memories are forever the Ghost Dancer's."

Cameron recalled Black Hawk telling him that, along with other things he had thought a bit hard to swallow. It was all so unbelievable, yet he could no longer dismiss her power. He didn't understand it all, but, this time, he would not push her away and laugh. Instead, he would stand by her, supporting her in this strange, mystical world he now found himself embroiled in.

Not really sure of what to say, Cameron pulled Ghost Dancer to him and held her. It was all she needed, to be held close in the strength of his arms. To know that now, no matter what, he was there.

Slowly, the wood burned down into red coals, aglow in the dark, silent night.

"Is this it?"

Ghost Dancer turned to Cameron and looked at the small, bushy tree he pointed at. "No." She turned her attention back to her own search, her breath foggy in the cold morning air. "It is very gnarled and the bark almost black."

With great patience, she hunted for the tree. Their footsteps were marked on the frosted ground and, as the sun rose, gaining strength, sunlight danced off the crystal prisms that covered the bared branches of the trees. Dark clouds rolled in like a great beast threatening to devour up the slight warmth offered by the sun. Ghost Dancer quickened her step. It would not be good to get caught in the cold rain so soon after her sickness.

"We'd best hurry," Cameron called out. "I don't want you to get soaked in the storm that's coming."

Ghost Dancer could not help but smile, their minds were so close in thought, and this left a pleasing warmth within her heart. "I will hurry."

The thunderheads edged closer and just as she began to doubt that the tree and its precious roots would be found, it was there. Delighted, she began to dig into the hardened ground, the cold night making it difficult. Cameron joined her, and with his help, they uncovered the dark, rooted fingers that grew deep in the earth. Careful to do no damage to the tree, she cut a few of the roots and placed them in her bag.

"What is this for?"

Ghost Dancer glanced up from her work. "It is a very special root containing a certain drug. When consumed, it will cause strange dreams and imagined things."

"A sort of hallucinogen," he added, more to himself than to her.

"Yes, I believe that is the right word. I will make a powder and it must be given to Jack Bender. The more he consumes, the more control I shall have over him. He will be susceptible to my calling. My nightmares will become his. In time, my thoughts will influence him. This will be the time for us to entrap him at his evil game."

"Wow," Cameron muttered, impressed and just a little frightened. "Remind me not to ever make you mad."

Ghost Dancer chuckled, the glimmer of humor in her bright eyes. "Yes, you would be wise not to do so."

Cameron grabbed her and pulled her close. "I suppose you'd turn me into a snake or a toad."

"That," she teased, "I cannot do. But I could make you think you were one."

"Did you know that you are truly the most beautiful woman I have ever seen?"

Her chuckling turned to laughter. "What a timely turn of conversation, Cameron Wade. But, still, it pleases me."

He snuggled even closer. "Does it now? What if I were to tell you that I love you? Would that please you, too?"

"Greatly," she replied, her head tilted up to look into his face. "More than greatly."

Unable to resist her tempting cherry lips, Cameron brushed them softly with his own. "We had better not dawdle, Angel. I just felt a raindrop, maybe even two."

"If you insist."

"I insist." He grinned, taking her hand in his.

"Lone Wolf," Ghost Dancer said, drawing his gaze to her. "You do not have to leave."

His head hung in despair. "My grandfather betrayed you, I cannot stay. His shame is now mine."

"That is not true," she argued. "You have always been faithful, I know *you* would never betray me."

"I would die for you, my Ghost Dancer. Never would I do as Broken Arrow. His hatred drove him, as my love drives me."

"Then stay." She offered her hand in welcome. "I need all my warriors beside me now. Especially one so devoted."

As if a great weight had been lifted from his shoulders, Lone Wolf sighed. "The strength of my arm is forever yours."

He accepted her forgiving hand and smiled.

Chapter 24

"You may enter," Black Hawk called in answer to Cameron's scratching at his tepee.

Cameron entered, careful to place the flap back down to keep the cold air out. Red Bear and Black Hawk were sitting near the crackling fire, passing a pipe leisurely between them.

"Have you seen Ghost Dancer?"

Black Hawk nodded. "It was time for her to prepare for the dance. She has gone to the sweat lodge to cleanse her soul."

Cameron felt a bit lost without her by his side. "I guess she did mention that, but I forgot."

Red Bear watched Cameron, shuffling nervously by the entrance. He motioned to him to sit, then handed him the pipe. "It will calm you."

Cameron gratefully accepted the handmade bowl. "Yeah, I could use a drink." He looked down at the smoldering pipe. "Or something."

He took a long draw and felt the heat burn deep in his lungs, the haze of smoke stinging his nostrils with its potent smell. "Lordy," Cameron wheezed, hoping the fire in his throat would ease. "What the hell is that?"

Black Hawk and Red Bear both laughed, their white teeth bright in the darkness of the tent. "Our tobacco"—grinned the older of the two men, his brown eyes twinkling—"is not as smooth as what the white man grows."

"I'll say," Cameron agreed readily, exhaling the strong smoke. He passed the hot pipe back and relaxed on the pile of furs, a bit lightheaded.

Red Bear puffed on the pipe, then turned back to his white brother. "You are to be honored tonight."

Cameron looked confused and asked, "What do you mean?"

"No man of your race has ever seen the Ghost Dance. It is a great honor."

Black Hawk's head nodded in agreement to what Red Bear had said. Then his mind took a sudden change of direction. "You love my daughter very much. I can see that."

Cameron blinked, wondering if he had missed something during the conversation. But he answered honestly, "I love Ghost Dancer very much. She is my life."

"It is a lot to ask of a man, to go against his own people for hers." Red Bear's words spoke the plain reality of the situation. "Yet you are willing to do this for my people?"

"I've got to admit, I fought the idea. But even my stubborn streak had to give way to the truth." Cameron's voice grew soft and tender. "Ghost Dancer is the most beautiful, the most special woman I've ever known. And, when I look around the village, I feel differently than I did. I'd like to think I know what keeps her here, with the Sioux. Everything's not so black and white after all."

Both men were pleased by his words. Cameron had proven himself to them and to the Ghost Sioux. Black Hawk once again gave Cameron the wooden pipe.

"As I said, you would understand with time. And you have." He nodded wisely.

Cameron shook his head in disagreement and to clear his head of the sudden dizziness he felt. "I don't know, Black Hawk. There's still so much I don't. Understand, I mean."

"What do you need to understand?" Red Bear coughed as he blew out another deep puff of the potent tobacco.

His head lolled back, and Cameron gave in to the urge to close his burning eyes. "I'm not sure I understand this Ghost Dance thing." He raised his heavy head and, with difficulty, opened his eyes again. "Yet, on the other hand, I'm not so sure I really want to."

Black Hawk seemed to know what he was trying to say. "Sometimes it is best to believe with a blind faithfulness, until the time comes when the truth of it all does not bring with it fear."

Cameron's mind was buzzing, and he had to concentrate hard to make sense of Black Hawk's words. But, slowly, he did. "Perhaps you're right. I'd better ease into this whole thing nice and slow. Too much all at once could scare the hell out of a man."

"To fight our enemies," Red Bear exclaimed, his words slurred the slightest bit, "is an easy thing. To endure pain, to accept grief—it is all a simple thing for a man. But to face the unknown, this is the greatest of challenges. I admire you, Cameron Wade, and I am proud to claim you as my brother."

"As I am to call you my son," added Black Hawk, his arm reaching out to clasp Cameron's.

"I thank you both for your vote of confidence, and I promise to do my best by the Ghost Sioux. I just hope Ghost Dancer knows what she's doing." Cameron felt too warm, the room seemed to move about him in a waving circle. He needed some fresh air. He eased his cumbersome body up, suddenly uncertain if he could stand at all. Somehow, he managed but was none too steady on his feet.

"I think I need some air." On shaky legs he made his way to the flap. "I'll see you later, at the lodge."

The damp, cold air brought immediate relief to his head and he walked off the hazy effects of the tobacco. The one question he had wanted to ask and couldn't continued to plague his mind. Over and over, it rang in his head.

Was the Ghost Dance dangerous?

For some reason, he believed it was. How could it not be? Yet, he really knew nothing about it. Most likely he was imagining the worst. He was making a mountain out of a mole hill.

Yeah, that's what I'm doing.

The steam drifted like low-lying clouds in the sweat lodge, the air thin and difficult to breath. The humid heat caused perspiration to roll down her face and over her bare body, leaving her long hair dripping wet.

Ghost Dancer's thoughts were wild and undisciplined, wandering about haphazardly. She thought about Jack Bender and her people's freedom from his evil doings. She thought about what lay ahead and of the dance. She thought of Cameron and of the love they shared. Ghost Dancer rushed from one thought to another in haste. There was so much to think about. Then she tried to pray.

She began to chant, the words of prayer slowing the clamor, easing her thoughts from her head. As the sweat cleansed her soul, the soft droning quieted her mind, the silent flurry chased from her in the wake of song.

An old woman waited outside for Ghost Dancer, and was ready with a blanket when she came out. She was quickly rushed to a nearby tepee for her preparations. There, another woman waited, and each was ready to do her duties. Without words, they performed their assigned tasks.

Ghost Dancer was bathed, her skin scrubbed until it was glowing and her hair combed until it was sparkling in the fire's yellow light. Carefully, one applied her face paint, the artwork age-old in striking black and white. On her upper and lower lids the woman drew charcoal lines, the azure color of her eyes the center. White was filled in over and under her eyes and out to her temples. Black, the color of night, covered her cheeks, lips, and the rest of her face, creating a powerful look.

As one woman made her up, the other prepared her costume, the same as the First wore hundreds and hundreds of years before. Next, she was dressed, each item placed upon her with extreme care and precision. In generations gone by, the Ghost Dancer had been a male, and the dress suited for him. A black skin of the softest fur was used as a breech cloth, her long legs and shapely hips exposed the full length. A finely quilled breastplate, the pride of a warrior, was pulled over her head and fastened in the back, barely covering her full breasts. Bands of feathers and fur dangled down her slender arms and about her ankles, images of the sun and the moon mingling among the markings. Feathers of the sacred white bird were braided into her silvery, blond hair and several were placed in her earlobes and dangled to her white shoulders.

The sound of the distant drums announced it was nearly time for the dance, the beat touching deep within Ghost Dancer's soul. She felt her heart quicken, the pace matching the drums.

Again, she prayed. Then she was ready.

The two women escorted her to the Great Lodge, the sounds of people and celebration greeting them. They left her alone, and, abruptly, the night grew silent.

The sudden quiet that ascended upon the crowd told Cameron that something was about to happen. He waited, holding his breath, anticipation building inside him. Slowly, gently, the drummers again stroked their instruments, the beat gathering strength with each second that passed, on and on, faster and faster. He was reminded of a locomotive, huffing and puffing with exertion as it started, then finally reaching full speed. Completing the image in his mind a great cry rose, sounding like the steam whistle. The huge fire sparked, flames leaping into the air, and a screen of smoke rose.

When the haze cleared, she was there.

The vision before him mesmerized Cameron. The noise, the smell, the heat. It all played on him, sending him into her world of mystery. She remained still, unmoving, all her beauty and glory before them. He waited. For what, he didn't know.

With deliberate slowness, she began to move to the heady rhythm. With conscious prolonging, she swayed, then worked up into the faster-paced dance. Sound reverberated through Cameron and the whole crowd, their eyes never leaving her. Steady and strong, Ghost Dancer kept time with the drumbeats.

Once again, Cameron felt lightheaded because of the haze that filled the large ceremonial hut. The dance took her away, claiming her by the unseen mystic power he felt about them. Suddenly, Ghost Dancer's voice rose above the din, its soothing tone subduing all but her words. Only the drums and her chanting could be heard. Powerful, yet distinctly feminine, her voice held them enthralled.

Sweat glistened off her near-naked body, the flames of the fire highlighting her every curve. Cameron could see her muscles flex from exertion as she danced. Her movements were sensuous, their meaning intoxicating. Emotions drowned him, and he was drawn to her. Desire fevered his blood. Admiration flooded his thoughts.

Like an infectious laughter, the excitement stirred him, then leaped through him like a wild fire. His heart beat erratically, the movement hard within his chest as it reeled out of control.

She was beauty. She was power.

Like a gathering storm, Ghost Dancer quickened her movements. On and on she danced, never tiring, never missing a beat. Cameron was out of breath just watching, but her energy never wavered.

She whirled about, again and again, her hair billowing out in a silver fan. Her eyes were closed and her face tilted upward. Still, she kept on. Still, she called out.

Time passed, yet Cameron did not notice. For him, only Ghost Dancer existed. Nothing more. He felt a numbness overtake him, and all other noise faded into the background, all the other people were no longer near. Only Ghost Dancer existed.

Her head turned toward him, her eyes opening to reveal the clearest, brightest of spheres. He felt himself being drawn to her, and into her. Blue mated with green, seducing him, pulling him further into her world of magic. Ghost Dancer called to him, her chanting becoming his name. He wanted to go to her. He wanted to. . . .

Ghost Dancer whirled away, the touching of their gazes broken. She stretched her arms upward, reaching for the Gods Above, reaching for the powers they claimed as their own. She called to them. She beseeched them.

Others took up her cry, their voices adding strength to hers. Cameron did not know what it was he yelled, only that he wanted it for the Ghost Dancer. He wanted it for the people. A great weariness descended upon him and he became aware of a heavy exhaustion. The heat was unbearable and beads of perspiration ran down his face, the salt burning his eyes. Yet he cried out. They all cried out.

Cameron felt hypnotized, unable to break away. He could only watch her dance. She never slowed the burning rhythm. Her voice never weakened.

Suddenly, Ghost Dancer's hand came up dramatically to her face, and she drew her fingers down over her cheek.

Ugly red marks appeared where she had touched her skin, and drops of blood ran through the black paint on her face.

Something deep in Cameron's gut twisted. It was at that very moment that Cameron believed.

Jack Bender's eyes flew open, his mind pulled violently from his sleep. He sat up and stared into the darkness. Something close to fear lurked within him, and he swallowed the disgusting taste of it.

What had awakened him, he didn't know. Only one thing stood clear and defined in his mind.

He muttered the name, "Ghost Dancer."

Sudden awareness came, and he felt pain in his cheek. The scarring scratches on his face began to throb. Slowly, he rose from his bed and lit a lamp. Taking it, he crossed to his bureau, and hesitantly, looked into its mirror.

Shock bolted through him, and he nearly dropped the light. Huge, ugly welts, swollen and infected, festered on his face. But mostly, it was the blood that oozed from the sores that kept his eyes riveted to the horror. This time, the fear leapt up inside him. With a shaking hand, he touched the mottled flesh that had been his face. Pain tore at him.

Quickly, he sloshed some whiskey into a glass and drained it. Then followed it with another.

Ghost Dancer knew of his fear and smiled.

When Cameron came to her, she was once again in the sweat lodge, washing away any impurities of the dance. It was almost morning, the night lost in the dance. She heard him shoo away the old woman, her childlike giggles echoing in the distant night as she sought her own tepee and sleep. He entered and moved to her side. Words seemed unnecessary between them.

Energy still surged within Ghost Dancer, an ethereal high still clinging to her spirit. No defined thoughts came to her mind, only the remembered beat of the drums remained. Tenderly, Cameron took the soft cloth and began to wash away the smeared paint that remained on her face. Even in the fire's scant light he could see the smoothness of her cheeks, the ugly marks of the dance no longer there.

Cameron closed his eyes a moment, recalling so vividly the feeling that had touched him as the blood had run down her face. He was not surprised, he did not question that they were gone. He merely believed. Without further thought, he tended to her, as one would a child, bathing away the remnants of the dance.

Ghost Dancer slowly moved back to reality, the gentle strokes upon her flesh soothing the turmoil that remained in her heart. Desire rushed in its place, taking her by surprise.

When the paint was cleaned away, Cameron continued washing the sweat that still clung to her body. Each curve was diligently tended to. He rinsed fresh water through her hair, cradling her head onto his arm. Chill bumps covered her nakedness, her nipples hard as the cold water washed over them. After the heat of the dance, it felt good. The passionate heat churning inside her kept her warm.

Several moments passed before she realized that Cameron was no longer bathing her, that his hands were massaging her tired muscles, easing the tension from her. Like a rag doll she grew limp and languid, leaving only the arousal within her to keep her awake, to keep her in need.

Soon, his hands were replaced with his burning lips, wet against her flesh, setting it afire with his teasing. When he came to her breast, his tongue, hard and hot, darted out to trace a damp line about the rosy tip, promising to suckle only when she whimpered for it. Ghost Dancer felt the heat tingle inside her, and her hips arched in a lover's rhythm. She grasped his head between her hands and pulled his warm lips to hers, demanding the surrender of his playful tongue to her own. A wild desperation grew inside her, leaving her trembling with its intensity. She recalled vividly the moment in the dance when their eyes had locked, much as their bodies did now. Never had she wanted him more.

He lifted her to him, and Ghost Dancer wrapped her legs about Cameron's waist. His own need locked with hers. Her mind still played the beat of the drums, and her body kept time with it. She found the sweetness of his mouth, drawing the plunder from it as she danced once again. Only this time, she danced for love, her body entwined with his. As with her dance, they began slow and easy, before climbing to the point of frenzied ecstacy.

Ghost Dancer's nails dug deeply into Cameron's back, but the pain only pushed him further into the magic of passion. Perspiration glistened off both their bodies, mingling with the moisture of love. They climbed, one step at a time, one beat at a time, to that point that drew them until their release came in unison.

Cameron held Ghost Dancer firmly in his arms. They clung to each other, unwilling to let go, unwilling to accept it was over. They both trembled from their exertions. Still, no words were spoken. The spell remained unbroken.

* * *

Ghost Dancer lay curled on her side, her mind flooded with fresh remembrance of her dream. Tears washed down her cheeks and she smiled, her hand laying tenderly upon her flat belly. Their remarkable passion had given her a son.

Chapter 25

Jack Bender straightened his overcoat and pulled on his fine leather gloves. He walked to the front door, but paused and stepped back to catch his reflection in the long mirror. A narcissic smile touched his hard features at the perfection he appraised openly. But it disappeared, the stiffness of his healing cheek making him turn his face to examine the damage once again. What he now saw was not what he'd seen last night, and momentary confusion touched him. What the light of day revealed was healing scratches, a touch of red still showing, but none of the horror he had witnessed hours earlier.

"Must have been a bad dream," he mumbled aloud, pushing the disturbing memory from him. He tilted the hat on his head just a fraction further, then satisfied, walked out the door.

The wind whipped his coat about and the cold gently slapped his face. Outside his gate, he met Lillian and her faithful sidekick, Mary Beth. His mood brightened when his gaze fell on the radiant redhead.

"Good day, ladies," he said, tipping his hat to

them, but his attention remained on Lillian.

"And good day to you." Lillian preened at the man.

Glancing from Bender, Mary Beth caught sight of a friend and waved, politely excusing herself.

Bender gave her retreating back only a second's notice, then turned back to Lillian. "And what brings you out on such a brisk day?"

"When a girl's got a proper fur, she doesn't feel the cold." Her long fingers brushed the fur of her cape affectionately.

Bender smiled, thinking to himself that this was more his kind of woman. Not that . . . that Ghost . . . He stopped himself, as a surge of hot anger threatened to spoil this pleasant moment. "I agree," he said absently, trying to gather his concentration.

The sudden silence brought a slight blush to Lillian's cheeks, and she shifted uncomfortably. Adding to her discomfort was the sudden apprehension she experienced from the look of pure violence that had entered Bender's eyes. That was now gone. She saw Mary Beth returning and tried to think of something to say. "I had hoped . . ." She couldn't finish.

"I had hoped," Bender finished for her, "that we could see each other again. A bit more privately, I mean."

She certainly knew what he meant. She started to say no, but instead said, "I would like that."

For a brief second Lillian wondered why she had acknowledged Bender's invitation. Then quickly, most determinedly, disposed of her doubt. He was a man, a handsome man, a rich man, a *single* man. "Until then, Major Bender."

"Yes." He bowed elegantly. "I shall count the minutes." He turned to Mary Beth as she walked up. "It was a pleasure to see you both again."

Mary Beth coolly nodded in return. She put her hand on her friend's elbow and guided her down the walk, away from the disturbing man.

"I swear, Mary Beth," Lillian pouted, acutely aware of her friend's scowl. "You certainly are prissy sometimes."

"And I swear," Mary Beth stressed, "you are a dangerous friend."

Lillian stopped and turned her own frown upon her. "And what does that mean?"

Mary Beth was uneasy under her glare, but bravely finished what she had started. "That man is evil and you know it, deep down inside, you know it. Yet, you insist on toying with him like you do all the others. That, my friend, is dangerous."

"Oh, pooh," Lillian declared dramatically with a delicate wave of her gloved hand. "You are a worry wart. Jack Bender is as harmless as the others, and as eligible."

Mary Beth clucked at her.

"Oh, don't be so holy. You should be thinking like me just a bit more. You're not getting any younger, and I really don't want my best friend to be an old maid. I just couldn't bear it."

"Old maid," Mary Beth cried out in indignant anger, her face turning a dark shade of rose. "Better an old maid than giving myself to that . . . that awful man."

Lillian was sincerely contrite. "Oh, really, Mary Beth. I have no intention of giving myself to him. I know just how far to go. Far enough to get a proposal of marriage, but not so far as to ruin my reputation."

Mary Beth replied, doubt showing clearly on her face, "I don't know. It doesn't feel right. Promise me that you will be careful. Even more so than usual."

"That's silly," she objected, but seeing the look on her friend's face, Lillian gave in. "All right, I promise. Now, if you are satisfied, shall we go?"

Mary Beth felt better and resumed walking. "I bet Mrs. Dawson is feeling lonely now that Angelique is gone."

Lillian smiled, looking forward to the afternoon. "Well, we shall perk her up if she is." She paused, then added, "You know, Mary Beth, I rather liked Angelique. She was strange in ways, but I liked her."

This confession shocked Mary Beth. "I do believe there is hope for you yet, my friend. You've a kinder heart than you ever let on."

"Nonsense."

"I liked her, too, Lillian." Mary Beth smiled. "Maybe we'll see her again soon. Perhaps Cameron and Angelique will get married."

This made Lillian's smile disappear. "Married!" Then she thought better of what she was about to say. She could no longer deny the obvious. She had witnessed the way they had looked at each other at the dance. There was more to their relationship than even she knew. "Yes, perhaps. They would make a handsome couple."

"Yes, they most certainly would," Mary Beth agreed, pleased by Lillian's change of heart.

The first flakes were light and airy, the morning's cold bringing the dampness down upon the small band of riders. Black Hawk and his son led their warriors, with Ghost Dancer and Cameron just behind them. Fort Laramie lay a short distance beyond the hill, and at first light they would ride in.

The Ghost Sioux would stay outside the fort easily blending in with the camps of Indians who, because of the winter, had come for food and water. Cameron and Ghost Dancer would let the colonel know they were unharmed.

As they rode into the camp, the presence of the Nahhe Lahkota warriors caused many to stare in curiosity, but, when Cameron's presence was noticed, all went about their own business. Their lives depended on the military, and they would not interfere in what was obviously an Army matter.

Ghost Dancer slid from her mount and crossed to her father, who had already dismounted. "I shall return later, my father."

His dark head acknowledged her. "We shall see that all is made ready."

She turned to leave, but he stopped her. "Be careful, Ghost Dancer. As long as he lives, he is a danger to you."

"I will be careful."

Red Bear whirled her up into the air, as he had since they were children. "You had better be, my dancer. I will not be there to watch over you."

A smile lit up her face, and she clung to her adopted brother. "I promise. I promise."

Red Bear handed her to Cameron. "Take care of her."

"I will." Cameron grinned. "Well, I'll try."

"It is a difficult task," Red Bear agreed. "To try is all I can ask."

The two men clasped hands in newfound friendship.

"Come on, Angel. Let's go see Wilma. She's probably worried a few more gray hairs while you've been gone."

Ghost Dancer kissed him on his cheek. "I will see you at the house."

A worried frown creased his forehead. "Are you sure you can get in unseen? We have guards posted all over the fort."

She smiled again. "It is child's play."

"Sorry." He chuckled. "I must have lost my mind."

"Yes, you must have."

Cameron laughed out loud this time. "I will see you there."

Wilma's face showed immediate relief and happiness as she pulled Cameron into her arms, giving him a hug that left him breathless and a bit red-faced.

"Come in, come in," she said, then yelled, "William."

The colonel walked into the room to see what it was his wife needed. "Cameron," he hollered in much the same way, crossing to stand by his side. He grasped his hand warmly. "Cameron, tell us"—he looked about—"where is Ghost Dancer?"

Cameron had sent word earlier that she was well, and their anxiety was eased. At that moment, a soft knock sounded and it was Cameron who answered it, admitting the very woman they asked about.

She was immediately embraced by the older woman, with tears and laughter. Wilma placed her hands on Ghost Dancer's cheeks and looked deep into her bright eyes, her own filled with tears.

"You are all right?" she asked, needing further assurance.

Ghost Dancer placed her hands over hers. "I am fine."

Wilma hugged her again. "I can see that."

"Now, Wilma, give the girl a chance to breath." The colonel's voice was a bit lecturing, but his eyes showed humor. "Come, sit down everyone."

In a matter of minutes, they were seated, a cup of hot coffee in hand, their laughter warmly drifting through the room.

Wilma's gaze kept moving to Ghost Dancer as if she were still uncertain that she was truly safe. Ghost Dancer gave her hand a reassuring squeeze.

"Wilma, the worse is over. It will all be over soon."

This prompted a question from the colonel. "Why do you think it will be over soon?"

Cameron set the china cup aside and answered. "We know who's behind the massacres. We know who tried to kill Ghost Dancer."

A grim look replaced the colonel's joy of seeing the girl alive. Now he had to face the problems at hand, again. "You have the proof I need?"

Cameron shook his head, "No, but we will."

"I sure hope so, Captain. I've had a difficult time of it, keeping a lid on this tense situation." He sighed, tiredness showing through his gruff exterior. "Who is doing this? Who the hell wants the Ghost Sioux out of the picture and why?"

Cameron looked only briefly at Ghost Dancer, her calm eyes giving him the confidence he needed. "Major Bender killed Samuel Smith. That was the start of all this."

"Bender!" The colonel's look was one of incredulity. "An Army man?"

Cameron raised his hand. "I know. I found it pretty damn hard to believe myself. But the truth is, he had his men leave Ghost Dancer to drown in a hole in Smith's mine. If I hadn't gotten there when I did . . ." He let it drop, his point made.

"But why?" the colonel urged.

"For the gold. Old man Smith found his dream, Colonel. Bender found out and killed him, but there was still the Indians to deal with. The mines are in their territory."

"So, he attacked the wagon train and the homesteaders, laying the blame on the Ghost Sioux."

"And in turn, the Army would do his dirty work and rid the hills of the supposed offenders." Just the thought of what they had nearly done brought the heat of anger. "Damn his black soul to hell," Cameron ground out through clenched teeth.

"I still can't court martial Bender," the colonel said, bringing all eyes back to him. "I *need* proof, Captain, *substantiated* proof. If he was brought before a board, it would be his word against hers. No offense, Ghost Dancer, but you're a white woman living with Indians . . ."

"And my word would mean nothing to them," Ghost Dancer finished with a whisper.

"Then we must let Ghost Dancer give us the evidence of his guilt."

The colonel raised his white eyebrows in amazement. "And how, might I ask, is she to do this?"

"Bender thinks that Ghost Dancer is dead. Now she is free to do what she does best."

This time it was Wilma who threw out the question to her. "And what is it that you will do?"

Ghost Dancer wasn't certain she knew what to say. "What I must do is difficult to understand, and even more difficult to explain."

Coming to her rescue, Cameron said, "Believe me, Wilma. It's probably best that you, that both of you, don't know."

"Yes," she agreed readily, her curiosity suddenly cut short by a twinge of uneasiness as she sought her husband's agreement. "I think you're right. I shall ask no more questions of you."

"I thank you, my friends."

Cameron came up behind Ghost Dancer and slid his arms about her waist, pulling her tight against his chest. The sweet smell of her hair filled him and the gentle curve of her back, rounding provocatively to her buttocks, felt good against him. She seemed to fit so well against his body. So perfectly.

"You are quiet," he whispered in her ear, his warm breath tickling her. "Are you all right?"

She turned and smiled. "I am all right."

"Just have a lot on your mind?"

"I suppose I do," Ghost Dancer agreed, snuggling closer to him, always content to be held in his arms.

For a long moment, Cameron said nothing. Then he asked, "What's next?"

Her deep sigh drifted to him, making him regret his question. "We must get the powder into Bender's drink."

"How are we going to do that?"

"First, we must make a plan."

"That would be a good idea. Remember, Angel, no matter what, we'll manage. So you need not worry."

Ghost Dancer once again tilted her head up to look into his forest green eyes. "I am not worried, my Cameron. With you by my side, I cannot fail."

"Come on," he said, taking her by the hand and pulling her along behind him. "I have a plan."

"I'm sorry, Captain, Major Bender is not here."

Cameron looked at the pinched-faced woman and, despite her uppity air and dour look, he smiled one of his most disarming, alarming and charming of smiles. "I'm so sorry to hear that. Do you know when I might catch him in?"

The woman was taken aback, his manner so different from the last time he had been there. "I'm not sure I know when he will return, but I will certainly let him know that you have been by."

He heard the difference in her tone, saw the harsh lines of her face becoming softer. "I wanted to apologize for my rude behavior the other day." Again, he flashed the brilliant smile, taking her breath away. "It was unworthy of an officer and a gentleman."

She blushed and waved a hand in the air. "We all have our bad days, sir. So don't you worry about it another second."

"Well . . ." Again, he smiled, the wider the better as the older woman literally began to glow under his warm gaze. "I'm certainly glad you are such a forgiving woman. It takes a tremendous load off my mind."

"Come now." She tried to suppress a girlish giggle, the color of her cheeks deepening to a rosy hue. "It was nothing to fret about. I assure you."

Ghost Dancer heard the ongoing drollery and had to stifle her laughter. Cameron had the woman carrying on like a blushing virgin child. Quietly, she slipped into the library and within minutes, she had poured the powder into the crystal decanter, the drug mixing easily with the amber-colored brandy. With a singleness of purpose, she moved back to the door, pausing only a second as impressions of the room fluttered through her thoughts. A tear fell when she saw the limp body of the young Sioux woman who had tried to help her. Determinedly, Ghost Dancer walked on, again seeing another vision. This time of Broken Arrow. She had no doubt that he too was dead. But she did not feel the grieving sorrow that came when she thought of the other victims of Bender's evil cruelty.

Returning her thoughts to the business that had brought her here, Ghost Dancer moved to the staircase, her eyes looking up. She could hear Cameron starting to stumble over the conversation, and quickened her step. Upstairs and in Bender's bedroom, she made certain she did not linger. Finding another decanter, she put the rest of the root powder in it, mixing it thoroughly.

She made a fast retreat, nearly running down the stairs, and quickly disappeared down the hall, to the back of the house. Just as she opened the door to leave, she heard the front door close. Their timing could not have been better. She breathed a sigh of relief and made her way back to the colonel's house.

"Jack Bender," Ghost Dancer whispered. She reached out and opened the window. The cold wind rushed in and blew her hair around her. She stood in the darkened room, only a smidgen of faded light washing over her from the moon that bravely peeked out from behind blackened storm clouds.

Bender came awake when the balcony doors crashed open, the harsh wind slamming them back against the wall. He got out of bed to close them against the cold rain.

"Jack Bender," she called again, her voice the softest of murmurs.

He heard his name called. Clearly and distinctly. He could not explain it, yet he could not deny it. A chill rushed over him and he quickly closed the doors. The sudden need to cross himself disturbed him as much as hearing things. He needed a drink. Maybe two—or more.

Chapter 26

She was beautiful.

Jack Bender could feel the warmth ignite within him, dispelling the chill of his heart. Slowly, she walked toward him, the smile that blessed her face causing his pulse to race ahead in an erratic beat and the blood to pound in his head. He reached out, his hand to hers. He welcomed her beauty, he welcomed her soft body to his yearning one.

He reached out, and she was gone. Sad, he turned away, but froze in horror. A pool of icy, blue water stretched out to infinity and in the dark depths lay his beauty. Dead. Drowned, by his hand.

Bender jerked awake, choking on the feeling of horror at what he had done. Remorse was an unknown feeling to him, and it prompted a battle of confusion in his sleep-muddled mind. Hot, violent anger took control, forcibly ridding him of all unwanted emotions. Throwing back the heavy cover, he got out of bed and made a straight line for the bottle of brandy.

He poured himself a healthy drink, but, before

lifting it to his lips, he raised it in salute. "Here's to you, witch. May you rest in peace."

The liquor burned his throat, the feeling a welcome one. He slammed the snifter on the table and turned to his bed, hopefully to sleep. Suddenly, she was there.

He saw his own reflection in the large mirror, but he also saw Ghost Dancer standing behind him. Her long hair fell about her shoulders like spun gold, the thin satin gown revealing all her womanly virtues. Bender spun around on his heels, but she was not there. No one and nothing was in the room.

"Christ," he muttered to the empty room, "I'm going mad."

"What's the matter, Angelique . . . I mean Ghost Dancer?"

Ghost Dancer turned away from the mirror and looked at Wilma. Her eyes were half-closed in sleep as she leaned against the jamb, the door opened just enough to poke her head into the room.

"Nothing, Wilma. Nothing at all."

"I heard you up." Wilma yawned widely. "I could make you a cup of hot chocolate. It would help you sleep."

Ghost Dancer smiled and returned to her bed. "No need. I'm sure I'll sleep now."

"What the hell are they doing here?" Bender demanded.

"I don't know, boss," Mac said, shaking his head

in emphasis to his confusion. "All I know is that there's a band of them Ghost Sioux right outside the fort here."

It took a moment for Bender to consider all possibilities, then he shrugged his shoulders in a nonchalant attitude. "It doesn't matter why they are here, it doesn't matter one way or the other."

"Why's that?" Jim wondered aloud, surprise mixed with curiosity.

"Perhaps," Bender mused, an idea forming in his head, "we can use this to our advantage. The colonel seems to be siding with those red-blooded savages, so I think we'll have to give him more reason to want them out of the hills. Something that will hit close to home."

"Meaning?" Mac questioned, still unclear as to what he was thinking.

"We've raided some settlers, now it's time to strike at the Army itself. Nothing would cause a stir more than killing some soldiers, maybe even their families."

"You can't mean it!" Jim shouted before he had time to think. The black glare he received was his answer, causing him to shift uncomfortably. "I mean to say, wouldn't it be too dangerous?"

Bender had to draw upon his reserve of patience, something he had so little of lately. "Of course it would be dangerous to attack right here within shouting distance of the fort. But what better way to achieve our objective? This would have to make them stand up and take notice, and do something in return."

"What about the Sioux?"

Dark eyes bore holes into him. "What about them?"

Mac felt uncomfortable under his look. "Shouldn't we keep an eye on them or something?"

"I don't see the need." Bender smiled. "Their precious Ghost Dancer is dead. What can they do to threaten us?"

Both men shrugged. They really didn't know, but they were nervous nonetheless.

"You are both being ridiculous. Now get out of here, I've got to think about this awhile. Just make sure the rest of the men will be ready when I give the word."

Bender waved them away with his four-fingered hand while the other massaged his temple, his head splitting with pain. Once again, he sought relief from the decanter of brandy.

"Lillian," Jack Bender called out, then quickly corrected himself. "Miss Thomas."

Lillian stopped dead in her tracks, her heart lurching. What on earth had gotten into her? With the greatest aplomb, she put on a pleased smile and turned to him. "Why, Major Bender. What a surprise."

"A pleasant one, I hope." He smiled in return, his thinking wishful.

Suddenly, she recalled Mary Beth's words of fear and her own promises. Lillian had never known such trepidation, but managed to keep it from her voice. "Of course it is."

"Good," he declared, a triumphant note in the singular word. "I was wondering if you might be free for dinner, perhaps tonight?"

The tall redhead suddenly felt small and vulnerable. Desperation plundered her thoughts, jumbling them together. What would she say? What could she say?

Bender was aware of her sudden confusion, but did not become overly concerned. The woman had made it perfectly clear what she wanted from him, and understood what he wanted from her. "Is tonight not good?" He could no longer bear the silence.

"No," she said, quickly pulling together a thought. "Tonight is not a good night, Major Bender. Perhaps another evening we could . . ." *Could what?* she wondered, then shuddered as a vivid image came into her mind. "Another evening perhaps."

"Of course." He smiled again, and as always, the movement never reached the black hardness of his eyes. "I shall hold you to your promise, Miss Thomas. I am not a man to be put off."

That, she believed. "I shall remember." With a braveness she did not know she possessed, she looked straight into the abyss of his eyes. "I am not a woman to take such an offer lightly."

With a gallant gesture, Bender took her gloved hand into his and pressed it to his lips. "Until then."

He turned and went on his way, leaving a shaken and frightened Lillian to stand forlornly on the street, unconsciously wiping the back of her hand on her skirt.

"Lillian."

She jerked around. "Mary Beth," she cried in relief, waving her hand in the air in reply. "Where have you been?"

"I told you—" Mary Beth was stopped short as Lillian grabbed her arm and pulled her along beside her.

"Never mind." She hurried her step. "Oh, Mary Beth, I've never been so scared in all my life. And I don't even know why."

"Scared. What happened?"

Lillian stopped her harried pace, causing Mary Beth to have to step back. "He just stopped me."

Mary Beth's eyes grew round. "He?"

"Jack Bender," Lillian whispered, almost afraid to say his name. "He stopped me right here in the middle of the street. I didn't know what to say."

"Did he ask to see you?"

This time Lillian's eyes grew large. "Yes. Oh, Mary Beth, you were right. He *is* evil. I could feel it. What am I going to do?" Panic put a hard edge to her lilting voice.

Mary Beth drew herself up, taking her friend's hand in hers. "For starters, you should not go out alone anymore. If you are always with someone, he will not do anything. I'm sure of it."

Lillian felt a little better. "You're right, of course. I'm just flustered. I don't think a man has ever done that to me before."

"Well." Mary Beth laughed. "There's always a first time."

"Yes," joined in Lillian, her fear gone in the face of her friend's companionship. "Now, let's go shopping."

* * *

Bender went into the saloon, a feeling of irritation grating against his tightly strung nerves. From the first moment he had seen Lillian Thomas in the street, he had wanted her. Fiercely. Sweat broke out on his forehead, and he dabbed at it impatiently with his handkerchief. He had been angry that she would be unable to see him, unable to relieve him of his "needs."

Suddenly, he found himself wondering at his own thoughts, questioning his strange behavior. Perhaps his Sioux squaw had affected him more than he'd thought. Especially when it came to satisfying his lust, at any moment or time.

Yes, he decided, that was what it was. He wasn't used to being celibate, even for a few days. Well, that was certainly something that could be cured before he had to return to the fort. And he was already in the right place. His dark eyes moved up the stairs, and his mind rolled through the possibilities, each face of the girls who worked upstairs popping up. Recalling the pleasing talents of a young girl named Anna, he came to a decision. Then, with extreme anticipation and a smile on his face, he climbed the stairs, two at a time. The beautiful, redheaded Lillian could wait, but Anna could not.

A low growl came from Bender, his head hanging into his hands. Anna's soft crying made his teeth clamp together, then grind as she whimpered.

"Quiet, damn you," he yelled, but it only caused

her to cringe at the edge of the bed, the comforter hugged to her for protection. "Get out." He couldn't stand the sight of her any longer. "Get out, now."

Anna did not hesitate a second, and pulling the covers with her, she stumbled from the room. Soon, the echo of her howling ebbed. Bender lay back on the bed, his mind whirling fast and furious. He continued to stare blankly at the ceiling.

What on earth was the matter with him? Never before had he been impotent. Never! Even with the lowly Sioux, he was always filled with need, never lacking, never failing to reach satisfaction. But today, he had found only frustration and anger. The anger was appeased momentarily by beating Anna—that always helped. But the frustration remained.

Shame, if not a touch of fear, scourged him like an evil plague. Then the question he could have done without struck him. *What if it happens again?*

This thought brought him off the bed in a instant, his heart beating too fast within his broad chest. It wouldn't! It couldn't! Desperation made him reach for the bottle of whiskey that sat on the girl's dressing table. In one, long drought, he nearly emptied the bottle, the terrible burning on its way down to his stomach killing the dreadful coldness he felt inside. Then, like a child in a fit, he threw the bottle at the mirror, at the reflection which did not meet his satisfaction. He looked like hell. He felt like hell.

Maybe he was in hell.

* * *

"Are you all right, boss?" Mac asked, rubbing his whiskered chin and studying Bender.

He cast a black scowl at Mac, but his reply was, with effort, even. "I'm fine, old boy. Why do you ask?"

Mac shrugged. "Nothin' in particular. Just look a bit peaked's all."

Trying to convince Mac otherwise, Bender made an effort to smile, but it was half-hearted at best. "Don't waste time worrying about me." He wiped at the sweat that covered his brow, the smile dying away as quickly as it had come. "Are you in or out, Mac?"

Mac turned his eyes back to the cards he held, putting his mind on his bet, not his boss. Whatever was bothering Bender was the man's own business and certainly not his.

The subject seemed to drop, but Bender remained uneasy. His thoughts rambled about with no purpose, his nerves drawn too tight over a hair-trigger temper. He drummed the table with his three long fingers, then moved his cards around with no real order in mind. Impatience grew inside him, and he did not know why.

Absently, he fingered a poker chip. Over and over he flipped the chip, not really seeing the object his eyes seemed to be focused on. Finally, he stopped his fidgeting, the chip laying unheeded in his palm.

Bender's eyes burned, and he closed them to ease his discomfort. When he opened them again, he was looking at his hand, the chip still in it.

Suddenly, it was no longer a painted, wooden token, but a large, woolly spider. It moved, then scurried up his arm.

"Christ!" Bender yelled, nearly falling backward in his chair as he swatted at the foul creature. "Get it off me!"

Mac looked at Jim, who sat across the table from him, their exchanged looks showing concern, if not a bit of wonder. Bender was acting strange.

His glazed eyes stared at the red chip he had flung from him and slowly, his dulled mind realized it was just a harmless round object for playing cards.

"I need something to drink, Mac," he mumbled, running his hand though his hair. "I need a drink!"

It was dark, as dark as coal. Bender walked in the blackness, not knowing where he went or why. Only that he could not stop, nor could he go back to where he had started.

He was looking for someone. Again, he wasn't sure who, only that he needed to find that person. So, on and on he went, his mission unending.

When he came upon the grave, something strange and frightful gripped him, causing a knot to form in the pit of his stomach. Slowly, he moved to read the words carved upon the granite headstone.

"Here lies the Ghost Dancer."

An odd tightness came to his throat and a misting to his eyes. He couldn't remember ever crying before, not for anyone or anything. He knelt down, his head bowed in sadness and grief. Vivid images of her beauty came to mind.

"Ghost Dancer," he whispered, his trembling hand reaching out to touch the damp soil that covered her.

Through the dirt, a hand darted out and clamped onto his own, pulling him down into the thick mud. "No!" he yelled, fighting as the powerful grip dragged him into the earth, into her shroud of death, and into her cold embrace.

Bender flung himself out of the bed, screaming, "No!"

Never before had he known such fear, such horror. And he hated himself for it. But most of all, he hated Ghost Dancer.

"Damn you. You haunt me, even in death, you witch woman!" Feeling defeated, he sat on the edge of his bed, his head in his hands. "How can I fight someone who's dead?"

Chapter 27

"Looks like winter's here, Wilma."

Wilma nodded at the comment, her gaze taking in the snow that was beginning to fall outside. "Thanksgiving's going to be cold, with lots of snow. Always is though."

"Yes," sighed the woman who stood across from her, fingering a bit of lacy material that lay on the table. "This country can be harsh, but we go where our men are stationed."

"Laramie's better than most forts, Jane. We do have our blessings to count."

Jane felt a bit guilty for complaining and knew that Wilma was right. "What are you and the colonel planning for Thanksgiving?"

"Bill and Katherine Robins have asked us to join their family for dinner."

"Oh, how wonderful. John and I are going to be there, too. Imagine, all those children."

She didn't need to elaborate any further, as both women were able to envision it quite well. Wilma laughed. "It should be fun."

"Yes, it will be," Jane agreed readily. "Well, I

need to be going. I'll be seeing you both at the Robinses' then?"

"We'll be there with bells on." Again, she laughed.

Black eyes watched Jane leave the store, then his gaze returned to Wilma. He took a step forward.

Wilma turned and came face to face with Bender, a small gasp of surprise escaping before she could stop it.

"My, oh my," she whispered, out of breath all of sudden. "You startled me, Major. I hadn't realized you were standing there."

An evil smile curled his lips. "My apologies, Mrs. Dawson. I had no intention of scaring you."

"Of course not," she mumbled, unsure that he really was sorry. Unable to resist, she moved a few feet away.

"May I help you with your packages?"

Wilma met his dark gaze. "That's kind of you, but I haven't far to go, nor much to carry. There's no need to trouble yourself."

"It's never any trouble, Mrs. Dawson." He took out his handkerchief to dab at the moisture gathered on his upper lip.

"Are you all right, Major Bender?" Her sharp eyes took in his slightly rumpled appearance and the milky paleness of his skin dotted with perspiration.

Irritation pricked at the edge of his foggy mind, but with some effort, he held it back. "I assure you, I've never felt better."

Anyone could see it was a lie, but Wilma said,

"That's good to hear. I have everything I need, so I must say good day."

Bender bowed slightly, the gesture stiff and somewhat forced. "And I have duties I must tend to. Have a pleasant day, Mrs. Dawson."

"Thank you, Major, I will." Wilma turned to leave, not taking to heart a single word he uttered.

Bender's eyes stayed on Wilma until she was no longer in sight, her short, round figure disappearing into the falling snow. His four-fingered hand clenched into a fist at his side.

Ghost Dancer swished the brandy around in the crystal decanter, dissolving the root powder in the fiery liquid. She set it down, then looked up at her reflection in the mirror. Angry impatience touched her, and she knew what Bender was feeling at that moment. She also read a sense of danger about him, and understood that his thoughts were evil. Ghost Dancer glanced about the room, where everything spoke of the man, from his overly large bed, to the dressing table she stood in front of. She closed her eyes and gently ran her fingers down her cheek.

"Bender," she called to him, soft and sweet.

Bender's head jerked up, his hand moving to his face. He felt the caress.

"Jack Bender."

He heard it. He heard her call his name.

"Ghost Dancer," he said beneath his labored breathing.

"Did you say something, Major Bender?"

His black eyes locked onto the clerk, and he saw the odd look plastered on the older man's face. "Did you say something?" he repeated.

"No," Bender snapped. "I didn't say anything."

The look told the clerk to move away and not to bother him again, and he gladly did so, almost stumbling in his effort.

Without saying another word, Bender left the store. The cold wind that slapped at him felt good, clearing his heated mind a bit and cooling his sweat-dampened face.

"Ghost Dancer," he called out.

He all but ran to his house, a strange desperation guiding him. Bender slammed the front door open and ran up the stairs to his bedroom, unheedful of the cold wind that followed him in.

"Ghost Dancer!" he yelled, so certain she would be there, waiting for him. Quickly, he searched the room, throwing things aside in his haste. But he found it empty.

"Witch." Bender felt near tears, disappointment mixing with the potency of anger. "Witch!" he screamed.

He tore at his hair in fury. He could even smell the sweet scent of her!

Bender was disgusted with himself. He desired a dead woman! Ghost Dancer was driving him beyond reality. She was pulling him toward madness, and he felt helpless to stop it. Exhausted, he slid to the floor, pathetic and damned.

"You may have committed me to this hell on earth, but I will have the last laugh, my little witch woman," he swore as he rested his head against the polished cherry wood, his eyes closing. "I will have what I want. Even the dead cannot keep me from it."

"He looks absolutely horrible," Wilma exclaimed, her eyes round with wonder and curiosity. "What on earth is the matter with him?"

Her question was directed at Cameron, but Ghost Dancer knew it was really meant for her. Still, she failed to answer. What could she say?

Cameron cleared his throat, uncertainty also written clearly upon his face. "I don't know, Wilma. Even I don't ask for explanations."

"In other words, my nosy wife," the colonel said, hoping to ease the difficult situation, "it's none of your concern. At least, I believe that's what has been said."

Ghost Dancer felt Wilma's disappointment. "I do not mean for you to be left out. It is something that cannot be explained. Your culture does not understand much of the Sioux beliefs, or our shaman. Once again, I must ask you for your trust and leave it at that."

Just the word "shaman" created a chill on Wilma's skin, and she decided, once again, they were right. It was none of her business. When would she ever learn? "Of course, dear. I'm just a curious old fool, that's all."

"You are not a fool." Ghost Dancer gave her a reassuring hug. "I have asked you to deal with something quite strange. It is no wonder that you ask questions. I am sorry that they cannot be answered."

Wilma placed her hands upon her hips. "I don't know what it is you're doing, but it seems to be working. The man is on the edge. I was talking with Jane about Thanksgiving, and then he was there, like an evil omen. Scared the living daylights out of me, he did. I was certainly glad to get out of there and out from under that black-eyed stare of his."

"What about Thanksgiving, Wilma?" her husband asked.

Wilma's lower lip pushed out. "You haven't forgotten, have you? We're expected for dinner at the Robinses'. It's been planned for some time now."

"With all that's going on, Thanksgiving just hasn't been on my mind. Are you sure we should go?"

Wilma shot him a disapproving look. "Of course. Katherine's been planning this for weeks now. We can't disappoint her."

The colonel looked appropriately guilty. "I just thought. . . ."

Her hands went into the air in mock exasperation, only the twinkle in her eyes told the truth. "That's the trouble with you men. You think too much." She moved off, her mind already on the evening meal she needed to prepare. "Should leave the thinking to us women. The world would be a better place for it. That's for sure." She disappeared into the kitchen, the door swishing back and forth in the sudden silence of the room.

"There is no reason for you to forgo your celebration of Thanksgiving," Ghost Dancer said, feeling responsible for their argument.

A seldom seen grin claimed the colonel's face. "Now, don't you pay no mind to that hot-headed woman of mine. I married her for that fire in her eyes." He laughed, a warm, gentle memory of times past. "And I do my best to keep those flames ablazin'."

Cameron couldn't help but chuckle at that. "I can see you do. Better watch your step, William. Looks like she could be a handful."

"Certainly is," he agreed with feigned seriousness. "I'm in command of a fort and hundreds of soldiers. I can do without taking charge of that little spitfire."

Ghost Dancer did not take part in their joking. Her mind was on other things. "This dinner you are to attend, when is it?"

"Next Thursday's Thanksgiving. Why?"

"You will be going to the Robinses' house?"

"That seems to be the plan," the colonel answered. "Why?"

"I have a thought, and soon it will be Bender's."

"Boy, oh boy," the colonel muttered. "I don't understand you most of the time, young lady. But like my wife, I'll mind my own business and keep my nose out of yours."

"And I don't understand you much of the time, but I, too, will keep my nose on my own face."

Their laughter filled the room, and Ghost Dancer enjoyed the light moment in the darkness she knew was yet to come. To fail would bring disaster for them all.

* * *

Bender slept the fitful sleep of the damned, visions of the dark disturbing his drink-induced slumber.

"Witch," he cried, again and again. "Witch woman."

Ghost Dancer stood at the end of his bed, watching the man as he fought the silent demons of his nightmare.

"Bender," she whispered, drawing his red-rimmed eyes open and then to her. He blinked but made no other move. "Bender."

"Go away," he finally responded, his throat dry and raw from the fiery liquid he had imbibed too frequently in the past few days. "Leave me be, witch."

She did not stir.

"Be gone with you!" he yelled, impatient with his own dream. "You'll not win this fight, my ghost of the Sioux. I'll not let you."

"You cannot win, Bender. You fight a losing battle."

Her voice was sweet, like sugar, her smile beguiling, but false. He felt the heat of anger and, to his dismay, the heat of passion's fire. "I'm not some old fool medicine man whom you can scare. Leave me, I'll not listen to you again." His voice was strong, but he shook in spite of himself.

"You will not harm my people with your lies. I will see to that."

His laugh was a harsh bark, and his smile was that of a man who courted madness. "Your people will feel the burning hatred of the white man. *I* will see to that."

"Your words are empty, they hold no venom."

Her manner and speech taunted him, and he felt control slipping from him. "Be gone, witch! I'll not let you invade my mind! Be gone!"

Bender leaped from the bed and lunged at her, his arms grabbing for his vision. They caught only air. "Witch!" he screamed, turning in circles to find her. No one was in the room. "Witch!"

Bender's cries followed Ghost Dancer down the stairs and out the back of the house. For the briefest instant, she felt sorry for him. He had no chance against her power. Then, determined, she squashed all pity as she recalled those innocents who had perished at his evil doings. His own black nature would be his death. She only fueled the fire that would take him.

Within minutes, she was back at the colonel's house and without a sound, she made her way to her bedroom.

"Where have you been?"

Cameron's voice came from the darkness, stopping her. Her eyes searched the blackened room, but could only follow the sound. "I went for a walk." She heard him shift in a chair and moved toward him.

"In the middle of the night?"

A slight strain affected his words and Ghost Dancer was keenly aware of his worry. "I am sorry to have caused you concern."

A deep, slow sigh touched her ears, and her

heart ached at his sadness. "I am truly sorry, my Cameron."

"I know that," he replied, trying hard to understand her ways. "You went to him, didn't you?"

Ghost Dancer considered lying, but thought better of it. It would serve no purpose except, perhaps, to hurt him. "Yes. It was time."

Fear, anger, horror. All these things struck out in full force, leaving him speechless for a long moment. "Time for what?" he finally managed to ask.

"It is time," Ghost Dancer said, laying her hand upon his shoulder. "For the end."

Cameron closed his eyes as thoughts of what the end would bring sprung violently into his mind. He pulled her to him, his head pressed against her ribs. He wanted only to hold his Ghost Dancer close, to hear the soft beat of her heart in his ear, to feel her safe in his arms.

"You heard what I said," Bender ground out, his irritation great, his patience nonexistent. "Thanksgiving, we will ambush the colonel and his wife, on their way home from the Robinses' place. No one will miss them until morning."

Mac knew he had heard right, but still objected. "That's just outside the fort, not even half a mile."

"Damn, Major," added Jim. "The colonel?"

"Yes." He made it clear with his hard-lined look and stony voice. "Kill the colonel and we solve two problems. One, we get rid of the very man who's holding the Army back, and two, with the colonel out of the way, I am in command, then the Army will most certainly retaliate in force."

Mac pulled his gaze from Bender and shook his head in doubt. A chill grazed the back of his neck and raised the hairs on end. The look he saw in those black eyes was the gleam of insanity. He knew it. He had seen it before during the war, but recognition still left him powerless to stop it. "It's too dangerous, Jack." He used his boss's familiar name in hopes of reaching his lost mind.

"It is what has to be done."

"He's right, Mac." Jim knew it was crazy, but they had gone too far to stop now. "This would stir up things for sure. No one would think twice about us killing a few Injuns."

Bender started to make his plans. "They will be alone and easy prey. It will be simple. It's just an old man and an old woman. Nothing to fear, Mac."

"What if Cameron Wade's with them?" Mac questioned further.

"What if he is? It would give me much pleasure to kill him."

"I'll see to roundin' up the men." Without any further complaint, Mac gave in. "Just in case we need them."

"We won't." Bender smiled, the look in his eyes a flash of danger. "Trust me, Mac. It will go perfectly."

Chapter 28

The carriage wheels had been replaced by runners, making it glide over the crusty snow with ease. The horse's harness jingled from the tiny brass bells that shook as he trotted along, his hoofs clamping loud and steady in the hushed silence of the dark night.

A harsh beauty painted the landscape. Heavily laden clouds rolled above, threatening the world with more snow. Even now, the first flakes floated down to earth, whitening the thick furs that covered the two passengers' laps.

The colonel bent his head to break the chill of the wind from his face, his gloved hands guiding the horse home. Beside him snuggled Wilma, her face hidden in the blankets of wool and fur.

Ebony eyes became alert at the faint sound, still some distance away. Bender felt the thudding of his heart within his chest, anxiety prompting it to beat faster. Blood rushed through his veins as he waited, thoughts of victory marauding through his mind, and like an elixir, made him feel a lightness in his head. Flashes of another time, of another war, mingled with reality, leaving him confused as to what was real and what was not. The sounds of battle imposed on the unnerving silence, and his face flinched at the harsh noise. His mount sensed his mood and the beast shifted nervously beneath him. Having had little to no patience lately, Bender's hand tightened on the leather reins, pulling the horse's head up, causing the bit to jerk.

"Be still," Bender threatened in anger. "Be still you sorry son of a bitch or you'll be glue in the morning."

His threat was mindless, the words holding no meaning to the dumb animal. But feeling better for saying it, he continued to cuss the big black.

It took an eternity, but finally, the sleigh appeared, rounding the corner in a swish of ice that crackled and crunched beneath it, the ring of the bells following behind like an afterthought. Bender's horse snorted, much the same way as he did in satisfaction, the feel of triumph close at hand.

His spurs dug deeply into the horse, prompting the stallion to jump forward in a wild leap, the animal's cry mixing with that of the other men, their faces painted, their weapons held high. They rode out in force, death their only intent. Bender felt the joy of it all.

But his joy was short-lived, like a thought cut off as the Ghost Sioux made their countermove, their own weapons ready. By their side rode the Army, and together they swarmed around Bender and his band of men. There was the briefest of moments when all became silent, every man squared off, every man holding his breath. Then hell fell upon them in all its fire and brimstone.

Guns were fired and arrows spent, the cries of pain mixing with the yells of the true warriors. Vindication and vengeance were theirs, the glory of the moment carried in their hearts, these strong emotions no longer known to Bender. Surprise lurked with the ultimate fury of defeat. He whirled his horse about as survival became his foremost thought. He looked for the opportunity to flee.

Suddenly, Bender felt the terror of the dead upon him. Ghost Dancer sat before him, high upon her great white, as his evil sparred with her good. She looked so real, so alive. Yet, he knew that she was a vision of his mind. The Ghost Dancer was dead, this he knew and believed to be certain, even if all else remained unclear.

"Damn you, my witch woman," he cursed her above the din, then leveled his pistol at her. "You and I shall tumble into hell together. I killed you once, but I shall do so again for my own peace of mind."

From the corner of his eye, Cameron saw Bender, and he realized with a sickening clarity that Ghost Dancer was in his direct line of fire. Fear choked the warning in his throat, so instead he lunged his horse forward at Bender. It was too late.

Bender pulled the trigger, but instead of Ghost Dancer, another fell from the bullet. His eyes grew wide with anger, their darkness bulging from his overly pale face. "No!" he screamed in total and complete outrage and disgust. "No!"

He twisted his black stallion around just as Cameron reached him, their horses colliding, nearly unseating each man from his saddle. Before Cameron could regain control, Bender was racing off. Without hesitation, Cameron rode after him.

Ghost Dancer was torn between the desire to follow Cameron and the need to go to Lone Wolf, who now lay upon the ground, his body having shielded her from certain death.

Her tears blinded her as she jumped from her horse and ran to her friend. She turned her head up to the storm-laden sky, the blackness promising even more wickedness to come. "Grandfather, surely You will not forsake me now. We have come such a long way."

She quickly said the prayer for Cameron, who followed Bender. She pulled Lone Wolf's body into her arms. His eyes opened, but there was no light in the dark brown depths.

A bloodied hand caressed her cheek, wiping away her tears. "The Ghost Dancer is no longer needed by her people, the truth has been found and justice has been done. Go home and wait for your man, as the woman he has taken to his heart."

"That was a foolish thing you did, my friend." Gently, Ghost Dancer wiped the smudges of dirt from his face, as her tears continued to fall.

"I have always been the fool when it came to you, my Ghost Dancer." He shuddered, drawing a ragged breath.

"Never," she denied, then corrected his words, "always the bravest of warriors."

"Because of my great love for you, I gladly die for you." Slowly, his eyes closed in weariness.

"And the Ghost Dancer shall always remember." She cradled him to her breast as life left him and sought the spirits in the sky. She would always remember.

For the first time, Ghost Dancer noticed that the fighting had stopped and it was silent. The dance was done, and all had been brought to this end. Except for Cameron Wade and Jack Bender.

The snow came down in dense sheets of ice, the wind freezing and strong. The storm lived up to its promise and left a deep covering of snow upon the ground. Ghost Dancer looked out the window, as a strange darkness descended upon them, her mood just as bleak. Cameron was somewhere in the storm, and she only allowed herself to think that he was alive, and Bender dead. That was the way it had to be, at least it was all she could cling to.

She feared to sleep. She feared the truth of her dreams. They might bring her happiness and relief, and then again, they might bring her grief and sorrow. She saw too much in her visions, and right now, she preferred not knowing, one way or the other. This was something that the Ghost Dancer could not face. Not now.

Wilma came up behind her and placed a comforting hand upon her back. "Dearest, you must get some rest."

Ghost Dancer shook her head.

"I insist," Wilma argued. "You don't have to sleep, just rest."

"I am fine, Wilma. But I will lie down for a bit."

Ghost Dancer allowed Wilma to take charge, easing all burden of thought from her own shoulders onto Wilma's capable ones. Wilma's calm chatter seemed to keep Ghost Dancer's mind from Cameron.

"There now," Wilma said, tucking the comforter more snugly about her charge. "Isn't that better?"

Ghost Dancer tried to smile but failed. She turned away, as her tears threatened to spill over. "It is much more comfortable, Wilma. Once again, you spoil me."

Wilma patted her hand. "He'll be fine, Ghost Dancer. I just know it."

"Of course he will," she agreed softly, afraid to think otherwise. "He will come back to me and all will be well."

Ghost Dancer's eyelids became heavy, the warmth that spread through her making it hard to stay awake. Her head snuggled deeper into the softness of the large feather pillow.

Wilma stood, giving her hand a final squeeze. "Cameron will be home soon and it wouldn't do for him to find you all red-eyed."

She moved across the room. "You sleep now, and I'll have something warm and filling when you wake up. Maybe I'll just pop a few biscuits in the oven. I know how much you like them."

Wilma continued to bustle about the room, her work like a soft tune, lulling Ghost Dancer into that space somewhere between sleep and awareness.

She didn't want to sleep. With sleep came her dreams.

The wind whipped and tore at the trees, the bared branches snapping, while the evergreens bowed to its strength but held. Snow continued to cascade down in thick, heavy blankets of white, leaving a deep covering of ice. It was cold, so very cold.

Ghost Dancer shivered and pulled the warm quilt tighter. The wind whistled its eerie howl of might and somewhere a shutter banged in protest.

Cameron thought the cabin had to be close, but the driving snow made it difficult to see. The blizzard raged full force, and he knew he needed to find shelter soon. His hands and feet were numb, his face frozen into a grimace of pain. He urged his horse to move on, it had to be nearby.

Above the whine of the wind, he heard a distant clanging of wood on wood. Cameron followed the sound, as his animal trudged through the deep snow drifts with effort.

"Come on, boy," he encouraged. "It can't be far."

The banging got louder. The shack had to be nearby. He was on it before he really saw it. The old building sagged beneath the storm's heavy hand, but it stood like a beacon of hope, drawing Cameron to its meager warmth.

He rode his mount to the old miner's homestead. Memories flooded his mind. The last time he and Ghost Dancer had been here, he'd proven himself to be a judgmental ass. What strange events had transpired since then, bringing him full circle. Hadn't everything begun with Sam Smith's murder?

He tipped his head upward at the falling snow. Damn weather. If the storm hadn't turned so vicious, he would have caught Bender. Moving like an iceman, Cameron slowly slid from his saddle to the snow-covered ground.

"Come on, Red." Cameron led his horse up to the cabin's icy steps, and kicked open the rickety door. The loud squeal of objection caused him to jump. "I don't think anyone would mind if you came in."

The dimly lit interior showed that the cabin was the same as he had left it. "Certainly couldn't mess it up none." He led the chestnut into the one-room shack, and Red practically filled it. Looking around, Cameron grabbed some broken furniture and snapped it into small pieces that would fit in the stove.

"A fire would be good." His teeth chattered loudly. "Real good."

He located some dusty matches and struggled with his trembling hands to strike them against the floor. Finally, the flame took to the old, dry wood. Cameron had just let out a sigh of relief when the door burst open. Snow, light, and a man tumbled inside. Cameron stared first in shock, then in potent fury at Bender.

Yelling, the man lunged at Cameron, slamming into him and knocking them both onto the littered floor. The air rushed from Cameron's lungs, and he grunted in pain. They grappled without doing much damage. Their stiffened fingers had a hard time clinching into fists. Both struck out randomly, landing ineffectual blows, leaving their knuckles split and bloody. Within minutes, they both struggled for air, their lungs burning in the freezing temperature.

Bender's look was glazed, lost to another world. Cameron realized he was battling a man touched by madness. The madness strengthened Bender. Ghost Dancer's magic had worked, perhaps too well. Bender's fingers closed around Cameron's throat, denying the air his burning lungs screamed for.

"She would have been mine, Wade." Bender's voice trembled. "She should have loved me and not you. I gave her my love and she gave me *nothing.*"

Cameron's ears rang and his face felt as if it would explode from the blood that gathered there. He felt for a piece of wood, his numb fingers curling around it. He struck Bender a solid blow, but it only loosened his grip. Still, Cameron took advantage of his opponent's momentary weakness and broke free. He fell against Red, forcing his horse to crash against a table.

Bender jumped back and pulled an ominous knife from his boot. An insane light sparkled in the depths of his eyes, and an evil smile played upon his mouth.

"Well, Captain," Bender sneered. "I'm going to be generous. I'm going to let you share eternity with your Indian witch."

Cameron laughed casually, clearly catching Bender off guard. "As soon as I'm finished with you, I plan to marry Ghost Dancer."

Comprehending the meaning of Cameron's words, Bender's eyes bulged. The blood drained from his face. "You can't marry her. You can't marry the dead." His words came out barely above a whisper.

"She's not *dead*, Bender. The woman you saw today was very much alive. You just failed one more time to kill Ghost Dancer."

"You're lying!" he screamed, obviously terrified to believe the truth.

All Bender's horror and anger focused on the steely-edged blade he held. Like a coiled serpent, he struck, his rasping breath sounding similar to a hiss, his smile agape like an open-mouthed viper.

"Say your prayers, Wade. You're about to meet your Maker."

"You couldn't even kill a defenseless woman, what makes you think you can kill me?"

Cameron continued to push Bender, taunting him with words of ridicule, each syllable taking the man closer to the brink of insanity. Each swing of Bender's arm became wilder.

With a final burst of energy, Bender used his body as a battering ram and plowed into Cameron, sending him sprawling. The knife plunged toward his heart, and Cameron twisted. The deadly blade caught the flesh beneath his shirt. Pain lanced his side and blood flowed from the wound. Bender whirled about, victory alight upon his maddened features. Cameron leaped toward his horse and saddle. His rifle was still in its holster. Jubilation changed to fear when Bender stared down the barrel of the twenty-two.

Throwing back his head, Bender roared his frustration. Cameron's horse shifted nervously and bumped into his master. Bender took his chance and crashed through the age-weakened boards of the cabin door. Cameron fired, but hit only wood and falling snow.

Bender stumbled through the blizzard, making a straight line for the mines. One thought remained clear in his hazed mind. Ghost Dancer had to be dead. Mac and Jim could not have failed. They had assured him the entrance to the shaft had been blocked. There was no way in hell she could have gotten out.

She was dead.

At the mine entrance, he took down a torch from the wall and lit it. The oil-soaked rags flared immediately. He moved into the darkness, his meager light casting shadows on the damp rock walls. He almost ran, his steps shaky and uneven. Every once in a while, he stumbled in his haste.

"She is dead," he repeated.

Soon the howl of the wind was no longer heard, but he continued on, moving deeper and deeper into the old tunnels. His single-minded purpose drove him onward. He didn't think of Cameron following him. Nothing mattered, nothing but reaching Ghost Dancer's resting place. He had seen her grave and knew she could not have escaped.

"She is dead. . . ."

He knew it, was sure of it. But he did not stop and turn back. He had to see for himself that Wade had lied. When he finally reached what should have been a wall of rubble, Bender stopped, dead in his tracks. He held up the torch, its flickering light showing him the awful truth. Before him was the hole, the beams that had blocked it were moved and the dirt that had clogged it were pushed aside. No power on earth could have wrought the scene before him.

"She's not dead. . . ."

"No," Cameron replied, coming up behind Bender. "Ghost Dancer is not dead."

"Why?" he whined so pathetically, his gaze turning to Cameron. "Why?"

"I found her and got her."

"No. You couldn't have known."

"I knew, Major." The reminder that the man was an officer brought a flash of pain to Cameron. Had the Army and its way been the cause of Bender's insanity? No, he decided. The military life had merely been stepping stones for the madness that lurked within the major's evil nature.

"You're going to hang for what you've done, Bender." It was beyond Cameron's understanding. "All those innocent people you killed—and for what? Gold?"

"Yes. For gold. A hell of a lot of gold, a mountain of it."

The memory of the women and children Bender had murdered washed through Cameron's mind. The burning pain in his side grew, and for a moment his knees weakened but anger kept him standing. Bender dove for the gun, crashing into Cameron. The jolt caused the rifle to go off. The gun's blast echoed down the long, narrow shafts of the mine. Both Bender and Cameron froze, listening, afraid even to let the air out of their lungs. For a precious moment, all was silent.

Then the horrible sound of timbers cracking reached them, followed by a slow shifting of the earth beneath their feet. The weight above them groaned, raining down dirt. A light shower at first, it quickly worsened to a wicked storm. Both men let go of each other. Their instincts kicked in, with survival foremost on their minds. Bender moved first, striking at Cameron almost as an afterthought before scrambling away.

Cameron landed hard and was almost immediately covered with falling dirt. He pulled himself up and ran through the choking dust, dodging rock and old splinters of wood that became deadly daggers. The avalanche smothered his torch, and his eyes stung from the thick dust. He moved on blindly, stumbling over Bender's body. The man's torch barely burned as it lay on the ground, still in his hand. Bender's body lay pinned beneath a ton of rubble with only his head showing.

"Help me!" he screamed, his eyes round with fear and pain.

Against all reason, Cameron tried to pull the man free, but he couldn't budge him. Large support beams had fallen beneath hundreds of pounds of earth and rock.

As the mine crumbled above them, more dirt fell. Bender spit the damp ground from his mouth, but it was replaced by more.

Cameron pushed at the beams with all his might, but he fought a force greater than himself. In the dimness that surrounded him, he saw Bender's face disappear beneath the growing mound of earth, as if a hand had descended, smothering all life.

Gasping for air, Cameron reached for Bender's hand. It was flaccid, limp. A loud moan filled the tunnel, its aged beams unable to withstand the sudden shift of the earth. Like a wailing woman, the mountain determinedly reclaimed its possession of the land. Cameron crawled forward, inch by inch, foot by foot, choking for air that was no longer there. Then he saw it, the meager light that marked the mine's entrance. He was going to make it.

The roar caught him by surprise, deafening him. A wave of rock and earth knocked him to the ground. Cameron knew only the blackness that swallowed him.

Ghost Dancer cried out, calling Cameron's name. Tears dampened her face, and she felt the fear that her mind would not make clear. She did not know what she had been dreaming. For the first time, she could not remember.

Chapter 29

"My father, I know something terrible has happened to Cameron."

Black Hawk reached out and smoothed back the hair that had fallen across her forehead. It was obvious how distressed Ghost Dancer was and he was glad that Wilma had sent the colonel to get him from the camp. "Have you *seen* this?"

Tears filled her eyes and spilled down her cheeks. "I . . . I have, I think, but I cannot remember."

Red Bear stepped forward and tried to comfort her. "Cameron will come home and your worry will have been unnecessary." He sat beside her on the strange pallet, taking her hand into his. "My dancer, you must rest."

Wilma stood behind them both, wringing her hands. "You're brother's right, dear. You've been up all night—ever since your nightmare wakened you."

Ghost Dancer smiled weakly. "Thank you, Wilma, for bringing my family to me. But it was unnecessary."

Black Hawk handed her a bowl filled with a dark, thick liquid. "Drink this, it will calm you."

"No, my father, I cannot sleep until Cameron returns." Once again, she tried to get out of bed.

His look became stern and Black Hawk gently pushed her back. "Drink."

As upset as she was, Ghost Dancer knew better than to disobey her father. She drank the bitter liquid.

"Now you will sleep, and no dreams will disturb you."

Her father's voice was soft, soothing her frayed nerves as much as the potent mixture. The herbs were quick, almost immediate in their relief. "You will wake me when he comes?" She wanted to be optimistic, yet she couldn't keep the tremor from her voice.

"Of course, we will," Wilma said. "As soon as he gets back."

"Yes," Ghost Dancer murmured, already feeling sleepy, her eyelids drooping. "You will not forget, Wilma?"

"No, I won't be forgetting." Wilma once again bustled about the bed, tucking and smoothing the coverlet. "Not this old girl. My memory's sharp as a tack."

Black Hawk met his son's gaze and nodded. They moved back and allowed the woman to care for Ghost Dancer. Red Bear stopped at the door and spoke to Wilma. "We will be back later, after she has rested. You are a generous woman, Wilma Dawson, and you will not be forgotten by the Ghost Sioux."

Wilma waved her hands in the air. "Oh, pish, haven't done anything I didn't want to. Now you go on, I'll see to Angelique, er . . . Ghost Dancer."

Black Hawk and Red Bear smiled at her chattering, then nodding, they left.

Wilma turned to Ghost Dancer. "You get a nice long rest, and when you wake up, Cameron will be home. You just wait and see."

Cameron felt a weight upon him, pushing the air from his lungs. Anger surged, giving warmth to his numb body and purpose to his pain. With agonizing slowness, he moved his arms beneath him, then with all the strength he could muster, he pushed himself up. Like a creature breaking free from its cocoon, he shoved the dirt and rock away and rose. Unleashed fury pumped through him like a powerful drug, and he fought the darkness of his grave, scraping for the light of day.

He wasn't ready to die!

He stood, sucking in a gulp of dirty air. Stumbling forward, he stepped out into the raging storm. He coughed to clear his lungs of the filth and breathed in snow-laced wind. He could not contain his euphoria, the excitement of being alive. Cameron turned his eyes to the mine entrance. It no longer existed.

A smile twisted his cracked lips, and he winced at the sudden pain. He felt the bleeding start again. For Bender, the mine seemed a fitting tomb.

A shiver touched Cameron, and he turned his mind to other matters. Like getting back to Ghost Dancer—alive.

* * *

This time when Ghost Dancer woke, her thoughts were distinct, her purpose clear. Remembering what she had seen in her dream, she got out of bed. All too vividly she saw Cameron and his horse struggling through the blizzard that raged about them, his face covered with ice crystals as he slumped in the saddle, his weariness so plain it sent her heart to her throat.

She must go to him.

Ghost Dancer dressed and quietly left her room, careful not to disturb Wilma or the colonel. She knew she must do this alone. It was her quest to find Cameron. She rode her great white out into the eye of the storm, the snow falling fast and furious about them. Determination made her oblivious to the numbing cold, and only one thought was in her mind—Cameron.

Then, with a startling suddenness, the snow stopped, and the wind calmed its madness. Ghost Dancer paused and watched as the threatening black clouds rolled across the night sky, the break allowing the full moon to peek through. Its white light reflected off the snow that covered the earth, making the darkness seem bright. Distant images became clear as the whole world turned into a wonderland of crystal and ice. So beautiful, yet so very deadly.

Something reached inside Ghost Dancer and touched her. Stiffly, she dropped down from her horse and started off on foot. The snow was deep and difficult to walk through, but she did not turn back. She had gone only a short distance when she saw the horizon move. Excitement, hope, and relief, surged through her, giving her the will to run on.

Cameron felt the numbness and realized the danger. He fought the fatigue, as his head nodded on his chest, but the constant jerking of his horse's movements pulled him back to awareness. He yawned, then shook his head to rid himself of the sluggishness. He couldn't give in; he wouldn't give in.

Thoughts of Ghost Dancer gave him the energy he lacked. His mind drew a picture of her beautiful face, and he imagined her soft skin beneath his fingertips. He loved her. He would make it back to her, to his love, to his life.

His blurry gaze was drawn to the distant white. It took several minutes for his chilled mind to realize what it was he watched. Then, slowly, he began to smile. He called out to her.

"Angel." It came out a hoarse croak, not carrying to her ears. Instead, he urged his mount to move a little faster. "My Ghost Dancer," he called again. And when he drew closer, he slid from his saddle, then stumbled on.

They fell into each other's arms, overwhelmed with joy. Tears froze on their faces as they clung to each other.

"My Ghost Dancer," Cameron whispered. It was all he could say. "My dear, dear Ghost Dancer."

Ghost Dancer placed her hands on each side of his cheeks and looked directly into his eyes. "My

Cameron, we must go home."

"Yes, yes," he agreed, feeling a great tiredness of the body as well as of the soul. "Let's go home."

Ghost Dancer touched Cameron, laying her hand upon his shoulder, deriving a feeling of pleasure from the simple act. Since returning to the fort, they had settled into a comfortable companionship. Neither seemed willing to face what was to come. Ghost Dancer knew that her father and brother waited anxiously to return to their village, but she forced this thought from her mind. "Are you coming to bed?"

"Yes," he replied, taking her extended hand into his. Then he hesitated, and a devilish glint came into his eyes. "On one condition, my love."

She giggled at the look on his face. "And what would that be, *my love*."

"That you marry me."

The light disappeared from her face, and sudden doubt grabbed her. She had feared this moment and knew the time had come for them to part. After all they had been through, they still had not resolved their relationship. Lone Wolf's words came back to haunt her. "He will never understand . . ."

"We have discussed this before, and we ended up hurting each other."

Cameron held up his hand to keep her from saying more. "I was a fool. I expected you to stay in my world as my wife, unaware, or perhaps a better word is unwilling . . . I was unwilling to see what it was that I asked of you. I am seeing clearly now, Ghost Dancer. I know that if we are to share our lives, it must be with the Ghost Sioux. I won't . . . No, I can't give you up, you are my life." The look on his face was convincing enough, but the sincerity of his words made it even clearer. "And if it means leaving my world for yours, then that is the way it will be."

This touched Ghost Dancer beyond description. "It is too much to ask of you."

"It is nothing to ask," he refuted easily. "Where we live does not matter. What matters is that we are together."

"What of your career in the Army? It is so very important to you." Ghost Dancer was hearing everything she had dreamed of, but she was too cautious to accept it readily.

Cameron's look turned a bit sad. "I had a lot of time to think, out in the storm. I discovered some things about myself, and my all-important Army career. Suddenly, *your* goals, *your* duty to the Sioux had more importance and reason. I asked myself, to what end is the Army working?"

"And what answer did you find?"

"One I didn't like, Angel. Suddenly, everything I believed in was being replaced by ones that do not deal with killing, but with survival." Cameron stopped, sorting out his thoughts before going on.

"When I thought I couldn't go on, I did. I thought of you, of our life together. It gave me strength. I want you to be my wife and to bear my children. I never want us to be apart again. Never again."

"Yes. Never again." Her eyes blurred from tears of joy. "But, Cameron, among my people, we are already considered married."

His dark head shook in disagreement. "I want you to marry me in the way *my* people do. In your customs, should you tire of me, you only need to place my things outside the tepee and it's over. We are divorced. I don't want it to be that easy. I want to be married by a preacher, for better for worse, till death do us part. The whole works."

The tears ran down her cheeks now. "The whole works?"

Cameron threw back his head and laughed, feeling the soreness of his body. "Yes," he yelled. "Will you marry me, Ghost Dancer? Will you pledge to spend the rest of your life with me and never throw my clothes outside?"

"It would make me very happy to share my life with you, Cameron Wade," she said from her heart. "And I will never declare us unmarried, and your clothes shall always remain by mine."

Delighted, Cameron pulled her to him, his lips taking hers in a silent vow of love. He kissed her long and hard, his tongue playing with the sweet softness of her own. Easily he ignored the slight twinge of pain in his side, but with great effort, he pulled back. "You had better rest now, Ghost Dancer. I want you well rested for our honeymoon."

Disappointment glowed strong within her, and she pouted. "Honeymoon. What is a honeymoon?"

"It's also a white man's tradition. Generally the bride and groom run off somewhere to be alone, spending their wedding night and many more in blissful lovemaking."

"The Sioux also honeymoon." She looked mischievous, as her fingertips traced an unseen line along his muscled torso, side-stepping the bandage that remained wrapped about him. "Sometimes before *and* after the marriage is declared. Couldn't we mix some of your customs with mine?"

"Such as?" he teased.

"Could we not share the blissful lovemaking before and after this 'whole works' wedding? I will be most careful of your wound."

Cameron slowly pulled her back into his arms, this time with no intention of letting her go. "I think that would be a wise compromise. We must always be willing to consider the other's feelings."

"Yes," she whispered into his ear. "It is a good thing to remember."

Chapter 30

Cameron rose from their bed, and went to his wife. She sat by the fire, its flickering light dancing off her as she knelt near its warmth.

"Ghost Dancer." He reached out and turned her delicately shaped face to his. "Why are you crying? It's over, my love. Bender's dead."

She sniffed. "I know that he is dead."

"Then what has you so sad? Was it having to say good-bye to Wilma and the colonel?"

"It was a difficult thing to do, and I shall miss them. But we are where we need to be, with my people." Again, she did not go on, her eyes unable to look directly into his curious gaze.

"Tell me what it is, Angel. I can't read your mind."

Her sigh reached his ears, and he felt a tightness of his heart. Once again, he lifted her chin so that he could see her better. "Tell me. It can't be all that bad."

"It is," she whispered. "It is not over. Bender's death is not the end."

Cameron did not want to believe what she was

saying. "What do you mean? The mine was totally lost when it caved in. The Army knows he did the killing, and it's settled."

Ghost Dancer was silent a moment, her head hanging in despair. "I had a dream. I saw what is to come."

A chill ran over Cameron, but he said nothing, he just waited for her to finish.

"A man with yellow hair will come into the hills, with your Army. He will find the gold Bender died for. It is everywhere. Many will soon follow. Our land will be overrun with the white man and his greed for this stone of gold."

Cameron was stunned. "No, it won't happen. They wouldn't break the treaties."

Tears came again. "It will happen. More grief than you could ever imagine will befall the Sioux and the entire Indian nation. What we have been through is only the beginning of the end for a great people. The ground will run red with our people's blood. The white man will do this letting, and all is doomed. It cannot be denied."

"No," Cameron muttered in disbelief. "It can't be."

"I would give anything for it not to be." She placed her hand upon his. "It is not all that I have seen this night."

Cameron was afraid to ask more.

"I saw a hidden valley, a beautiful lush paradise, somewhere to the west and north." She took a deep breath, then finished. "I must take my people there."

His eyes met hers, and he knew she was serious.

That was what frightened him. "Leave the Black Hills?"

She nodded. "To stay would bring the end of the Nahhe Lahkota. We *must* survive. That is why Grandfather has given this vision to me."

Cameron pushed back his hair. "What of the other tribes?"

"They have their own shaman, chiefs, and holy men. They will guide their own people, and their word will draw each to his own decision. I can guide only the Ghost Sioux."

"Since we know what can happen, couldn't we stop it?"

Ghost Dancer's shook her head, the sadness in her eyes painful for him. "No. This is a scourge too great for us to stop."

"When must we go?" he asked, still not sure about this whole thing.

"A morning will dawn with three suns in the eastern sky. It is then that we must go to this secret place."

Something fled from Cameron, much like relief chasing away his apprehension and fear. He fought hard to keep these feelings from showing, keeping a straight look on his face. "Come back to bed, love. That could be a long time in coming."

Ghost Dancer understood what he was thinking, even more so than he did. "It may come sooner than you think, my Cameron."

Spring was not too far off, the days grew longer and warmer. Cameron was drawn from his sleep, a wanting stirring him. He felt the emptiness of his arms and finally woke. Over the months, he had grown used to her warmth as they slept, the warmth of her heart as well as her body. They had spent the long winter months in a blissful world, their love growing much like the babe Ghost Dancer carried within her womb.

Cameron pulled a buffalo robe over his naked body and went outside, knowing she would not be far. He saw her standing a few feet away in the quiet stillness before dawn.

"Ghost Dancer." He came up behind her, wrapping her in the warm robe with him, his hand sliding over the roundness of her belly and locking his fingers in front. "What are you doing out here? It's cold."

"The time has come for us to go."

Cameron brought his gaze from the top of her head to the eastern sky. On the horizon, three distinct, fiery suns rose into the darkened gray of the night, throwing an eerie glow upon the earth. In that moment, he did not doubt what they had to do.

"We must go," he said quietly.

She turned to look up into his eyes. "Are you certain you want to go? We will not be coming back."

Their eyes meshed, just as their hearts beat in unison. "Oh, my Ghost Dancer. You are my love, you are my life. How can I not go with you?"

She smiled up at him, a wondrous light in her eyes. "Yes." She then laughed, soft and sweet. "How can you not?"

The Legend

It is said that Ghost Dancer and Cameron Wade led the Nahhe Lahkota to the hidden valley of her dreams. Some say they live there still, safe from the outside world.

It is also said that many children were born of the Ghost Dancer's union, but no one can say to whom the Spirit passed. Some say she was the last, for now her people were forever at peace. . . .

Author's Note

Though the Ghost Sioux and the Ghost Dance religion existed, the Ghost Dancer, her particular tribe, and the portrayal of the Ghost Dance are purely fictional.

I thought it might be of interest to my readers to know that the man with the yellow hair who went into the Black Hills was George Armstrong Custer. He led an expedition in 1874, and this, in turn, led to the discovery of gold and in the years that followed, to the downfall of the Sioux Nation.

Also, the three suns that Ghost Dancer predicted would appear are in fact a natural phenomenon known as Sun Dogs. It is a parhelion effect which occurs when sunlight is reflected off ice crystals from the clouds, creating the image of more than one sun. This event has occurred over the Dakotas.